ARTIST'S NOTE ON THE COVER

The illustration shows a close-up of a Halifax II of 233 Squadron RAF during the run-in to the target. The enormous explosion above the aircraft is a scarecrow rocket, intended to demoralize British crews by giving the impression that a bomber had received a direct hit by AA fire or night fighter. The mauvish or lilac searchlight on the back cover is a radar-controlled master-light and guides the other searchlights on to the illuminated target. Also shown on the cover are the latecomers who naturally received close attention from the German defences.

ONE OF OUR BOMBERS IS MISSING

Dan Brennan

NEW ENGLISH LIBRARY/TIMES MIRROR

For
BILL MAISENBACHER
Flight sergeant air gunner
No. 10 squadron
Royal Air Force
and
HENRY PAWELSKI, JOHN KOLTON
Art Beaudoin and Saul Schneider
Sergeant air gunners
406th Bombardment squadron
USAAF

First published in Great Britain by Allen & Unwin in 1944
under the title *Never So Young Again*

© 1946 by Dan Brennan

First NEL Paperback Edition March 1979

NEL Books are published by
New English Library from
Barnard's Inn, Holborn,
London EC1N 2JR.
Made and printed in Great Britain by
William Collins Sons & Co. Ltd
Glasgow

4500 4275 8

CHAPTER ONE

It was spring when I arrived in Britain, and that afternoon, with Glasgow wet and dismal in the rain, I came on down across England in the dusk, past the neat, small, green fields and trim stone walls, to a town on the south coast. I lived in a big grey-stone hotel that overlooked the sea. Once the town had been a popular resort. But now the hotels were closed and the windows were boarded up and every night somewhere along the coast there was an air raid. I sat on a high wall by the sea, watching the gun flashes, feeling lonely, wishing I were flying, while from high overhead came the sound of British bombers setting course for the Continent. What would it be like up there? Would I be afraid? I felt damn lonely, looked at the sea and moonlight, and walked back to the hotel.

There was little to do during the day. On parade in the morning, and afternoons everybody went to the tea-dance at the pavilion that overlooked the sea. The war, except for searchlights and gun flashes in the dark over the sea at night, was something unreal, ike a movie, and still very far away. The town was full of air crews, all very keen to start flying operationally. One spring day I was ordered to change to another hotel, and carrying my two kit-bags, and sweating in my wool uniform in the hot April morning, I marched down the street in a column to another large grey-stone hotel. It was a much newer hotel and the floors and walls were not so worn. I went into a room on the sixth floor and dumped my kit on one of the fine empty beds and sat down on the edge of the bed and looked out the window at the ocean and barbed wire running along the beach. I sat there until it was time to go to lunch.

After lunch I returned to the room and sat on the bed again, unpacked my kit and looked out the window, and then lay on the bed in the sunlight and slept. It was three o'clock when I woke, and I washed and shaved and prepared for the tea-dance. The door was open and I was tying my necktie when I heard someone coming upstairs and then along the hall, and still tying my neck-tie I turned my head towards the doorway. Ed Fournier, with whom I had enlisted, came in the door. He was smiling and he held out his hand as he came across the room.

'Mack!' he yelled. 'How the hell are you? Heard you were over.'

'My God, it's good to see you, Ed. How are you?'

He clapped me on the back and I clapped him back.

'I'll be damned,' I said. 'Never thought we'd run into each other again.'

'Say,' he said, grinning, 'it's a tough war, isn't it? Beer and blondes. Tennis and tea-dances so far. Jees, it's good to see you, boy.'

'Good to see you.'

'Who's kidding who, brother? Sounds like we're both trying to soft-soap the other guy into buying the first five rounds. What've you been doing here?'

'Nothing. Marching. Waiting.'

'Browned-off?'

'God, yes. Like to get on flying.'

'Who wouldn't? Same all over. Schools full, so we rot here until a couple more crews up ahead of us are trained. What kind of kite you like to go on?'

'Doesn't matter, anything. I'm going nuts here just sitting around.'

'Don't get on Whitleys if you can help it. Burn like a bastard if they prang. Talking to a fellow other day. Said they're really deadly if you crash. Met any of the local females yet?'

'Few.'

'Brother, let me tell you. Stay away from these service club dances. Lady something-or-other runs one here. Gets all the local nice girls. What a collection of goons. All about twenty years old and they all go in for leading Girl Guide troops or breeding rabbits or some damn thing.'

'Thanks. You're a great help.'

'Okay. Just try it and find out. Let's go to the Pavilion this afternoon. Bags of stuff there. Not bad either. Met some really nice stuff there yesterday.'

'Let's eat first. You've certainly been having yourself a time, haven't you?'

'Brother, it is not fair. Blondes, brunettes, redheads. What a wonderful country. Wah,' he imitated Roosevelt's voice, comically rolling his eyes. 'Wah, ah loves wah. Sistie loves wah. Buzzie loves it. Hallelujah, brother. Pass the ammunition.' Then, in another tone, 'God, I wonder when we'll get out of here on to

6

flying. I'd give anything to be flying.'

'Sure, sure,' I said, and got a clean pair of socks out of my kit-bag. Each day everybody talked only of their desire to return to flying.

'You ought to see these English women. The ones at the Pavilion, I mean,' said Ed. 'They aren't bad. Not too much buck teeth and tweeds, if you know what I mean.'

I slipped on fresh socks, my shoes, got up and combed my hair. Ed sat on a chair smoking a cigarette, his cap on the back of his head. It was good to see him again, someone I knew. He blew out a jet of smoke, arced the cigarette out the open window, and straightened his cap.

'Had any leave yet?' he asked.

'No.'

'We'll have to get some together, see a little of the country and London.' I put on my cap, straightened my tie, and together we left the room. Outside, walking to another hotel, where everybody ate, Ed said, 'We'll go to London for the blondes and brandy, my friend. A few days of that. Then a few days recuperating in the country. Okay? Lady what's-her-name, who runs the service club dances, will fix us up to stay with some family in the country.'

'Some family,' I said. 'Okay.'

Ed smiled. 'Some family, brother. Come on, let's get a beer before dinner.

At the dance at the Pavilion that night I danced with a Waaf who was home on leave, and who, as she said, was trying to enjoy herself. Did I like England? she asked. Yes, I liked England. My God, what was I supposed to say? How long have I been over? she asked. I told her. What did I think of English women? Was it very different from America? What part of America was I from? Minnesota. No, she had never heard of it. It didn't matter. How were people different in America? No one could ever explain that, I said. Why not? she asked. Anyway I couldn't, I said. Maybe she would meet someone who could do it, I said. Or try the newspapers. They were explaining the difference every day. She asked my age. What had I done before the war? Wasn't the war rotten? Yes, I agreed, the war was rotten. And where the hell is this getting us? I thought, feeling alone in the crowded dance-hall, wondering what all this led to. To where tomorrow? And where in the days to come? Had I travelled in England before the war? she asked. No. Well, one ought really to see all of England, then one would understand what England really was. Didn't I agree? Yes, of course. Yes, she said, one had only to live in England to know what England meant. England was a feeling. One had only to be an English person to understand it meant a feeling. What the hell, I thought, bored and tired. I'm an American, but no one's going to string together a lot of pretty poetical pictures and make me believe that here now this is America. England was always many things but never any one thing.

On leave that spring with Ed, England was the trains running fast into Southampton, and along the tracks, the roofless houses, and the bombed rubble on the station platform, and the sunlight beyond the glassless depot roof with the barrage balloons silver-grey and motionless in the windless blue afternoon. It was that, and for the first time the fields of London rooftops rushing past blurred in the rain beyond the carriage window, and me excited and happy, and Waterloo Station, and the Bond Street whores in their coloured slacks standing in doorways out of the rain, holding their bright parasols and leashed lap dogs. It was not Westminster Abbey, nor Parliament, nor the Tower of London, nor all the places I had been taught to see. It was all people's faces and Leicester Square and tube stations and taxis and pubs up in Chelsea, and finally tired and ready for the country. And in the country a great stone house in a valley in Buckinghamshire, and an old woman who wore hats and long dresses like Queen Mary and asked polite questions about America, in a long drawing-room with the french windows open and May sunlight on the terrace. It was that, and on the table a picture of her son, long dead, among the lost forgotten dead of Flanders.

It was that, and bored with polite drawing-room conversation for which everyone, teacup in hand, seemed to have an accepted tried and tested set of questions and answers. But it was also May and spring, and a wood to walk in where sunlight came through the leafy branches of tall trees and in the damp cool air of the woods, walking slowly over the dry dead leaves of another year, and an old stone bridge where in the early mornings Ed and I leaned and looked at ourselves in the water, and then beyond at the hills green with trees, and the long still valley, or suddenly maybe a rabbit running across the dusty road that wound through the town between stone houses, small and old, and on out, climbing to stop at a gate in a wall in front of the old stone mansion where the days went quickly with people, kind and considerate to me because I was a long way from home. But England did not mean this. That those people were not England, for England was many other places, and I say this now only because so many have used words to explain, as England, places which they lived in and loved, and they were always pleasant places. I had not seen the unpleasant places yet. But I knew they were there, as surely as I felt the meaning of America was not in some of the rhapsodic poems of Sandburg, Lindsay, and Whitman. Not words evoking so easily emotional tugs at the heart about life in American states and towns where life could never be distilled in words, where the meaning of each life, for that life, was truly only a series of immediate instants of being awake or asleep, and not any poet's feeling or conception of time, and the earth and God and the moon. It was all, as I knew, only a commonplace discovery, but then there seemed many who were credited with understanding and wisdom, many who knew how to use words, who continued only to roll up nice word-pictures and label them Here is England, or Here is Democracy, or Here is Beauty, or Here is America, or here is typical this and typical that. I thought of this on the train returning from leave. But then in those days that was the way the thinking went.

And I was thinking of it the next day when Bijur, a friend from training days in Canada, came up to my room and said he was posted to a Wellington Bomber Operational Training Unit. But when I went to the train to see him leave I was not thinking at all, and later there were times when I could see no point in considering anything. But now at the train I still cared about many things. I cared about Bijur, and he was a friend going away. I shook hands. He went into a compartment on the train and opened the window and leaned out. I stood on the platform, and leaned against the outside of the carriage by his window.

'Well, I'll see you around, Mack,' Bijur said.

'Okay, pal. Take care of yourself.'

'Write when you get time.'

'Sure,' I said.

'Yeah, now I'll tell one,' Bijur grinned.

'When do you think you'll be in London again?'

'Don't know.' Up ahead the whistle trilled shrilly.

'Well, so long, pal.'

'Good luck, Bob.'

'See you around, Mack. Take care of yourself.'

'Okay, boy. So long.'

'So long, Mack.'

The train jerked and hissed steam and then slowly moved.

From the crowd I watched it move gradually out of the station. Bijur leaned out of the window and waved. He was grinning, his head stuck out over the top of the window. I waved to him. Then his carriage disappeared around a bend in the track and I went outside and back to the hotel, where Ed would be waiting to go out to the Pavilion and a pub.

That was the last time I ever saw Bijur. That was good-bye to Bijur. But it was not until a year later I heard he was killed over Bremen.

CHAPTER TWO

But there were always good-byes. There was the good-bye the day I left home. For me there would always be that day. The day I woke early in the morning and looked out between the spindle columns of the porch railing at the empty street and the green lawn. I lived on a wide paved avenue with many elm trees. The houses were big and wooden, and there was an elm tree to shade each house.

The water-sprinklers were turning on the lawns along the block. It was quiet and not too hot yet, and occasionally a car passed. Lying there I thought I didn't want to leave. In the early morning everything was different. There were green lawns and big trees and the nice sound of sprinklers turning, and everything was all right. Maybe I had made a mistake in deciding to go to Canada and enlist in the RCAF.

I rolled over and closed my eyes and heard the front door open and knew it was time to get up. I heard someone step on to the wooden porch.

'Mack.'

It was my mother. Half the porch was enclosed in screens. She stood on the open part of the porch looking in at me through the screen door.

'Hello, Mother.'

'Mack.' Her hand rested on the door handle. She paused, looking in at me. I knew what she wanted to talk about.

'Look, Mother,' I said. She didn't open the door. She stood

10

outside looking in at me. 'There's no point in going all over it again.'

'But, Mack – '

'We've been all through it before.' Did she have to drag through it again?

The evening before had not been easy. I came in late and she was sitting at the kitchen table. When she looked at me it was hard to tell whether she knew. Her bags, unpacked, were on the floor. Mary had picked her up at the station. And now she was home again.

'Have a good trip? How was California?'

'Fine. I had a lovely time.'

Then I was at the sink washing my hands and I could feel her looking at my back. I turned around, towelling my hands, and her chair was turned all the way around and she was looking at me. Well, this was it all right. I went on wiping my hands, looking at her. What the hell was the use of smiling, asking if she had enjoyed her trip?

'I've lost some weight, Mother.'

'Ten pounds,' she said.

'Mary told you?'

'Yes.'

'Had my physical exam. Okay too.'

'Oh, Mack,' she said slowly. Her face was sad and she looked then as if she could cry. A long time ago I had seen the same look on her face when the house caught fire, and something that was part of her life was being taken away from her. She had cried that time. They had put the fire out, but she was a long time getting over it. Now she did not cry. Just sat across from me at the kitchen table and put her hands to her face. I felt terrible but I felt it was the only way now. My old job was behind me, finished. To hell with this life.

And in the morning now she said, 'But, Mack, if you're not happy here – '

'It's not that.' What could you tell her? She had done everything for me always. All my life.

'Mack, what is it?'

'It's being restless and wondering what the hell everything is about and not able to find out here.'

'It's yourself, Mack.'

'No,' I said. 'It might be, but I wouldn't be too sure.'

She shook her head and looked sad. Her hair was black, her

11

features were straight and clear, and though she was over fifty she kept her good looks. Her eyes were dark-circled. Why had she had to cry? Why couldn't I stay? She was fond of me, and though we never agreed on anything there was a strong bond between us. No, it was all over, this life here. I must go.

'It's yourself, Mack. I've told you before.'

'No, it's you. You want me to grow up a nice young man with a nice office and business or a successful career or some damn thing everybody works for.'

'What's wrong with that?'

'Nothing. I just think it would be more interesting to understand why everybody works for those things, why they go on doing it. What their point is and has it any value?'

'You'll get yourself killed.'

'I don't feel that way. What time is it?'

'After six.'

'I'm going swimming.'

I leaned down to kiss her forehead. She moved away. She was angry. She tried not to show it but it was there, and she went into the house looking angry and sad.

In the cold water all the sleep came out of me. I dived under the safety ropes and opened my eyes. The water was still and clear and I could see the sandy bottom. I swam and got up on the diving dock. The planks were cold and damp and there was a cool breeze blowing. I dived in quickly to keep from getting cold, and came up blowing water, swimming towards the small headland about a quarter of a mile away. Swimming, I tired. Slowly treading water I looked around at the kidney shape of the lake, the tree-lined shore, and far across on the other side the high cliffs that seemed to hold in the lake, and the small shape of a locomotive moving fast along the edge of the cliff, blowing puffs of white smoke against a clear blue sky.

After a while I turned back. I came out of the water and it was time to go for breakfast. The leather seat in the car was almost too hot to sit on, and I did not have time to rub myself dry. When I pulled away, the popcorn wagon was opening for the day. It was parked beside my car, and a dark man opened the wooden panel that became a counter on the side of the truck and set out a jar of mustard.

Well, that was over too, I thought. That and a lot of things. And drove around the lake to the lake with the islands, and along the shaded streets, on which the tar was already soft and hot, to the busy street with the traffic signal, and across it, and past three street intersections to the corner where I turned down to the street on which I lived, and to my house with a dark Buick coupé parked in front. Inside, my sister was sitting in the living-room reading a magazine, the shades were drawn against the sun. I looked at her and went upstairs.

There in my room was my travelling bag. It was time to go. Tomorrow morning I would be in Canada.

CHAPTER THREE

Those early days in England were pleasant sunny days that passed easily. It was a clear sunny spring and in the mornings there was only one parade, and in the beginning, before people began to skip even that one parade, the day was mine and I walked and read and sat in the park or lay on the beach until lunch, and in the afternoons played tennis with Ed. The court was in a long green park. On all sides were high shady trees and through all the branches I could see the ocean beyond the cliffs that bordered one side of the park. In the evenings I drank heavy dark beer in a pub with a low roof of old oak beams. But like everyone else I was anxious to begin flying again. And later, with the entire company losing privileges because a few skipped parades, the days were not so pleasant.

So one morning I decided to ask a few questions. Three ranks of men were lined up in the early morning on a gravelled parking lot behind a theatre across from the hotel in which I lived. The roll had been called, and the men were being dismissed. The officer in charge was talking to the Station Warrant Officer.

'Sir,' I asked the officer, 'do you know when we'll be posted out of here?'

'No, sergeant. Don't bother me.'

'Where can we find out?'

'I don't know, sergeant. I told you I don't know.' He had not been looking at me, and now he suddenly turned away from the Warrant Officer and faced me, as I turned to leave.

'Sergeant, haven't you been in the habit of standing to attention when addressing an officer?'

'Yes, sir.'

He was a little man with a moustache, and a last-war campaign ribbon.

'You Yanks don't believe in discipline, do you?' The Warrant Officer stood stiffly beside him, looking straight ahead.

'As much as we feel is necessary,' I said. 'Why? Have I committed some breach of discipline?'

'Hickey,' he said to the Warrant Officer, 'take this man's name and number. Put him on guard duty all today.'

'Well, Sergeant, what are you waiting for?' said the Warrant Officer after taking my name. 'You're dismissed. Report to my office.'

'Nothing, only . . .'

To hell with it, I thought, it was never any good arguing with these people. I walked away, leaving them talking, looking very military, the Warrant Officer standing rigidly to attention. They were probably all right out of a uniform, I thought, but put them in a uniform long enough and they become something that was not truly – themselves. But perhaps they did not even need a uniform to change, perhaps what they were they had always been, and the type of clothes they wore only brought them out a little more clearly. And though there were many like them in the Air Force, there were just as many unlike them. But now it did not matter much what anyone was truly, I thought, angry and humiliated.

Later in the Warrant Officer's office, with the officer gone and just the WO and me alone, I stood in front of his desk.

'What the hell's bothering that officer?' I asked, wondering where the WO would stand now that he was free of the officer's presence.

He did not even raise his head. He was looking down at a letter on his desk.

'Stand at attention, Sergeant.'

'What am I "joed" for?'

'Report as guard on the hotel door.'

'Right, sir,' I said, and went up to my room and got my webbing equipment for carrying a sidearm. The guard watch was not difficult. I was on duty two hours, then off half an hour, then on two hours. It was a bright hot day and I stood in the hotel doorway and watched the traffic of factory workers on bicycles going past. I came off duty at six o'clock that evening.

After supper I went to the pub across the street from the hotel. Ed was leaning against the bar with a pint of bitter in one hand.

14

He was watching a darts game between four sailors. I went over to him.

'Hey! Hey!' he said, smiling. 'Hear you got the nice rough end of a very rough stick today. How about going to the Pavilion tonight? Met two pretty good ones last night.'

'Think I'll see a show.'

'Hell, there's not a decent picture in town, unless you go in for Tarzan's latest adventure. Come on.'

'Okay. Wait till I have a pint.'

'Here. Have one on me.'

The pint came, I drank it off. Ed finished his and we went outside together.

Walking, Ed said, 'Let's stop some place and have a scotch. How about the White Horse?'

We went into the White Horse pub on the next corner and up to the bar. I ordered and the drinks came.

'No, no water,' I said. Ed was holding the decanter of water.

'Okay,' he said. 'Here's looking at you.'

'All the best, old boy.'

'Bung ho! Ectually.'

'Cheerio! What! What!'

It was a cheap scotch, harsh, and it burned going down, but there was nothing else.

'Beer?' Ed asked.

'Half,' I said. After we had finished the beer we went outside and walked through the town to the Pavilion by the beach. In the twilight the air was soft and cool, and a breeze came in off the sea. The sky seemed greenish blue, and far out on the water I saw a freighter going past with a barrage balloon suspended above it. The streets were crowded and everybody was going some place, the square full of troops and all the buses crowded. We went upstairs in the Pavilion to the ballroom. Inside Ed looked around among the tables. After a moment he spotted someone and waved. We saw two girls in ATS uniform seated at a table across the room. One was smiling and her hand was slightly raised. She lowered her hand. We went across the ballroom to their table. Ed said hello to one of the girls. I stood there by the table.

'Diana,' he said to the other girl, 'this is Mack Norton. Mack, Diana Foreshaw.'

'Hello,' Diana said. 'You and Ed are rather good friends, aren't you?'

'Oh, rawther.'

15

I looked around for Ed. The girl and he were gone. I saw them dance past, talking and smiling. I sat down.

'Why did you say that?' Diana asked.

'What?' I asked.

'Oh, rawther. Just the way you said it. You really didn't have to say it as if you were making fun of an expression like that, did you? It's very childish. Why did you do it?'

'I don't know,' I said. 'You answer it. What would you like me to say?'

She looked at me. 'I say,' she said. 'You are rude.'

'Let's dance.'

'I say, can't we just have a nice evening?'

'Certainly. Let's dance,' I said. 'I'm sorry.'

'Really. You don't have to stay if you don't want to.'

'I'm sorry. Honestly. Let's dance.'

She laughed.

'Actually, you are ridiculous, aren't you?'

'Are you engaged or married or just what?' I asked.

Diana was dark. Her uniform appeared to be tailor-made, not standard issue. Her eyes were blue, her skin quite pale and smooth. I thought she was the best-looking woman I had seen in a long time, and because of that I felt as I often felt with a beautiful woman – at some kind of a peculiar disadvantage, as if I was perhaps a little too impressed. Yes, I thought, I had succumbed to behaving towards her in a ridiculous way, because of that idea.

There was a diamond ring on one finger of her left hand. She saw me looking at it.

'Don't let that bother you. I enjoy myself. He's on Canadian squadron.'

'Just wondered, that's all.'

'He was with the first Canadians to come over. We're going to wait until after the war. They're having hell's own trouble right now on these Norwegian raids.'

'Wish I could hurry and get on ops.'

'Are you really keen to go?'

'Certainly.'

'You're all like that, at first,' she said. 'You'll be very different after a while. Sometimes I hardly seem to know him when we see each other. He's not at all like he used to be.'

'What do you mean?'

'He doesn't seem to care about anything in particular. He can't even sit quietly for more than twenty minutes.'

16

'Why not get married now?'

'No,' she said. 'I don't want that now. Not that I don't love him enough. It's only that – '

'Only that you want to enjoy your own life and still feel you have someone?'

'No, you don't understand. You don't see that it's possible to have a good time with other people and still love someone. Haven't you ever been in love?'

'I don't know. I thought I was a few times,' I said. 'Should we dance?'

We got up and started to dance. She was very close to me, there was a soft perfume in her hair.

'You're a lovely girl,' I said.

She smiled. 'Nonsense,' she said. 'But thank you, sir.' She nodded, then added, 'But don't think I don't know it.'

'Counteracting an approach?'

'Why not?'

'You don't have to.'

'No, I know I don't have to. No more than you have to attempt an approach. But don't worry,' she laughed. 'I wouldn't mind kissing you, if that's what's worrying you.'

'Thank you,' I said.

Dancing, I looked at her.

Well, what do you know, I thought, fine if she wants to play it this way. We danced on.

'That's the trouble with all of you,' she said. 'If you can't kiss her, you run away like a lot of little boys. Angry as if you'd lost a game.'

'Oh, I don't know.'

'Rot, of course it's true. And you know it.'

The music ceased. We went back to the table. Ed and the other ATS girl were not there. The dance floor was empty. I could not see them at any other table.

'Where do you think they went?'

'Out,' Diana said. 'Where else do people go but out nowadays. I hope he's nice. She's very young. Just out of school.'

'Oh, he's all right. I wouldn't worry.'

'I'm not worrying,' she said. 'He's quite older than she though, you know. Still, it's probably what she needs. Honestly, I don't think the girl's ever been kissed in her life.'

'She hasn't missed so much.'

'I hardly think you believe that. What did you do before the war?'

'Worked on a newspaper. What do you do in these brown uniforms?'

She laughed.

'We're supposed to be frightfully busy people. Plotting enemy aircraft and such. Sometimes I wish I weren't when I see how easily we pick up their planes coming in over the coast. Makes one think of John's chances on crossing the German coast. On getting past their defences.'

'Maybe their radio equipment isn't as good as ours. I don't really believe anything would upset you very much,' I said.

'One can't afford to be upset or unhappy,' she said. 'It's hardly worth while. I do worry terribly about him though. God, I should feel terrible if anything happened to him. I don't know what I would do.'

'You'd probably get over it.'

'No.'

'Why not?'

'It's the only one thing I care about now.'

'Well, the war won't go on forever.'

'It might. Four or five years is just long enough to represent ever in my mind.'

'We have to beat them,' I said.

'Why?'

'It's very simple. Or they'll beat us and run us.'

'Do you honestly believe that?'

'Certainly. You have to find reasons to believe in this war after a while. Everybody has to have his or her personal reason. I guess mine'll just have to do for me.'

'Seems too simple,' she said. 'No answer can seem that simple and still be correct and true.'

'Well, don't try to think out other reasons. No one else can without telling lies.'

'You don't sound very logical,' she said. 'But I don't mind. I'm damn tired of logical people who are so sure their answers have everything taped perfectly.'

Ed and the other girl came across the dance floor towards the table. Diana said the other girl's name was Pat. They sat down. Ed was smiling.

'Awfully warm in here, isn't it?' Ed asked.

'No, just right, I think,' Diana said.

Ed smiled. 'I think it's terribly warm.'

'Well, go on,' I said, participating now in a kind of hinting

18

game Ed was trying to create. 'Say what you mean.'

'I mean it's warm in here,' said Ed. He was still smiling. Pat beside him sat very still and quiet.

'You mean why don't we all rush into the park and make love, don't you?' asked Diana. 'God, you are a tiresome little boy, Ed.'

'Let's dance,' I said.

'No. No.' Diana shook her head. 'Let's understand this. I don't mind Ed's suggestion at all. Doesn't bother me in the least. But I'd rather dance now, if you don't mind. But honesty – I really wouldn't mind the park at all on some nights with a nice person. The park aspect of it doesn't bother me at all. Damn silly to be bothered by anything like that. In fact, by anything.'

After the dance we walked to the hotel where Diana was billeted. I said good night and standing for a moment in the doorway kissed her and held her close. Nice, detached, impersonal pleasant kiss. But walking home it was different. Thinking of her now, not so easy to be detached. Now that I was away from her, not so easy to put her out of my mind, and as I went along the hall to my room Ed opened the door of his room and said, 'How'd you make out, fella?'

'Okay,' I said, not wanting to speak of it in an easy cocky way, in a way ashamed and disgusted with myself for having talked about it at all.

But later, alone, I was myself again; what the hell, she was only another girl, attractive, yes, gay, understanding, yes, but why get involved? What the hell is this? I wondered. I wouldn't see her again anyway, I decided. Easy as that to turn it all off. And I fell asleep hoping I would see her the next day.

CHAPTER FOUR

I did not see Diana for several days. I called at her billet but she was not in. Then one morning while I was walking along the street after a parade I saw her in an army lorry parked up the street on the next corner. Diana was sitting in the driver's cab behind the wheel. I hurried along towards the lorry and came up alongside it and tapped on the window. Diana saw me and smiled, and rolled down the window and put out her head. 'Hello,' she said, smiling, 'where have you been keeping yourself?'

I explained I had called several times but she was not in.

'You don't expect me to believe that, do you?' she asked, smiling.

'What the hell. It's true.'

'Good heavens, don't be so serious about it,' she said. 'Do you always look so grave when someone asks you a ridiculous question?'

'Okay, Okay,' I said. Then: 'How about doing something tonight? Say a few drinks or a show?'

'I'd love to, Mack, only I'm scheduled for a perfectly bloody evening at home. If you don't mind the expression. My home's here, you know. Why don't you call at the billet next week?'

'Sure,' I said. 'Or the week after. Or maybe next armistice day. Very nice. Many thanks.'

'Don't talk nonsense,' she said, wrinkling her nose. 'Honestly, I have to spend the evening with my fond parents. Haven't seen either for weeks.'

'Can't you escape after dinner?'

'No, really, Mack. I have a terrible lot of things I simply must do at home.'

'Tomorrow night?'

'Oh dear. This is complicated.'

'Quite simple. Really.'

She shook her head. 'No, it isn't. You don't understand.'

'Well, I'll see you around. Cheerio,' I said.

'Cheerio, Mack. Do call really next week.'

'You bet. So long.' I nodded and went on along the street. Well, if she did not want to see me again at least she was neat about the whole thing and I was a fool not to catch on sooner. What the hell. Maybe, it was all for the best. Still, she was very beautiful, and I was disappointed. I went on towards the tennis court. But maybe she did want to see me. Maybe I was only imagining things. Ah, sure, maybe, maybe anything. What the hell. Forget it.

That afternoon it rained. I stayed in my room and read. It was becoming increasingly more difficult to find ways of occupying my time. But I could stay in when it rained, and down the hall there was always a good dice and card game. At night there was the cinema, dance, and pub. I thought of learning French, or

Italian, or some foreign language. I often planned to go to the library and read all the books I planned to read when I had the time. There were many things I planned to do and now when there was time I did none of them. But in a way there was not really time. I tried once to do one of the things I planned to do, to read all Thomas Mann's books, but when I tried there seemed always a feeling of urgency, as if my life was hurrying towards something, and I could not concentrate. Perhaps it was only an illusion, but living that sense of urgency seemed much more an important reality than reading or learning anything out of a book.

So late that afternoon I walked down town to the park. The sun was out, and though the grass was wet the evening air was bright and warm. The park was crowded. Old men and women, their eyes watery in the fading sunshine, leaned on their walking sticks, where they sat on the benches around the bandstand listening to the thick sad waves of Scriabin and Massine. Nursemaids in white dresses played with children by the wading pool. A Spitfire passed low overhead – sound dying across the treetops. I sat in the park and watched the sun set over the ocean. When it was dark, I went along to a pub and had a few drinks. When I came out the moon was high and full and the sky was clear and light beyond the treetops. The streets were almost deserted.

There was time yet to go to the dance, but when I reached the Pavilion I didn't feel like dancing. Inside it was crowded, hot, and noisy, and the band's rhythm was poor. It looked as if there was nothing left to do except return to the billet and read in bed. I started back, walking slowly along the path on the cliff above the beach.

Suddenly there was the rising, falling, rising, falling wail of sirens across the night air. I heard an aeroplane low overhead in a gliding dive, its engine cut off, and while I was looking up trying to see it against the moon a flare fell on the beach below the cliffs. Suddenly it was alight around where I was standing. Just as I started to run another flare came down in the street behind the houses that fronted the cliffs, and from overhead came the rushing sound of bombs, and almost at once the dull heavy *boomf* as several fell a few blocks away. Then again there was the long, high, far, faint sound of one coming down, then the rushing sound growing larger like the approach of a subway train, then the dull *boomf* and flash of fire and dust above a row of trees ahead, while I felt the shock run along the ground under-

21

neath me. Ahead I saw four incendiary bombs fall in a row, directly across the path. On both sides of the path was sand covered with thick gorse. I lay flat in the gorse, and looking up, waiting for the sound of the next bomb, I saw two figures lying flat in the sand behind the bush next to me.

It was a clear moonlight night and I could see easily in the bushes. Diana was lying on her stomach with her head turned towards me and her eyes closed. Pat was lying beside her. I called, 'Hey! Pat. Hey! Diana!' Diana opened her eyes. They recognized me and, though they were only ten feet away, they raised their hands and waved. Pat got up, and kneeling on one knee looked around, then up at the sky.

'I don't know about you two,' she called, 'but I'm getting out of here. There's a shelter just down the road.'

'Wait a minute, Pat,' Diana said.

'If you're coming, come along. I'm going to make a dash for it.'

'It's safe here,' I said. 'It's all right. They're heading across town.'

'No, thanks,' said Pat. 'Are you coming, Diana?'

'Go on. Diana'll be all right here,' I said.

'All right. Only this place isn't my idea of where to be when they come out to cross the coast.'

You could hear the guns firing beyond the town.

'Take your choice,' I said. 'Safe now or maybe safe later. Or maybe not at all.'

'Safe all the time in a shelter, thank you. Cheerio, you two,' said Pat.

'Really, Pat. It's all right here,' Diana said.

Pat ran quickly up the street. I rolled on my back and watched her disappear under the trees at the next corner.

'Maybe she knows what's she's talking about,' I said. 'What are you doing here? Thought you were home.'

'My brave airman. Nonsense. I've been caught near here before. It's actually quite safe. I was just out walking with Pat.'

'Lightning strikes only one angle, I suppose?'

'You are scared, aren't you? Don't worry, you'll get used to it. I was frightfully frightened at first. They won't fall near here again.'

'What are they after here?'

'God only knows. Jerry doesn't. Probably the local maternity ward.'

'Do you ever shoot any down?'

'Sometimes. We got one the other night when I was on duty. Frightfully exciting.'

'I can imagine. Did it catch fire?'

'Blew up right in front of us. Terribly lucky.'

'I can imagine how the people in it felt too.'

'Not any different from you, darling,' she said ironically, 'if their load got a direct hit on you.'

'Wish there was some nice place we could go. No shooting. No nothing.'

'That is a nice dream. But it's nice here in the gorse too. Look at the ocean now.'

'I'm looking. There's a flare on it.'

'Stop complaining, Mack,' she smiled. 'Consider the moonlight.' She laughed. 'It is lovely even if a bit unhealthy just now.'

'Okay,' I said. 'Moonlight now under consideration.'

I looked at her face and eyes. I saw her lying close to me in the dark. Her body was long and I felt her lying against me. I put one arm around her shoulder and pulled her over close and she moved easily under my arm. I told myself I was a fool for feeling lonely and scared.

'Hello,' she said. She was smiling and my arms were around her shoulders. She looked up at me.

'Well?' I said.

She did not say anything, smiled, then moved her face closer to me.

I looked at her face, very close to me now. She closed her eyes and I put my arms all the way around her, and then with all of her hard against me, long and soft, her shoulders, legs, and throat, I kissed her slowly and on the mouth. She did not move for a long time. Then she opened her eyes and drew back her head and looked up at me. A slow smile came to her face.

'God, I am a bitch truly,' she said.

What the hell, I thought; it's her game, she started it, now she wants to moralize out of it.

'I don't care,' I said, and felt that, for me, I had said the wrong thing. For her it might be a game. For me with her it was not. But what the hell, if she were going to moralize out of it she didn't even have the courage of her convictions that she had voiced the first evening I met her, so now make her play up to her rôle.

'I know you don't,' she said, 'but I do. I don't know what it is.' She shook her head thoughtfully. 'It's just that I'm lonely and damn foolish tonight, that's all.' Then suddenly she laughed. 'It is pleasant though, isn't it?'

23

We laughed together in the dark.

'Come here,' I said. 'Come here and be pleasant then, and stop thinking.'

'No.'

'Look,' I said, 'you're a lovely girl. Hardly know you. I know this sounds damn foolish. Schoolboy line and all that. But you are lovely. But I'll be damned if I'll tell you you're lovely if you don't want to be told.' I was serious. Maybe too much so. Maybe it was being scared for a moment in the raid. Maybe it was only the feeling of kissing her, talking now from inside me. Maybe I was in love with her. I didn't know.

'I don't mind you telling me in the least. You are nice, Mack. Only please don't get serious. I couldn't stand that. Not now, anyway.'

'Don't worry,' I said. 'I won't. It is nice here, isn't it?' I looked down at the beach, white in the moonlight, and the moonlit sea beyond, and felt a cool breeze on my face and held my arm tightly around her. The guns had stopped firing and from far away came the sound of the all-clear.

'I say,' she said, 'we better go.'

'Wait a moment.'

'No. Really. Pat'll be wondering what happened.'

'Let her wonder.'

I put both arms around her, and when she lowered her head I took one hand away from on her back and took her chin in my hand and lifted her head. Her eyes were closed and her head went back and away from me, but I held her close and her head came forward again and I kissed her for what seemed a long time. She was quiet against me and after a while she put her arms around me and held me close and her lips became softer and opened a little. Then her eyes opened and she drew back her head and looked away towards the beach.

'Oh, hell,' she said. She shook her head. 'I shouldn't do this. I promised him I wouldn't. It's just that no one's held me or kissed me for such a long time. You don't know what it's like living among girls all the time. You can't even begin to imagine it.'

'I can imagine,' I said, and laughed.

She looked back at me. Her face serious.

'You don't know what I mean, do you?' she said gravely. 'We were so damn happy together while he was here, and now he's gone away and I haven't seen him for nine months. He can't get leave and neither can I. It's hell. Honestly.'

'You don't have to make excuses to me for all this,' I said. 'It's all right with me, however it happens. I'm just lucky, that's all.'

'Don't talk like that. You'll never be lucky with me.'

'I don't mean that,' I said.

She laughed. 'I didn't mean that either, what you're thinking. I didn't mean to misinterpret you. I must be tired. I'm getting irritable,' she smiled.

'I think we're both tired. Come on.'

'Oh, hell,' she said, walking. 'I hope you won't take this seriously. It was good fun though, I'm glad you were here to-night. I feel better now. I needed someone to kiss me. Someone nice.'

'I'm not particularly nice.'

'Well, no matter now,' she laughed. 'But you were nice when you kissed me.'

At her billet she would not kiss me. She said good night and I went on to the hotel. Ed was sitting out in front on the steps smoking a cigarette. He saw me coming up the steps.

'Hey, where were you tonight?' he asked.

'Had a few beers with Diana.'

'My God, don't tell me you're going back there again. You should have seen the lovely stuff I bumped into in an air-raid shelter. Tomorrow night – '

'No, thanks.'

'Christ!' he said. 'The young man's in love. This is awful. The young man goes soft on us.'

'Okay,' I said. 'So the young man goes soft. So what?'

'Forget it, Mack,' he said. 'Don't get sore. I was only kidding.' He laughed and slapped me on the back.

'Come on, let's go to bed,' I said. I got up.

'No,' he said. 'I'm going to sit out here a while.' He looked thoughtfully up at the sky and the moon.

'What's the matter?'

He blew out a jet of smoke. 'I was just thinking,' he said. 'Wondering how those Jerries felt coming in here tonight with everybody pranging away at them.'

'Don't worry,' I said. 'You'll find out soon enough.'

He sat on the steps smoking. I went on upstairs to bed. I lay in bed lonely and thought of home.

CHAPTER FIVE

Finally one day Ed and I heard we were posted to an Operational Training Unit for heavy bombers, and that we were taking the train out that night to an aerodrome near Oxford. After parade I went around to a phone box near the hotel and called Diana's billet, but she was not in. She was out on a gun site up the coast, said the voice on the other end of the wire. No, no one knew when she would be in. I phoned after lunch and she was still out. That evening, an hour before train time, I phoned and this time I recognized Pat's voice. I said hello and asked for Diana.

'She isn't well,' Pat said. 'She's upstairs lying down.'

'Tell her we're leaving tonight and I want to speak to her. Will you, please?'

'I'll see.'

'Thanks a lot, Pat.'

I heard Pat walk away, then in a few minutes someone else's heels tapping along a hall floor and then Diana's voice. It sounded strange, very tired and very far away, like a bad connection on a long-distance call.

'I just wanted to say good-bye, Diana. We're pulling out tonight. Just wondered if you could come down to the station.'

'I can't, Mack,' she said. 'I just can't.'

'Only be for a moment. I would like to see you before we go away.'

'No. I'm sorry. I can't. I just couldn't.'

Something was wrong all right with her voice. She sounded choked and almost on the verge of her voice breaking.

'What's the matter?' I asked.

'Nothing. Really. You're going tonight?'

'Yes. We're going up near Oxford. Say, what's the trouble?'

'Oxford?' Her voice was vague, flat, as if she did not even know she was speaking.

'Yes, we'll have to get together on leave.'

'Yes, yes, all right, Mack.'

'Diana.'

And then she was crying, her voice all gone, sobbing into the phone. 'Diana,' he called. 'Oh, God, Mack,' she said, crying, choking. 'He's been killed. I know he has.'

'John? When? Oh, hell, I am sorry, Diana.'

'I just heard from London. He went down on Trondheim last night. Oh, God, Mack! He's gone!' she cried.

'Maybe he bailed out.' Oh sure, I thought, and maybe he didn't.

What could I say? I'm sorry. No, there was nothing I could say. Nothing. Absolutely nothing that would help. But I went on talking, making words that were only meaningless sounds:

'Diana. I am sorry. Is there anything I can do?'

'No,' she said. 'It's all right, really, it's all right, Mack.'

'If there's anything I can do – '

'No,' she said. 'There's nothing anybody can do.'

'I have to run, Diana.' I felt like a fool, unable to say or do anything that would help her now.

'Good-bye, Mack,' she said.

'Good-bye, Diana. I'll send my address. Be sure and write.'

'Yes, all right. Good-bye, Mack.'

'Good-bye, Diana.'

She hung up. I went outside and stood on the sidewalk for a long time. Then it was time to go. I went back to the hotel, got my bags, and got in the column forming up in front of the hotel and marched down to the station in the evening rain that was beginning to fall. I couldn't have looked so well standing in the ranks waiting to get on the train. Outside the rain was falling and I thought of Diana, alone, crying back in her room, and John, whoever he was, somewhere in Norway either dead or alive, drowned, smashed, or burned, wandering in the hills or hiding. Ed was standing next to me.

'Hey, what's the matter with you?' he asked.

'Diana's boy copped it on Trondheim last night.'

'Thought you were her boy, my friend?' He laughed. 'Say, what're you kicking about? You're here and he isn't.'

'Shut up.'

I took off my kit-bag, threw it in the aisle on the train, and found a seat in a crowded compartment. Ed came in and sat down.

'You sore?' he asked.

'No, forget it.'

'Yes, that is rotten luck. Hope we're luckier.'

'We're not the first ones to hope,' I said. 'Plenty younger than us did plenty of hoping.'

27

'Don't be depressing,' he said thoughtfully. He had considered bad luck for the first time. Then: 'Yeah,' he repeated, musing. 'I guess you're right. Plenty of guys have.' His voice ceased.

The train did not move from the station for what seemed a long time. I sat in the carriage and looked out the window at the signs on the station wall advertising cough syrup and Austin, Reed tailored uniforms. Maybe he bailed out. Sure, he bailed out. Oh, sure.

The train gave a jerk and moved slowly out of the station. Beyond the town I looked back and saw the serrated roofs of all the big white hotels. I went up to London in the rain, looking out at the wheat now high and green in June, and the poppies red in the fields, and the rain falling steadily across the hills. I changed trains in London, bought a newspaper, read and slept and got off in the dark at Oxford. It was still raining and there was a lorry waiting at the station to take Ed and me to the aerodrome.

Only a week passed before Ed and I were flying together in the same crew.

CHAPTER SIX

That evening on the train to Oxford, how long ago it seemed then to final training days in Canada, to a December when another train ran across the cold, empty, snowy stillness of Saskatchewan, the steam from the engine hanging in great motionless plumes over the ditches beside the tracks, dissolving slowly beyond the level ground of snow, and I rolled smoothly on, watching the dead frame-towns of Manitoba pass, and on into the warm station in the dark at Winnipeg, and that night, in the dark, with the window shade up, I looked out into the fleeing countryside of starlit snow and moon-drenched snowy fields, all empty and still; then later in the dark at unfrozen rivers running fast under the bridges in the pine country, the forest's jagged crests now dark on both sides of the track. I was excited, far from home and young; there was a poker game in the next berth, and in the morning the forests were gone and dawn showed the skyline of Toronto, a dim serrated line of building tops in morning's faint grey haze.

In the afternoon the sun came out and I was on the train again, Quebec fields on all sides cold and snowy, the fine air full of sunlight, and then I saw the St Lawrence open and fast, taking glints of sunlight in spaces between chunks of ice, and far off high along the river I saw rising brown cliffs, and Quebec city on the tilted plateau, and the Château Frontenac silhouetted big against the fading western sky; and that night in the dark, among the sound of many sleighs' cold creaking runners I climbed the cliff's dark line of a foot-trodden path, hard packed, through the snow to another station and another train. There were always trains, and waiting in cold depots with my kit-bags heavy, and then running among troops and air crew for seats on the train. But then that was almost over for a while. For in the morning there was a town far up the river, and I got off and stood in an unheated depot among a lot of old Frenchmen huddled about a single cold stove. The air outside was filled with wind-blown snow, and I stood in the station, my feet numb, my face feeling burned with cold, while I waited for a lorry to come and take me to gunnery school two miles away. Ed was gone, sent away to another school, and in the station another airman came up to me and grunted something about a cigarette. I had none, and he went away and sat in a corner, slapping his arms, stamping his feet. Still the lorry did not appear. And I stood waiting in the cold.

And the next day, and for many days after, I was again living in a barrack-room full of twenty men, with snow piled against the windows, the air full of the stale stench of coal gas. And now I was not quite so sorry for myself so often. Now I could not quit and yet I hated to go on.

I slept in a top bunk of two iron bunks, and in the evening, when it was too cold and blowy to go out to town, they played cards on the wooden table beside my bed. No one ever won much, and I was lucky only once. It was here in Canada I first met Bijur. He was husky, cut his hair short, and had played football at three different colleges in the States. Almost everybody was there for a personal reason, bored, out of a job, too lazy to work hard, and a few romantic enough to believe it was all going to be something out of the movies. In the mornings, in the cold wet air that blew off the St Lawrence river, I lined up in two ranks to march off to classes. At first it was too cold to fly and none of the aircraft was serviceable, and in the endless days of snow, cold, eating, sleeping, and classes, with all the roads to the village blocked, and each night only a crowded room filled with the smell of coal gas and sweat, all grew to dislike each other and, to break their boredom, bickered, and finally often quarreled openly. So in the mornings, when the two ranks, heads bent against the wind, hands clasped over ears, ran gasping along the trodden paths between head-high drifted snow, Bijur and a friend from California amused themselves tripping classmates in the ranks, pushing everybody into the deep snow. Everybody tired and cold and still hungry and one morning tired and cold and still half-asleep, I was pushed, and I pushed back and flung Bijur on his back on to the hard ice-packed path. He got up raging.

'You sonofabitch!' he said. 'What the hell do you think you're doing?' He stood, feet apart, his fists clenched, his eyes hard, flashing.

'Pushed you. What the hell do you think it was?'

He got set and I thought he was going to swing. He was bigger than me through the neck and shoulders. I knew I couldn't beat him.

'What the hell,' I said. 'You pushed me first.'

'Don't be childish,' he said. 'I was only fooling, and you got sore.'

'Well, we're even then. Now, what the hell are you sore about?'

'You goddamn bastard!' He was still angry at being humiliated by being tossed on his back. And it had all been a fluke. I was certain he had slipped as I grabbed him and pushed. 'Do you want to fight here?' and again he got set.

'Now who's being childish?'

'I'm going to kill you, Norton!'

He looked that angry too.

'Oh, for Christ's sake, relax.' But I was afraid of him and didn't want to fight. His anger and the sudden almost insane glint in his eyes frightened me.

But in the end I had to fight, standing in the small square room used for a coat room, the window frosted and some of the class standing in the doorway, swinging and missing, tearing his hand away from my collar while he tried to hold me up close and get at my face with his free hand. And then I was free, only I was back up against the wall, sliding down my back on to the floor, where he had butted me with his head. And I was on my hands and knees getting up when he caught me with his right hand. I saw it coming, arcing up low from behind his hip, and I went down a little on one knee to move to one side out of the way, but it wasn't far enough and suddenly for an instant I saw the fist up close. It didn't seem to be moving towards me and then I was

30

out flat, with first the explosion and sparks in front of my eyes and then suddenly nothing at all. Just suddenly everything all gone, and later a black eye in the morning.

There were many fights during those winter weeks when the snow kept us indoors.

'Keerist!' everybody said. 'If we could only get overseas. Get this crap finished here.'

And during the days, with the snow piled high around the classroom windows, and the room always too hot or too cold, and seventeen faces around the tables that were set out horseshoe-shape about the small square classroom, with the corporal gunnery instructor squeaking instructions from behind his bifocal glasses, I wondered where everybody would be a year from now. New Zealanders, Canadians, Americans. Young, old, keen, and indifferent. And the Browning machine-gun parts lying black and oily and shiny on the tables, while the corporal's voice reiterated dully, above heads that tried not to nod, 'Third-position stoppage, gentlemen . . .' And Bijur would be aiming a piece of orange peel at somebody across the room, or Harris, bald, all-knowing, just out of the hospital with clap, would have his hand partly raised, always ready to debate any points with the instructor. The New Zealanders were all competing with the Canadians for the highest marks in the class. The Americans didn't care. They were all escaping from something in the States – a job, a wife, responsibilities. Everybody had learned how to express what they could not understand themselves – namely, why and whom they were fighting. All read the papers and magazines, so everybody knew the answers when anyone asked them why they were fighting.

Nobody had to think. The press did that for you. So no one ever told a bunkmate his real reason for enlisting, but in the barracks none were fools enough to use newspaper quotations as their reasons for going to war.

And the days passed. Cold, dreary, and ceaseless.

Christmas that year was not home, nor like any other Christmas. It was not the curtains drawn and the fire warming the living-room and the coloured decorations on the Christmas tree in the corner beside the living-room book-case. Nor was it my Aunt Mary, sitting, laughing, under the Christmas tree while her hands scrabbled at the bright wrappings of presents and her laughter filled the warm room. It was not a Christmas like that because now there was no time for home. There was time only for the

31

holidays in Rochester, New York, close enough for a three-day journey, all we were allowed at Christmas, and there a tall, silent blonde girl I did not know, in a country club bar full of people I did not know, who were nice to me only because I was there on invitation from a college room-mate. So that was New Year's Eve and Christmas, a bar stool and too many scotches, and a blonde blind date who kept asking who I knew at Yale and Groton, and other girls in their long dresses and well-cleaned faces and white ties who made remarks about RAF because they didn't like me in uniform among so many tail coats, and me wondering, where? why am I here? how? what for? Then the tall blonde, bored and glum, had gone away with friends to another ballroom. And later, drunk and alone, the party over, the cool sheets and pillow under me in the hotel room, telling myself in confusion: that I was a fool then, that I was fighting for the good of man, and knowing I got that one out of a book too, and that that was only excusing running away from my job and boredom, knowing that I wasn't a crusader, and feeling the cause was right, only feeling it was all more of humanity's foolishness. What the hell was I doing here? Alone in a hotel room in Rochester on New Year's Eve?

Then later it was good to be back at gunnery school in the barracks again and Bijur, sitting upon his bed, yelling, 'We're going overseas! Orders are through!'

'Gwan! You're dreamin',' said one Canadian.

'You're nuts! I saw the papers. We're moving out. It's all over. Exams tomorrow,' Bijur said. The odour of coal gas filled the room. Outside the wind blew and everybody sat on top of their bunks listening. The Canadian curled his lip in a dubious manner.

'You're full of crap, Bijur,' he said.

'I sneaked in the Wing Co.'s office, saw the papers. Wanna come down with me tonight and make sure yourself?'

'Okay. Only you shoot enough bull around here for ten guys.'

'Fourteen days' leave! We all get fourteen day's leave!'

As though still not believing, yet weighing his own doubt, the Canadian shrugged his shoulders. 'Oh, well,' he said.

'Hot dog!' somebody yelled. 'Fourteen days! England, here I come!'

'I still think you're fulla bull, Bijur,' the Canadian said.

But Bijur was right. He had sneaked in the Wing-Co.'s office, and the next day there were the exams, and the Canadians were highest in the class, and the New Zealanders were jealous because there was only one commission given and a Canadian won it. And a month later we sailed for England.

How long ago all that seemed on the train that night on the way to Operational Training Unit.

CHAPTER SEVEN

When supper was finished in the sergeants' mess at Operational Training Unit there was a crowd at the bar and in the lounge. It was the same every night. Ed and I bought beers at the bar and went into the lounge to watch the evening dice game. They were playing on a small card table and those who couldn't see over the shoulders of those around the table were standing on chairs looking over the shoulders of the players. It was a cloudy, cool July evening, and looking out one of the mess windows I could see on the aerodrome the aircraft my crew was scheduled, on their last training flight, to fly that night. I drank a few more beers, watched the game a while, then went to my room in a wing off the mess, put on my flying boots and flying sweater, and cycled across the aerodrome to the dispersal hut. Inside, everybody was talking, standing around the navigator's table. I talked with my pilot. Everybody was waiting for the weather to clear, he said. It was a bloody hell of a night to send anybody out according to the meteorological report. Cloud was seven-tenths, with severe icing. He said there probably wouldn't be any flying, but we had to stand by in case it cleared. They were always expecting it to clear and it never did. Same old story, he said; besides the kite we had was a hell of a ropey job. He hoped the weather wouldn't clear so we wouldn't have to take this ropey aircraft assigned to the crew.

'It's suicide landing on a night like this,' I said.

The pilot shook his head. He was afraid of the flight commander.

'You want to get us all in trouble?' he asked Ed.

'No, just trying to keep us all out of trouble.'

I went outside and got in the lorry that took the crew out to the aircraft. Sitting in the driver's cab with the pilot, waiting for the final word from the Control Tower, the pilot said he didn't want to go any more than anyone else, but what the bloody hell could he do about it! He couldn't just walk into Control and say he wasn't going because it was a hell of a night for flying. I said I thought it could be explained to them reasonably. No, he said, there was never anything reasonable about the Air Force. They had a quota of crews to train ready to send out by a set date and if the weather killed a few it was just too bad. If this weather killed you, he said, they figured you wouldn't be any good on ops anyway. Kershaw, in the back of the lorry, yelled that if this weather killed us we wouldn't have to be any good for anything anyway, and did we think there was a flight commander among the angels who would be easy about granting forty-eight-hour passes so one could go to hell on weekends? Just then the flight commander came out of the dispersal hut and ran over to the truck in the rain. We were to go to our aircrafts, he said. Control had phoned and everybody was still scheduled to fly. The gears ground into place and the truck rolled out in the rain along the runway towards the aircraft, and I looked at the flight commander running back to the dispersal hut in the rain.

At the aircraft I went back into the rear turret to check on everything. Everything seemed all right. I came out and sat on the floor in the rest position with the crew. The radio operator sat with his helmet and headphones on. I could hear rain on the metal fuselage. Nobody spoke for a while. Just sat and looked thoughtfully at the floor and wished they could smoke or that they were in their rooms or in a pub.

'Which runway we using?' asked Kershaw.

'North to south,' said the pilot.

'Bloody short run on a night like this, isn't it?'

'Hell of a cross-wind too.'

'Nice, eh?'

'Oh, damn nice. I think they'll scrub it though.'

'Really think so?'

'What's the trouble? Getting shaky?'

'Sure, why not?' Kershaw laughed. 'What am I supposed to do – put on a big not-worried act?'

'Ah, shut up, you guys,' Ed said. 'What the hell you worrying about?'

'For Crissake, relax, will you?' I said, feeling nervous myself.

'Why don't we play pretty games or something?' said Gibbon, the bomb aimer. Grinning, he glanced around at all the faces.

'We could read a series of inspirational editorials or some of Churchill's speeches,' Kershaw said. 'And feel heroic now.' The pilot laughed. I felt better.

'Mack, do you know how many crews they lost there last winter?' Kershaw asked.

'No. What are you trying to do – make us feel worse with a few statistics?'

'Come on,' said the pilot. 'Quit your beefing. You got yourselves into this and now there's damn-all you can do about getting out.'

'We can get killed, a nice quick form of discharge,' said Gibbon. 'Besides I did not get myself into this,' he smiled. 'Brother suckers, I was drafted.' He sat there grinning.

Kershaw was smiling. 'Not a patriot in the house.' He clapped his hands to his head, shaking his head from side to side. 'If only Hitler could hear us now,' he laughed.

'Call Control, will you, Gibbon, and see if there's any "gen" on whether we're going to fly?' asked Broughton, the pilot.

Gibbon nodded. He stood up and went forward to the radio table.

'I'm going back in the turret,' I said. 'So long.'

'So long,' said Ed. He stooped and went forward to the front turret.

I sat in the turret and looked out at the rain and darkness. Flames from the twin rows of flare pots that marked the runway flickered across the field. It was one hell of a night. I tested the guns for elevation and depression. They were all right. I would not need them probably, but you never knew. There was always the possibility of being followed by an intruder.

The intercom crackled and buzzed.

'Okay, Broughton,' Gibbon called. 'You can run up the engines. Flying's still on.'

I turned on the light in the turret and looked at the ammunition belts where they fed into the gun. All were in place. I switched the light off and looked out, on both sides other aircraft were starting up, I could see the bursts of flame from their exhausts. After a moment my own aircraft began to tremble and over the intercom there came the sound of the engines starting.

'Okay, Starboard,' said Broughton.

'That port engine,' I heard Kershaw say. It sounded as if he were addressing Broughton. There was no answer.

'Port engine boost, Jeff,' Kershaw yelled.

There was the splutter of the starboard engine starting, then more spluttering, metallic sucking sounds, then a sudden blasting roar as the engine turned over and started.

'How about that port-engine boost?' Kershaw asked.

'It's all right,' Broughton said.

'Doesn't look all right to me.'

'Bloody hell!' Broughton raised his voice, irritated. 'It's okay. Forget it!'

'Don't go if it isn't working perfectly,' I said.

Broughton was excited and nervous now.

'Anybody doesn't want to come can get the hell out!' he yelled angrily. No one said anything.

Down the field aircraft were taxi-ing around to the runway to take off. I saw their wing-tip navigation lights blinking in the rain. An Aldis lamp by the central tower was flashing a green light.

'All set, you blokes,' said Broughton. 'I'm going to taxi out. Kershaw, can you see anything on that side, old man?' His voice sounded better now, changed.

'Okay. Go ahead,' Kershaw said. I could picture them standing in the nose trying to see out in the rain. The aircraft started to move. Then suddenly: 'What's that?' Broughton yelled.

'Go on,' Kershaw said. 'It's only a tractor.' I felt the aircraft slowly moving, swinging around now.

'Bloody hell, I can't see a damn thing,' Broughton said. 'This windshield's covered with rain.' The aircraft stopped.

'Go on,' said Kershaw. 'Straight ahead. I can see. It's okay.'

Then the aircraft rolled slowly around the perimeter track and stopped behind another aircraft, waiting to take off. In a few minutes I saw it turn into the wind and go rushing along between the flare pots and take off. Then it was gone and Broughton was turning on to the entrance of the runway. I didn't know anything had happened to the aircraft ahead until I saw a flash of flame on the far side of the field. In the sound of my engines there was no sound of the explosion. Turning the turret I saw a fan of flame against the dark sky. Whoever it was had blown up on crashing. Broughton told everybody to wait. Maybe flying was scrubbed. I looked across the field at the burning wreckage and waited for a message from flying Control.

'Anything doing?' I asked after some time. No one answered. Then Gibbon's voice, 'Think we'll fly now?'

The aircraft did not move, engines idling.

'Sure,' someone said.

'All set, Broughton?' Kershaw asked.

The Aldis lamp near the Control Tower flashed a green light.

'Sure. What the hell,' said Broughton. 'Sure.'

I depressed the guns, so there was room to get braced, and

opened the turret doors: if anything happened I would not be caught with the doors jammed. The Aldis lamp near the Control Tower flashed a green light. The engine's roar deepened quickly.

'Okay, Mack?' Broughton asked. Then, 'All set, you chaps? Here we go.' I felt the engines suddenly accelerate. The fuselage trembled, shook. There was the sensation of moving a little.

Then the aircraft was rushing along between the flare pots. I watched the number of flares increase on both sides until there was a long twin row behind, then I felt the tail rise and I was riding high, looking out between the guns, knowing we weren't airborne yet, still rushing on between the flares. God, why doesn't it lift? Suddenly I was scared. I saw the long diminishing length of the flare path behind, I grabbed the butt end of the guns and got braced. Maybe nothing would happen. In my mind I saw the burning wreckage on the edge of the field. God, would this aircraft ever come off the ground? Darkness and flares rushed past on both sides.

'Blast!' Broughton panted. 'It won't climb! Hell! Blast!'

The aircraft bumped, rose, touched ground again, rose slightly again.

'Watch it! Watch it!' shouted Kershaw.

'Blast! Oh, blast!' Broughton yelled, panting.

I crouched and got my back braced against the wall of the turret, then I felt the aircraft rise from the ground, heard one of the engines miss, splutter, catch, then miss again, then sinking slowly. 'Oh, God!' one of the wings slowly going down, thinking terrified. 'Oh, God!' with the darkness rushing past underneath, then Broughton's yelling, 'We're going to prang! Get set! We're going to prang!' Then the shocking, tearing, jouncing impact, with the guns and glass perspex vanishing, everything whirling, roaring, faster and faster, and blurred rushing streaks of light, and then a smashing blow on the head and another on the back and across the shoulders. Then going up and up, bodiless, no feeling, no sight, only darkness and then something tearing at my face, knowing suddenly branches of a tree were clawing at my neck and bare hands and I was still falling, thumping. Oh, God, God, I'm dying, this is it. Then falling ceased and I opened my eyes, or rather I was no longer in a whirling, rushing darkness. I saw myself kneeling on the ground. I felt outside my body, kneeling looking over at myself. I stood up. On the other side of the field a jagged crest of flame made a roaring crackling sound. Then I heard the ammunition cans exploding. I started to run and fell down. I heard a big explosion, saw a pink flame mushroom suddenly in the middle of the white flame and the white flame expand. There was the steady crackling of the ammunition, and then I was standing again, running. I fell over something in the dark and reached out and felt something dark and lumpy and smelled burning flesh. I rolled it over and saw it was Ed. His flying suit was smoking and charred, and in a flash of flame from the burning aircraft I saw his hair was burnt off and part of his face was black. He lay on his back, his eyes open, and part of his nose gone.

'Ed!' I yelled, and grabbed him by the shoulders, 'Ed!' knowing he was dead. I held him by the shoulders and raised him a little off the ground, as if there were something I might do to help him. His head fell back and his eyes rolled white. He was very dead, and I knelt there and looked at the aircraft burning. Then after a long moment thinking started again, and I let go of him, stood up and ran towards the aircraft. The grass around it was on fire and I felt the heat from the melting fuselage. God, oh, God, why doesn't the crash wagon come? They're burning to death in there. I saw the flames grow higher, felt the heat, knew I could not get any closer. Where the hell was the crash wagon? I ran across the field, aware of the rain for the first time. My clothes were soaked, my face was wet, and I fell in a ditch and couldn't get up. I told myself I was all right, yet I had no desire to move. I lay in the rain and heard the crash wagon go clanging past on the road above. Go on, part of my mind said, get up, go on. I lay perfectly still in the mud and didn't care. I felt myself passing out and tried to hold my eyes open with my fingers. They were burning to death back there in the aircraft. All I had to do was stand up and yell. Somebody would come. I raised my head, opened my mouth on no sound, and heard someone hurrying behind me. Turning, somebody put the beam of a flashlight in my eyes. I got to my knees and stood up. They were back there burning to death. I moved, stumbled, someone caught me. I pushed them away.

'They're burning to death,' I yelled.

'Come on, feller. They've had it. The crash wagon's trying to get them out. Are you all right?'

'Get them out.'

'Don't worry. The crash killed them. How'd it happen? Are you sure you're all right?'

'Yes. I'm all right. Can't they get any of them out?'

'No. Come on.'

'Ed's over there.'

'I know. We found him.'

An oxygen bottle exploded. I must have jerked and stopped. 'Come on, Mack,' said a voice. I recognized one of the medical attendants. 'Come on,' said the voice.

'It's all right. Come on, Mack.'

'Maybe they're still alive.'

'Come on, Mack. They've had it.'

'You sure?'

'They're dead. Come on. I know.'

'Where we going?'

'Come on. You'll be all right in the ambulance.'

I didn't remember saying anything. Later they told me all the things I said, and how I wouldn't move.

'You bastards,' I said. 'Where've you been? You haven't even tried to get them out of there.'

'Come on, Mack,' said the attendant. 'It won't do any good standing here. They all had it.'

The ambulance, reflected in the glare of the fire, stood on the side of the road. I looked back. Small dark figures were running around the fire. I could not see the shape of the aircraft. Only fire. Someone said part of the wing and cowling were in the ditch up the road. I sat on the running board of the ambulance. Someone put a blanket around my shoulders.

The medical officer came up, looking tired and wet. 'Is this the only one? Why isn't he inside on a stretcher?' He bent down, put one hand on my shoulder, 'Are you all right?'

I did not look up. I could not move.

The doctor bundled the blankets around me.

A terrible chill came suddenly over me. I felt myself falling forward off the running board. The medical officer was shouting something in the rain. There was only the faint sound of the rain and in it his voice. Then everything whirled and rushed and turned dark, streaked and flecked with light, and I felt the blanket slipping off my shoulders and myself falling very easily and nicely into a kind of dark nothingness. It seemed lovely to be passing out.

CHAPTER EIGHT

That summer and fall they sent me to stay at a rest home, where I tried to stop seeing every now and then the picture of the crash and Ed's face. I stayed in bed most of the time because they said I was still suffering from shock, but some nights when the picture would come often to my mind I couldn't sleep at all. Often there were many nights like this, and no matter how hard I tried to think of something else, when the picture started to come it was no use.

I lived in a long room and the windows faced the sea, but at night, after the black-out curtains were drawn and the lights were out, there was nothing to look at, only to lie there knowing the picture was going to come and perhaps by thinking of something else for a while I could put off its coming. And so I would lie there thinking like this: Time I went swimming, long ago. Lake Calhoun. Seven years old. Hot July day. And everybody brought their lunch, and my bathing suit was too big for me because my sister wore it the year before. And Mary scolding me for staying out in the sun too long, and then the water blisters, painful and long and white, hanging on my arms and back like small withered dugs.

The yellow sand and the blue water and the white fat clouds and the sun. '25, '26. '27, '28, '29. Years going by. Holding my sister's hand and running all the way to school in the morning, and her white knee socks and straight hair, and always high grades in all her subjects, and running, me, holding her hand, trying to keep up with her. And my first bicycle, red and white, mine all that summer until someone stole it. And where was a letter from Diana? I had written. Why didn't she write? Where was she? Diana. My Diana. Where was she and why didn't she write? Diana, why, oh, why can't you write? Why do I have to be here and you wherever you are?

Diana! But thinking of her was almost as bad as the picture, but I could turn off thinking of her. I could feel myself starting to think about her and I would let my mind fill up with long ago again. Not that I forgot her. Only that I put her in the back of my mind, aware she was still there, but somehow turning off the loneliness for her.

And then I would think of my mother, and of how she looked, of a summer in a long-ago dead time, and she was wearing a blue silk dress and her hair was piled high on top of her head and it was Sunday afternoon. Oh, and they had me in short pants and my sister in white organdie, and mother saying, 'Now, Mack, it's your turn to ride in the back. Mary rode there last Sunday,' and then she would drive around the lakes. And how many thousand days ago was that? Sitting up high in a Hudson Super Six and mother's hat covered with artificial berries and flowers, while I held a toy aeroplane out the window and watched the propeller whirl around in the summer air.

Short pants and the story of Little Red Hen in a brown book, and a grey-brick building on a corner that was school, and a boy named John Junkin who could play hockey. Where was he now? That was in fifth grade. And a girl named Dorothy. First girl, and I put water tattoos on her arm and sent her a valentine and she married someone. Where was she? No, my God, don't let it start now. Yes. Hello, Ed. Oh, Christ. No, No. No. But maybe they didn't burn. Maybe the crash killed them.

Maybe Ed never knew what hit him. Maybe it didn't hurt him at all. And then it would go away and I would be lying in the dark room listening to the bombers on the way over that night, glad I wasn't with them, wishing I were out of the rest home.

And then on some nights that autumn I thought of the time my house caught fire, of my mother standing crying in the snow in the grey first light of morning, with the smoke coming out of the windows, and the crowd standing in the street while the fireman kicked in the windows, and my sister saying, 'Oh, God, my new dress will be a wreck.' But it didn't spoil the dress and the house did not burn down, and two nights later my sister wore her new dress to a party and maybe I would get over this too. Maybe things would return to normal for me. Maybe all this would go away. Just as the house was rebuilt.

Diana. Where are you? Why don't you write? Eh! No! Oh, God, they're burning! Again I was running and then the mornings my temperature, and at night the sound of the bombers going over. How long? Hello, Ed. How are you? You're all right, fellow. OK, Ed. You bet!

Then there were other nights when it was cold in November and there were winters at home to remember. That Christmas morning in Minnesota, the snow stuck to the branches of the

41

trees and the cars went rattling past with chains on, and the snow piled high along the walks and the trains coming home from school, the crowds standing in the smoky station. Christmas holidays. How long ago that was. Would it ever come again? The nurse came along between the beds, taking temperatures. Would you like today's *Mirror*? Here was the new *For Men Only*. Then day was finished and it was dark in the room. September, October, November. I counted the days. Maybe the picture wouldn't come again tonight. It didn't bother me so much any more. It came slower each night. It was fading. Maybe it would go away soon. But even that night it came again when I was almost asleep and I saw Ed burning, lying in the field with his eyes open, and the flame and explosion in the dark.

In December they brought someone new into the ward. The doors opened and whoever he was came in on a stretcher on wheels. He lay in the bed beside me and they put a screen around him. Sometimes he cried in the night. He was a month behind the screens and no one saw him. The nurses would not talk about him and after a while I didn't fear him. One night when there was the sound of engines going over again they came and took the screens away from round his bed and I heard him sit up in the dark. I could hear him drinking a glass of water. I sat up in bed, trying to see him, but it was too dark. He must have seen me leaning towards him in the dark.

'You don't want to see me,' he called from his bed.

'Hello,' I said. 'How are you? Who are you?' I heard him laugh.

'I'm fine – Jocko.'

'How come they finally took your screens away?'

'New face now. Can look at me now.'

'Swell. What time is it?' I asked.

'Don't know,' he said. 'Time. Don't care. Have new face.' He laughed to himself.

'What happened?'

'Plenty,' he said. 'Shot my face off with cannon shell. Twenty thousand feet.'

'Gees,' I said. 'That's tough. Wouldn't it be swell to be home now?' I was thinking of Christmas, wanted to change the subject.

'Home?' he said. 'I have no home.'

I didn't say anything.

'Know what that means?' he asked.

'Sure, I know,' I said glibly.

'My face. Beautiful. To my house. Warsaw. All gone. Don't

42

care. Where you from?' *

'America.'

'What did you get in the war for?'

'Fed up with my job.'

'Fed up?' he said. 'America?'

'Yeah. Fed up. America. You can be fed up in a lot of good places.'

'America. Where I want to go,' he said. 'Do you think they'll come in the war?'

'I don't know. Very few there have any feeling towards it.'

'You?' he asked.

'Sure, but I'm not anxious to die.'

'You have not enough war yet?' he said. 'Are no good in war until you don't care. Then you are good.'

'But not much good then after?'

'You all go back home.'

'Normal. Maybe,' I said.

'Remember things seriously?' he asked. 'Seem funny now, no?'

'You mean like who won a football game or something?'

He laughed. 'Yes. Never do anything but laugh at those people. Funny people now.'

'Maybe we all ought to get married and get very serious again,' I said.

'No,' he said. 'Don't need love any more. No good. A woman, you don't need all time. Only think you do. Don't need love any more. Plenty muscle and hate. Need.'

Then I felt it coming.

'Listen,' I said. 'Please. Just a minute.' I felt the picture coming on again, and I was frightened and started to sweat and feel a little crazy, as if everything were a long way off, all sounds faint.

'What's matter?' he asked.

'Nothing,' I said. Here it was. Ed! No. Oh, Christ, no! Forget it. Here it was and they were all burning. I knew they were all burning and couldn't get out. All of them. All of them back there in the aircraft and the flames were high and they couldn't get out. And no one was helping them. And they were burning. Trapped. I started to run and fell out of bed.

'Here now,' the nurse said, handing me water. 'Here now, drink this,' and she was supporting my head with her hand, and in a little while it went away and I was asleep, and by Christmas it was all gone. And everybody was asking, Had you heard the news? America was in the war. Wasn't it wonderful? Yes, it was wonderful. The Pole in the next bed was sure now the war would be finished in a year. I told him I hoped so. He was going back to his squadron to fly a Spitfire. The pictures did not come at night now. And I could sleep.

New Year's Eve I was on the train going to my squadron. The train was crowded, and I slept on the floor. All other New Year's Eves seemed a long time dead, and I thought of Diana and wondered where she was and why she didn't write. The gay days were gone all right. A lot was gone.

CHAPTER NINE

I could remember the gay days, the days when Bijur was still alive, the days after my class in Canada graduated and I knew there was no going home before I left for England. Home would only be my mother crying, arguing, everybody away at school and wondering what to do with myself. Besides there was New York, and I had plenty of money for two weeks there.

When I arrived in New York I went up to the Savoy-Plaza and got a room. It was on the fifteenth floor, and in the afternoon sunlight, looking out over the buildings' tops across the way, I felt excited. Twelve days of leave! I looked out the window far down on the street below. Where do I go from here, I thought. Below, the late afternoon crowd moved along the street. Lonely hour, workers going home. Twilight. What were they doing at home now? Mother? My sister? House under the elm trees. Twilight in Minnesota . . . New York! Twelve days!

The room was empty. No staying here alone; so unpacked, shaved and washed I went downstairs. The lobby was full of people standing about talking in small groups, and from the cocktail lounge came the steady hum of many voices and a band playing a last year's dance tune. I went into the lounge and found an empty stool at the bar, ordered scotch and water, and sat there wondering what I would do this evening.

At the bar they all knew each other. They were all talking. I was alone all right. Still, it felt good to be alone, away from camp, feeling as if I were on the edge of something quietly exciting. In the beginning of the war I always felt that way on leaves. Sitting at the bar I drank two scotches and ate some of the free popcorn in the bowl in front of me. People from the lobby came in and sat at the tables near the orchestra.

After I had sat there a long time someone tapped me on the shoulder. I turned round. It was Bijur.

'By God,' he said. 'Don't tell me how I knew it was you. What the hell are you doing in New York? The last fling or something?'

'How're you, Bob?'

'My God, how am I he asks! Damn good! Don't tell me you're still sore because of that fight.'

'No,' I said. What else was there to say? I shrugged my shoulders. 'No, guess it was pretty silly. Seems so now.'

'Sure. Sure. Come on. Have a drink.'

He hitched a stool up beside mine and called the bartender over.

'Just try and make me sore at anybody,' he said. 'Everything is wonderful. We're on leave.'

I told the bartender, 'Two scotches.'

'You know what?' Bob asked.

'No. What? You make it sound interesting enough.'

'Interesting? My God, you bet! You know what I'm going to do on this leave? Interesting? By God, you don't know the half of it! Drink and make love! You looked like the last rose of summer when I came in.'

'What the hell. I was just trying to think of something to do.'

'Love and liquor!' Bob lifted his glass. 'God bless 'em!'

I saw two girls, coming in through the door, stop and look about for a table. I turned for a better look. They were attractive all right.

'I give you the brunette,' said Bob.

I tried to catch the dark one's eye.

'Don't you think this long-distance approach is a failure?'

I caught the dark one's eye.

'Maybe I'm wrong,' said Bob. 'But not for long.'

He got up and went over to them. I sat on the high stool and watched them talk. The girls laughed and shook their heads. Bob came back smiling. I was ordering another drink.

'Any luck?'

'Luck? By God, yes. Just turned down by the two best-looking married women in New York.'

'What happened? You seemed to be doing all right.'

'Yes,' he said bitterly. 'Oh yes. Only it seems they love their husbands and their husbands are on their way here.'

'Come on, young crusader,' I said. 'Drink up.'

'My boy, you will have me thinking soon that I'm on my way to die for my country.' He put on a sober face, a solemn voice. 'Sir, it was only my job,' he intoned gravely. 'Yes, sir, a job we all have to do. Yes, sir, onwards and upwards with brotherhood, the little man, Mr Average American, my old grey-haired mother. But, sir, I insist, no medals. It was only my job. Yes, sir, thirty-two Messerschmitts.'

He grinned, then all of a sudden he stopped. We were a little tight all right. Knowing what had come to his mind all of a sudden . . . going away . . . really leaving here . . . maybe dying. No, impossible. Get talking again. That was it. Start talking again.

'You're mistaken, sir,' I said. 'It was thirty-four Messerschmitts. I saw the last two go down myself.'

'No,' Bob said. 'No, sir. Only thirty-two,' shaking his head. 'No, no, no, I won't take the medals.'

'But, sir,' I said. 'The *London Times*. All England. The world. Your old grey-haired mother. They insist. They wait. An answer, a word for the press, sir.'

'No. My principles. Tell the king no. He will understand.'

'Ah, but, sir,' I said. 'What of little Agnes, the girl you left behind? What of her? Surely, medals for Agnes?'

'To hell with Agnes,' Bob said. 'You can't prove a thing. The courts will throw it out.'

'Okay. Only I'm worried about her.'

'I wouldn't,' Bob said. 'Let's worry about us. You know, I'm sorry as hell we ever had that fight. You know I'm sorry?'

'You still kicked hell out of me.'

Bob laughed.

'Look. I will introduce you to the most beautiful girl in New York. I wouldn't do it for anyone else in the world. Most beautiful girl in New York City. She doesn't love anybody. Doesn't have to. Won't have you going away leaving no one behind. Figured it all out. We'll both leave her behind.'

He took a drink.

'Know what?'

'No,' I said.

'Let's get the hell out of here, and go over and meet her.'

'I feel good,' I said. 'Just like meeting her.'

'Come on!'

I paid for the drinks and Bob tipped the waiter. Outside it was evening. Twilight and car lights just coming on in the soft air.

Then later in a taxi passing an open space between a row of apartment buildings I saw the East River, bluish-green, and a black tug moving out towards the harbour, and on the other side a yellowish stone building that I was told later was the poorhouse.

'Who are we going to see?' I asked. Foolish. Maybe only something he dreamed up with the aid of the scotch. Doesn't know where he's going.

'Most beautiful girl in New York,' Bijur said.

Then the taxi stopped in front of one of the largest apartment buildings. It was very tall and new and impressive, and there was a doorman and an iron-grilled front door. Bob got out and paid the taxi driver.

Then the carpet went along a long hall to a small elevator door. The doorman followed. He closed the doors of the elevator. Inside I pressed the button. Seventh floor, said Bob. Then there was another long carpeted hall and a door at the end. I saw the number 707 on the dark wood panelling. I rang the buzzer for a long time, and then standing there in the hall I heard someone inside coming towards the door.

The door opened and my throat was suddenly thick, and there she stood. I turned over inside. Gloria! She stood in the doorway. No one speaking. Only something, regret, sadness, an open way long forgotten now remembered. Gloria!

We stood there looking at each other.

'You certain you two don't already know each other?' Bob asked. He looked puzzled, a little amused.

Gloria and I stood looking at each other. Soft hands, music at night, the back seat of a car, a country club dance, Gloria coming down to school on the train. Four years? Five? Summer night on a country club veranda, across the night air an orchestra playing what? What year was it? Where? Long ago.

'I'm going to get the hell out of here,' Bob said. 'You know each other, don't you?'

'Yes.'

'Mind if I go?' Somewhere Bob's voice.

'No,' turning to him, as if remembering now suddenly he was there. 'No, don't go. Stay.'

He laughed.

'Here she is. Best-looking girl in New York and you have to know her. My God!' He clapped one hand to his head and

47

started to walk away, down the hall.

'Hey!' he called back, turning his head. 'Don't forget what I told you. She doesn't love anybody.' He laughed.

Gloria laughed.

'Sure!' I yelled after him. Then he turned his head and got into the elevator.

I looked at her for a long moment, then followed her inside. She closed the door. We went into the living-room. There was a big window at one end of the room opening on to a balcony and I looked out, wondering how this had happened after five years, seeing the East River green and blue beyond the window. It was quiet in the room. I could almost hear and feel her standing somewhere behind me, watching, waiting for me to turn around. I looked out at the river, and hoped she did not see how this was affecting me. What did one say after five years?

'Hello, Mack,' she said quietly, after a long moment. She was standing behind me, touching my shoulder, and when I turned she was holding a glass out to me. 'Drink?'

I looked down at the ice floating in the glass. She was holding a glass of her own, drinking from it. She had not even been in the room. Not heard her leave, I thought. Gone for a moment. East River. Green blue. Gone mixing drinks. My God, long time. Everything gone, changed, I thought.

College. Five years ago.

'Darling, you know we couldn't get married.'

'We love each other, Gloria.'

'Isn't enough. Money.'

'I'll get a job. No, I won't work for your father, Gloria.'

'Darling, you're so silly.'

'I know what it would be like. I don't mind being owned as long as it's by you. Don't want to be owned by your whole family, Gloria. Blame me? Darling, take a chance.'

'It wouldn't work.'

'You've got to help me make it work, Gloria. I've got to have you.'

'Don't be foolish. You better go. It won't work out.'

'All right! To hell with it! You won't take a chance.'

'Oh, Mack, darling. I'm sorry.'

'Sorry! Hell! Good-bye.'

Gone – I had actually done it that day. Gone. Walked out. Regret, weeks, months after. Gloria! Gloria! Where are you? Why did I do it? Go back. No. Can't go back. Mr and Mrs Davis, announcing the marriage of their daughter, Gloria – 1936,

'37, '38, '39, '40. Five years. Gone, all the feelings taken away in those years. Good healing. Had to be. Mrs-what-was-her-name-now? What would it be? I couldn't remember her married name. Five years. It did a lot of things. Took care of regret.

Gloria, on the lounge beside me, was changed, older. She was still very beautiful.

'Haven't really changed, have you, Mack?'

The lighter flicked in her hand, flame touched the end of her cigarette.

'Some.'

'No, Mack. Not really.'

'You have.'

'Yes? How?'

'How does one tell a woman in just what way five years have changed her?'

'My God, we were young, weren't we, Mack?'

'In some ways, I suppose.'

'Still really a child, aren't you?'

'At least I knew what I wanted then.'

'You are funny. What are you running away from now in that uniform? What are you wanting now?'

'God only knows.'

'Just a moment,' she said.

She got up, and walked towards the hall that led to the kitchen. She was tall and dark and walked very straight, always very sure of herself. It was a kind of lovely miracle to watch her walk. She went out of the room.

I sat in the lounge and looked out the window at the East River. It was getting dark. Remote and sourceless, a horn on a boat blew two long melancholy notes across the gathering darkness. I sat on the couch waiting for her to come back. She came into the room carrying several bottles of beer under one arm, a bottle of scotch in one hand. She was smiling. Her eyes were smiling.

'Here,' she said. She opened two bottles of beer, handed me one, touched bottles, and put the bottle to her lips and drank. 'Darling, that's wonderfully lovely, isn't it?' She lowered the bottle, looked down at me, her eyes not showing what she was thinking, as if maybe she were thinking of me and something far away at the same time. A long time ago. Country club veranda in a dead time, old tunes across a summer darkness. Gloria, Gloria, I love you. I have to have you.

'Mack,' she said, and slid down on the couch until her head

49

rested on my shoulder, 'I wish we had married. If only for the happiness we could have had for perhaps say, two years. Don't you see what you really are?'

'What brings this on? My God.'

'All right,' said Gloria; 'but you do really want to hear, don't you? You're a romantic. Terrible. I never was. We'd never have made out. You'll probably wind up a long-faced, serious goop, always looking for a positive meaning in everything. Poor romantics.'

'Have a drink.'

Gloria sat up and reached for another cigarette. She lit one and leaned back.

'It's all gratification of one's ego. Self-sacrifice. Ambition. Any of it. God, don't you ever get just plain tired of it, Mack?'

'Need something new, don't you?'

Gloria nodded.

'Come here,' I said. 'Kiss me. It's unselfishness – you need.'

'I was that way that year at school,' she said.

'Oh, yes, you were – not. Or you would have come with me.'

We kissed. Everything seemed better. It made going to war easier. Everything easier. Killed loneliness. But not for her. I could sense that.

'What's happened?' I said, and laughed. 'Lost your taste for a few pleasant emotions?'

'Don't be silly,' said Gloria, 'of course not. But you don't expect me to slide so easily into ardency after five years.'

'Who did you marry?'

'No one you know. Knew him when I was a kid up in Greenwich.'

'Why'd you marry him?'

'Why not? It seemed like the best thing to do at twenty-one.'

'Well,' I said, 'you must have been more foolish than I thought if that was all you could think of to do at twenty-one.'

'You went away. I felt terrible.'

'You could have called me back. Let's get tight tonight. I feel wonderful seeing you again.'

'You could have come back yourself. Aren't you tight now?'

'Me?'

'Yes, you. Don't look like that,' Gloria said. 'It spoils it for me. I never could love a man who looked serious after beer.'

'Want to go some place and dance?' I asked.

'No.'

So we sat on the lounge with a phonograph playing old tunes.

I looked out at the East River. It was dark outside, and there were lights on the river. We sat in the dark listening to the phonograph, 'East of the Sun . . . West of the Moon,' on and on, saccharine, sad, and tranquil.

'What are you thinking?' I said.

'Nothing,' Gloria said. 'Nothing, really.'

I took a long pull at the cool scotch and water. In the dark room it was quiet, river beyond the window, phonograph playing, Gloria beside me.

'Gloria,' I said, 'what happened to him? Where is he?'

'He's dead.'

'Hell – I'm sorry.'

'No, no point in being sorry.'

'How'd it happen?'

'Started taking things seriously. Went to Spain driving an ambulance. Got himself killed. Fool. Bloody fool.' I thought maybe she was going to cry.

'Hell of a note,' I said.

'No,' she said. 'It's all right. I'm all over it.'

'Like you are about me?'

'Yes, like you are about me. Oh, hell, Mack. I was a fool.

'Mack,' she said, 'do you really believe all the things we said, all the things we felt?'

'That's a foolish question. No one can after the age of three.'

'Why three?'

'All right, make it seven. But they start changing you away from your real self even before they get you in school.'

'You better go home,' she said. 'It's late. I don't want to have to stop myself from running the old emotions. It would be too easy a way out, an escape for both of us, and it couldn't mean anything.'

'You're right there,' I said. 'It wouldn't mean anything. But does it have to?'

'Yes. You know you want things like that to mean something. Now. Especially when it's become increasingly more difficult to care. Good night, Mack. Call me tomorrow.'

'I'll call about noon. Would be nice though, wouldn't it, making love again?'

'Yes. Good night, Mack.'

'Good night, Gloria.'

I went home. When I went around to her apartment next afternoon she was ready to go out. Downstairs, waiting in front of the apartment in the sunlight for a taxi, she held my arm tightly, and we smiled together and were happy. It was good, alone in New York with her.

'Well, what should we do?' she asked. 'Where should we go?'

I raised my arm to hail a passing taxi.

'We can have a wonderful time together,' Gloria said. 'We can run around to the Biltmore just in time for cocktails.'

'God, you are a sentimentalist.'

'It's better than talking,' Gloria said. 'That's the trouble with you. You discuss everything until you find out you really didn't enjoy something you thought you enjoyed at the time or vice versa.'

'All right. The Biltmore.'

I hailed another taxi. It stopped and I climbed into the back seat. Gloria lit a cigarette and we sat close together. The taxi started up along the street.

'Hi, ho,' said Gloria. 'Here we are, aren't we?'

'Now for a bar.'

'Now for a bar, he says. Come closer, darling.'

'You're only imagining things, aren't you? Building new illusions.'

I looked out the window at Fifth Avenue going past.

'Just using an old illusion again,' she said.

We went along to the Biltmore. Later it was all gay and dancing and many night clubs, and laughing and dancing, and early morning at Longchamps with toast and marmalade and warm scrambled eggs.

I stayed ten days in New York and every day and night with Gloria was the same. In the day there was the theatre and lunch and cocktails and dinner. It was all a pleasure to return to after barrack life so I never tired of it and I was never bored, always excited and happy, and each day and evening was fresh, though we always did the same thing, and when it came time to go I dreaded the packing, the checking out, the last minutes in New York. We were happy together because there were always old experiences to talk about, to laugh over. But we were not in love, and on the evenings when I ran through all the old emotions I wished only that I might bring back the past, if for only the enjoyment of losing it again, with her. Twice I saw Bijur, and he also was enjoying his embarkation leave. He said he would call and bring a girl some evening and dine with us, but he never did. Nor did I ever see Gloria again. I kissed good-bye at the station, and both of us promised to write. But I never wrote, and a year later in a London Red Cross Club I read in a New York paper that she had married again, and her husband had been killed in Bataan, and now I can't even remember her second married name.

But the night I left on the train for the port of embarkation she stood on the station platform and waved good-bye. But now that's all gone too.

CHAPTER TEN

I would always remember my first 'op'. The elation over the unknown to come when I was in briefing. Then the empty hollow feeling for the first time, sitting later in the turret, the engines slowly revving up, the aircraft throbbing under the strain of the deep heavy rising and falling roar of the engines, while I looked out across the empty still meadow behind the dispersal point. The dusk was cold and tranquil. Great God, is it really me here? I thought, pulling on my helmet. The engines sounded roar on roar running smoothly. I checked the bulb in the ring sight.

Here it is really, at last. This is it. Alone in a turret in the Yorkshire dusk. God, where had the rest of the world receded to? My heart quickened. It had all seemed exciting and pleasant in briefing; then later in the mess, over operational tea, I had felt good among laughter and talk, jokes, flying sweaters and boots; tea-flasks to fill, casual laughing cheerios. Somewhere before in my childhood I had seen it all before, a story, a book, a movie. Hell, this wasn't real. Even in briefing, emptying my pockets, in case I was shot down or did not return, so there would be no tell-tale evidence for the enemy – even that was all another world, as remote from death or its possibilities. Even then I was not hollow or empty suddenly with the conception of what this truly was. 'Hell of a target for a first trip,' Gerald Barrett, the pilot, said. 'Dortmund.' Already he and Pop, a bald-headed Canadian navigator, had made a freshman trip with an experienced crew. Gerald was a smooth, round-faced young man of thirty, an RAF regular. Dortmund. It meant nothing to me. It might as well have been Keokuk. It had no significance. Only later I learned to judge each city in terms of danger, as everybody else judged them.

I sat in the turret, trying to adjust myself and the bulk of my heavy flying suit into a comfortable position. The engines idled. Gerald sat up ahead in the cockpit, waiting to turn out on to the perimeter track. My spirits were low. The meadow beyond in twilight was a lonely still sight.

I started thinking of what they were all doing up ahead in the aircraft; their feelings; feel heroic now, I told myself, think of all the fine inspirational editorials, American advertisements, political speeches, all about 'our brave boys' winging their way into the heart of the Third Reich, the simple little lad from Corn-crib Corners, Iowa, who loves the corner drugstore, a girl, and a movie. Join now, my boy. Still, no worse than all the egotistical twaddle in which I had indulged most of my life.

Up ahead Pop was bent over his table, a cone of light on his map. Already he was figuring, winds, drifts, courses. That's what I needed – something to do instead of just sitting here. Harry was in the tail turret. I swung the mid-upper turret around in which I was seated. I could see all over the aerodrome.

Harry called up: 'Everything okay, Mack?'

'Okay, Harry.'

'Righto, boy.'

I looked forward and saw Gerald's arm thrust from the side of the nose cabin. He was waving away the wheel chocks. His arm vanished. (Well, here we go.) The engines roared and the aircraft rolled very slowly forward.

We turned on to the perimeter track, rolling slowly around the field, and there behind us, each at spaced intervals, big-nosed, dark as bull fish, thick-winged, rearing big on their tyres, immense and impressive in the gathering darkness, came fifteen bombers. Then I realized suddenly I was to be the first to take off. We turned slowly into wind. Figures of aircrew not on the 'ops', the ground crews, and office staffs clotted darkly along one side of the runway. The wind sock blew rigidly from north to south.

Would Gerald have any trouble taking off in a cross-wind? We were using the east-to-west runway. Four tons of bombs, how many thousand gallons of petrol, and Gerald with his thirty-odd hours instructions on four-engined aircraft added to the tension and strain he must be undergoing at this moment. No man ever truly conquers and tames an aircraft, his own temperament, and the elements. They are all his enemies at various moments. Gerald had to face them now.

I heard the blasting roar of the engines opening up, the faint shudder that ran all through the steel frame of the aircraft. Then I was looking out; a green light winking blurred in the dusk; I felt the aircraft bumping along. I sat, tensed, remembering the crash before. God, would this aircraft ever leave the deck? I felt and saw it slough and drift a little across the runway; eight thousand pounds of bombs, one hundred and twenty-five miles an hour, sixteen tons of aircraft. I felt puny, as only flesh can feel, faintly goofy with the remembrance of the other crash, then suddenly I saw the aerodrome surface falling away behind; a green light blinking far away on the air.

Darkness swallowed the aircraft. Lights from the aerodrome vanished slowly in the smoky ground haze. 'Set course in ten minutes,' Pop called to Gerald. The aircraft climbed steadily, above haze, above darkness, into the soft green twilight.

Later in the dark it was strange cocking the guns; the metallic clash of the bolts sliding home; sweating in the turret with my flesh cold against the sweat; alone years ago in a dark cellar, feeling a lizard cold against my bare hand. A shiver ran along my back.

Below then was the coast, sea foam breaking whitely, far, far down; a friendly light winking good-bye from the last dark headland of England. So far, far away. Warm homes somewhere in Yorkshire. Then out over the dark sea. Is it all real? Are we really going? I was scared.

I looked out towards the west, the dying sun across the edge of the world. Dear God, that we must pass all this loveliness going where we are going. For there beyond the upthrust black lines of the tail fins lay a blood-red tranquil sky, slowly, so slowly, blending to purple and gold, soft and everlasting.

I sat gazing out, watching the sky turn dark, the stars began to blink, remote and cold.

I remembered suddenly my guns. 'Gerald,' I called, 'Okay to test my guns?'

Gerald: 'How far out are we, Pop?'

Pop: 'Fifty miles.'

Gerald: 'Okay, Mack.'

I depressed the guns and pressed the firing button, *rrrrrrr*, I heard the staccato explosions, long and red the trace arched out in the dark.

'Okay, skipper. Guns are jake.'

'Okay, Mack.'

I felt better. Thank God, there were no stoppages. I did not fancy wrestling in the dark with my guns.

Remote and lonely we droned on, the sky empty and dark, depthless and domed by stars. Then Pop saying, 'Fly a new course in five minutes, zero seven eight magnetic'; and Gerald, 'Righto, Pop, zero seven eight magnetic. Got it.' I opened a paper bag of raisins and slipped a handful under my oxygen mask.

'Hello, Johnny,' Pop's voice calling the wireless operator. 'See if you can get me a couple of fixes, okay?'

'I'm listening to base.'

Pop angrily, 'Oh, for Chrissake, bugger base. Get me some fixes.'

'Yeah! And what if we're recalled and I'm off the air?'

'Lissen, you dim-witted bastard! We're only fifteen minutes off the Dutch coast. I want to make damn sure we're on track.'

Johnny, whining: 'But I gotta obey orders.'

Pop: 'Do you want your bloody ass shot off or do you want to win the gold medal for being the model radio operator? I don't give a goddam if Churchill is duty operator at base, get me a fix! Understand? We don't want to go in over any defended areas.'

Johnny, in a hurt morose tone: 'All right.'

Then later Johnny giving fixes.

Then Pop's voice: 'We're dead on track, skipper.'

Gerald: 'Okay, old man. Good show.'

And so it went, swinging the turret from side to side, each moment a prolonged period of time. Darkness and stars, moving without seeming to move; seeing imaginary objects in the dark, frightened for a second; then to discover it was only a star blinking.

I looked at my wrist watch; airborne one hour. It seemed ages. Soon we would be crossing the enemy coast. Here was a danger area for night fighters; we had been warned at briefing.

I looked back at the dark sky between the tail fins. Then suddenly Harry's voice from the rear turret, 'Hey, Mack! There's a kite on our starboard beam! Can you see it?'

At once I strained my eyes to starboard, swinging the turret around. Yes, it is an aircraft all right, I thought, a vague dark shape flying level with us about six hundred yards away. I depressed the guns, centred the dark blurred shape in the centre of the ring sight, and watched it.

Then Reg's voice: 'Jesus! Look at the flak! We're crossing the coast, Gerald.'

No one said anything, then Pop's voice: 'Can you see the coastline? Can you get a pin-point?'

Reg's voice: 'No, we're past it.'

'Oh, bloody hell! Keep your eyes open, will you!'

Reg's voice, calmly: 'think we're just north of Amsterdam. There's a searchlight.'

A long beam, twice as long and brighter than any beam I had ever seen, arched across the sky ahead.

We were all worried, frightened. Here we were alone for the first time over enemy territory not knowing exactly what to expect.

We flew on, the searchlight behind us, probing, stabbing the night, looking for us. Far ahead we saw the target, a glow against the dark. Then we saw flares falling singly and in pairs among the searchlight beams. There were cones of searchlights dead ahead and on all sides. God, how would we ever get through it? It didn't seem possible. Flash after flash of bursting flak filled the glowing sky above the target.

Gerald said to Reg, in the nose, 'Okay, old man. Let's see you take us in there.'

Reg laughed. 'No promises about getting us out.'

We flew on. Flak began bursting all around. I was terrified. A sudden flash of light on all sides. I felt my heart and arms and legs constrict. Why aren't we hit? We did not seem to be making any noticeable progress towards the target. Just on and on towards the glowing fire; seemingly hanging motionless, unable to defend ourselves. But what if we were hit? Full bomb-load. We'd never know what happened. An aircraft went past, diving, its fuselage covered with flames, and then we were in over the area lit by incendiaries. How small and absurd all man's ambitions and desires seemed now. Clan or club, political party or religion; how silly and hopeless seemed the strength of people who took those things seriously.

Suddenly the aircraft lurched and dived and bumped upwards. There was a flash of light and the faint yet heavy sound of an explosion. I felt the aircraft heave skywards. I called into the intercom. There was no answer.

God, have we been hit? I saw we were plugged in. 'Hello! Hello! Hey, you people! Hey!'

Then suddenly a crackling sound in my ear and Reg's voice: 'Okay' Bombs gone. Let's get the hell out of here.'

Pop's voice: 'What the hell's wrong with this intercom, Johnny?'

My voice angrily: 'What the hell is wrong with it, Johnny?'

Reg's voice: 'Bomb doors closed.'

Johnny's voice, pettishly: 'I don't know. How the hell can I tell up here?'

Pop's voice: 'You ought to be able to. It's your job.'

Gerald's voice: 'Shut up, you blokes! What's the course out of here? Bloody hell! These searchlights!'

Pop's voice: 'Two eight zero magnetic.'

I saw one wing-tip down, felt pressed downwards, and knew we were banking away. On all sides searchlights groped towards us. One beam passed just underneath. If they ever got us in a cone we were done. Gradually the flak and searchlights were left behind.

Gerald's voice: 'Did you have a flare in the bomb sight?'

Reg's voice: 'Bang on, my friend. I think we really pranged the place.'

Everybody felt terribly relieved and pleased, exhilarated and anxious now to get home. All talking.

Returning we expected many things; being lost, attack by night fighters, engine failure. There was always those troubles. But nothing bothered us until after we left the Dutch coast.

Then suddenly Eddie the flight engineer's voice: 'Skipper, we're losing petrol out of number one tank.'

Gerald: 'Well, switch over.'

'I have, I think the main line and tank have been hit.'

'How much petrol have we?'

'Half-hour. It's been going fast. We must have been hit over the target.'

Then Eddie said excitedly, 'Blast! The starboard outer's packing up.'

The aircraft heaved upwards, then sank. Gerald brought the wing up that was going down.

Pop's voice: 'We're only fifteen minutes from the English coast. Enough petrol, Eddie?'

Eddie: 'Just trying to work it out.'

We flew on. Gerald feathered the engine. We hoped the weather wasn't bad on return. But it was. Grey misty haze off the sea. And then we saw the light winking from the headland. Home! We were filled with exhilaration. Tired, we leaned against the guns.

Then suddenly Eddie's voice, terrified:

'Skipper! The starboard inner engine's going to pack up. Oil pressure's going right off the clock.'

Gerald's voice, shakily: 'Eddie! Eddie! What the hell is wrong?

This other engine's going.'

No answer. God, so this is it! First trip. I knew Gerald did not have enough experience to land on two engines, let alone even fly on two, and looking down I saw the dark squares of the fields only a thousand feet below. The aircraft seemed to be sinking steadily.

Then suddenly there ahead I saw a circle of lights, an aerodrome. Gerald saw it too.

Then Gerald's voice: 'Hello, Beetle, hello. This is Broadmind W. William. May I land? Two engines are packing up. May I land?'

No answer. Lights twinkled prettily below. We were down-rushing in the dark, running parallel to a line of lights that marked the line of the flare path. At the end of the field we would have to bank and turn in and get square with the mouth of the flare path. If we had enough speed we would make it, if not, if another engine on the same side packed up, as the saying goes, we would side-slip into the ground. At five hundred feet there would be no chance for correction if we lost flying speed in a turn because of engine failure. But we were diving. Perhaps that would keep up the air speed.

There was nothing to do but sit there. It was no use trying to bail out at this height.

'Eddie!' Gerald's voice: 'Eddie!' – panicky now – 'the starboard inner's gone! Eddie! What the hell!'

No answer from Eddie. The aircraft lurched, sank a little.

Gerald's voice shouting: 'Hello, Beetle! Hello! Broadmind W. William! I am landing! I am landing! Do you hear!'

Still no answer from the ground.

Then I saw the lighted funnel-shaped mouth of the flare path appear just ahead and under the wing, and there ahead as we banked in was the neatly lighted street of the flare path. The aircraft seemed to sink perceptibly on one wing. Gerald brought it level. I felt drained and hollow and weak. Then I heard the sound of the engines throttling back. Below, the dark fields appeared to be fleeing past much faster than usual for a night landing. The lighted funnel-shaped mouth of the flare path slid underneath. We seemed too high at this point. With only two engines we would never be able to throttle forward and go round again if we overshot the field. Get down, Gerald, I thought, get down. Dark land slipped underneath. Now we were somewhere in that mile interval between the edge of the aerodrome and the funnel. The ground kept coming up faster, and suddenly I knew everything was all right. Gerald was going to make it. His intercom was open and I could hear him panting. And then suddenly I felt the first bump of the runway, saw the two lighted lines of the flare path slip past on both sides, and then we were running smoothly along the runway. Everybody started congratulating Gerald.

Joyous voices over the intercom: 'Good show, Gerald.'

'Damn good.'

'That was okay, Gerald.'

Gerald's voice: 'Phew!'

CHAPTER ELEVEN

The next morning when I went down to flights I heard there was a call on again that night. Harry, the other gunner in our crew, was sitting on the table in the gunnery office.

He sat there looking tired and glum, smoking a cigarette. I was tired, but there was still the exhilaration of being back. I felt slightly deaf in one ear and both ears squeaked when I swallowed. My eyes were sore, and felt bugged out with the strain of peering through the darkness the night before. We left the gunnery office and walked along the road across the field to the sergeants' mess. A heavy bomber droned overhead. The day had passed when we bothered to look up at an aircraft. We studied the sky. Cloud was low but blowing fast in the wind.

'Think this cold front will blow over?' asked Harry.

'Maybe. Your guess is as good as mine. Wouldn't be a call on, would there, if they didn't expect the weather to break?'

'Oh, I don't know,' said Harry. 'You never know. They'll send us out in anything if the chances look at all favourable. Suppose we gotta win the war sooner or later.'

And we looked at each other and laughed.

'How do you feel after last night?' I asked.

'Oh, all right, I guess. You?'

'Okay, I suppose. Going in town tonight if they scrub it?'

Harry laughed, arched his cigarette away.

'Brother, am I not?' He looked across at the grey dismal fields, then at me. 'Coming in?'

'You don't think I'm going to stay here, do you?' Harry laughed dryly. 'Remember the jolly comradeship of the men who fly, brother?' Then, 'God, could I use a beer right now.'

'Come on,' I said. 'They've got a new recipe for brussels sprouts at the mess.'

'How would you like to be meeting the most beautiful girl in the world tonight? And two quarts of champagne?' Harry asked.

'Funny boy. You are getting flak-happy,' I said.

'Do you think we'll go tonight?'

'Hell, I'm not running Bomber Command. Don't worry about it.'

'I'm not,' Harry said.

'Hell you're not.'

'So are you, Mack. Don't kid me.'

'No one is kidding anybody,' I said. 'I'd rather be going in town tonight than anything in the world.'

Now in my mind I saw the crowded, smoky bar in town where we would laugh and drink and talk all night if we were not operating.

'You watch up above tonight if we go, okay?' asked Harry.

'And you?'

'Down. I'll leave it up to you to watch the beams and above, okay?'

'Okay, fella,' I said.

'Think we'll go?' Harry looked up at the sky. Overhead cloud blew fast towards the South.

'Afraid so.'

Harry lit another cigarette. We walked on quietly.

All that afternoon grey low cloud continued to blow over in the direction of the Continent. Even in briefing there were bets made that the 'op' would be scrubbed before operational tea. As I came in the mess for tea Harry was just ringing off the telephone.

'Well, what's up?' I asked. 'Is it scrubbed yet?'

'There's a war on, my friend,' said Harry. 'Fat chance of a scrub. Just called Gerald, says Met says the front will be past the Rhine by midnight.'

Eddie came out of the lounge.

'Still on?' he asked. 'Heard the phone ring. Saw you answer it.'

'Met says it's okay,' Harry said. 'But you know what they are. Greatest optimists in the world.'

'So we're on?' Eddie asked. He didn't look too happy.

'We're on, brother,' said Harry, laughing. 'Hoy! Hoy!'

'Well, hell, let's eat then,' said Eddie, suddenly smiling. 'I hear the grub stinks in Stalag Four.'

After operational tea we piled into the bus waiting outside the mess and rolled along in the cold twilight, passing the briefing-room, then on between two ploughed fields, passing a brick farm-house on the left side of the road; two children and a woman waved to us from a side window. They were always there when we went past on the way to flights before a raid.

In the locker-room we stood around pulling on our kit, slipping into our flying sweaters.

'Wonder what Paulette Goddard is doing tonight,' Harry said, buckling on his chute harness.

'Brother,' called Reg, laughing from the other side of the locker, 'you should care. You're going to be dead by morning anyway.' Laughter, voices filled the room.

Outside the buses were waiting and we drove out across the aerodrome to the dispersal point on which our aircraft waited. The ground crew were waiting around the aircraft, smiling, friendly and cheerful.

'Tough target tonight?' somebody asked.

'Tough enough.' Bochum was the target.

'Don't forget we want 'er back.' They joked, grinning, taking the curse off the grin and joke.

'No bloody fear,' Harry smiled quietly.

I leaned against the starboard tail fin and looked at the aero-drome. Later how well we were to learn this place! How much it became a part of our lives. The wind sock rigid in the wind, the calm still moment all over the aerodrome just before the first engine started up somewhere would begin roaring; the windmill silhouetted against the fading sky, a line of geese trooping past from a near-by farm. Somehow in the beginning there was a magic in all of it. But later, in the end, we only grew to hate it, to hate all things that were near to or related to death.

But now from somewhere on the aerodrome came the sound of the first engine starting up. The tranquil evening had ended.

Saying cheerio to the ground crew we climbed into the aircraft and got up into the mid upper turret. While the engines were warming up I tested the ring sight, switching it on and off, checked to see if the gun-cocking toggle was in position, then waited, submerged in the sound of the engines and my own thoughts.

There was something now foolishly exciting about this trip. It was strange the various states of mind and moods you might be in. Tonight I felt happy, suddenly, now excited with anticipation, already the fear of the previous night was gone. Gradually this experience was killing emotion, hardening it, later after many trips I had no feeling at all about a trip, sometimes a dread, then after that just not caring, not even exhilarated on return.

At twenty thousand feet I felt cold and sleepy. I told Gerald I wanted more oxygen; he said the oxygen valve was full on. In my ear the radio crackled, and in the crackling I heard the muffled heavy voices of German night-fighter ground stations calling to night fighters in the air. Our crew began talking to Johnny, the radio operator.

'Jam the bastards, Johnny.'

Johnny's voice: 'Hell, man, that's what I'm doing.'

Then the snapping crackle of Johnny slamming his radio key up and down, then the intermittent cut-off German voices full of excited gurgles and exclamations, calling and yelling, trying to get through the noisy pandemonium Johnny was creating. Then it was silent.

'Anyone want some tea?' Eddie asked. He was feeling happy all right, mentioning tea at this early stage of the trip.

'Save it until we get off the target,' Gerald said.

Harry's sarcastic voice, laughing: 'Aren't we the confident bastards though? – knocking back tea on the way into the Ruhr. Dear! Dear! Well – la-di-da-di-da!'

We flew on in silence. A cone of searchlights stuck up stiffly into the sky on our starboard. That would be Duisburg. The next formation of cones would be Essen. I was looking at Duisburg when a lone searchlight, and then three more, shone on the aircraft from below, filling the turret with a blinding purple light, while I felt the nose heave, then felt one wing going down, and knew Gerald was doing a stall turn. I closed my eyes so as not to be blind later in the dark, then opened them as Eddie called from the astral dome that the searchlights were gone. Then a row of sudden yellow flashes burst directly behind and below, sending a quick surge of fear into me.

But in a moment it ceased and below it was all dark again. Reg called up to say he could see the target ahead and then we started to dive in under Reg's direction, hearing again the familiar: 'Left, left . . . hold it . . . just a little left . . . there . . . there . . . hold it, Gerald, steady,' while we hung in the glare from the fires and saw the searchlights catch and hold an aircraft, now small and delicate as a silver moth, high above us and on the port side. Turning and twisting, diving and climbing, the searchlight holding it while minute, white round balls of flak burst all around. I watched fire come slowly from one of its engines, a long lick of flame, then it fell slowly in wide circles, then flopping over on its back it went down into the searchlights. The searchlights swept away and went out. After a long moment on the darkness of the ground from where the searchlights operated there appeared a sudden smear of flame. In a moment the searchlights were on again, sweeping the darkness, but we were out, away from the target, free, flying on in the dark towards the Zuyder Zee. A thin cold film of moisture that was sweat covered my chest and back. I felt it drying coldly against my skin.

Darkness surrounded us, enveloped us. The moon was gone. I looked out, feeling worn out, but still keyed-up. The motors throbbed an even deep hum. Suddenly, without warning, the aircraft bumped and rocked violently from a shell exploding directly underneath. I felt the aircraft slowly saw off on one wing, diving, then Gerald pulled it level again.

We passed over the Zuyder Zee, then the searchlights of Amsterdam arched swiftly across the sky searching for us. We went for the coast in a long dive, and the darkness was filled with the flashes of bursting flak. The aircraft bounced and heaved: tossed this way then that by the explosions. Again and again Gerald fought to hold it in a controlled weave. The searchlights pointed fingers of light towards us, trying to spot us, while from outside came the fragile buckshot rattle of flak along the fuselage and the deep heavy *boompf* of each close explosion. One of the bomb doors dropped down, shot away, and we began to stall, with the feeling of all forward motion stopped; I was conscious of the aircraft standing motionless on its tail.

Then suddenly the stars wheeled and spun and the searchlights beam criss-crossed upside down, and then we were diving, Gerald gaining air speed again, pulling out of the stall. Level, we flew on.

No one said anything over the intercom. I estimated the machine was now down to four thousand feet, a dangerous height against light flak batteries. A long snaking thread of fire wound slowly up to starboard of the turret, and I could hear the phut, phut, explosive sound of the light flak shells. In a moment, if they were any good at all on the gun battery, they would be able to predict us and lay a pattern barrage around us.

Gerald dived the aircraft and then we climbed. There were shells bursting all around, smokeless black puffs, so after the first flash I could not see the white smoke puff, and I was unable to estimate approximately how close they were firing. Suddenly there was the sound of a loud explosion over the intercom.

Gerald called: 'The port outer's packing up!'

There was a pause. A long silence. Then *boompf*, a loud rocking explosion, and suddenly we were diving, apparently powerless, out of control. The stars wheeled directly overhead, wheeled, spun, vanished.

Pop yelled: 'Pull it out! Slowly, slowly, Gerald.'

I felt sick with terror, then suddenly resigned, very calm. I sat waiting. So here it was.

Then gradually the nose lifted and the stars returned to their normal position. I smiled wryly to myself and thought desperately. 'Oh, thank God.' Then without warning there was another flash and an explosion, and the starboard outer engine coughed and cut. I felt the aircraft falling to one side, then slowly the tail began to drop, and I knew we were stalling again, the controls useless.

Gerald's voice: 'Oh, blast! They've hit the tail . . . sorry, chaps . . . did the best I could.'

I sat there crouched, now badly frightened, mouth dry, stomach faint and cold and empty, my thighs stricken stiff as boards. Oh, God, I thought, get me out of this. I had never prayed before because I believed, as most air crews believed, that if you were doomed you were doomed. Neither prayers, sacred medals, nor a rabbit's foot would be of any help. But now I prayed. My God, I prayed. Please, dear God. I want to see Diana again. Please, dear God, get me out of this and I'll never disappoint anybody again. I'll stop whoring around and drinking. Dear God, please let me live. Oh, dear God, please. Dear God, I want to live! Live! Or, my God, how terribly afraid I was. I held tightly to the posts above the guns, waiting for the instinctive feeling that would somehow tell me for certain that now this was the end. But it did not come.

We flattened out, and below I saw the irregular line of the Dutch coast. Then searchlights far behind and the dark sea waiting quietly for us to fail to get home. We staggered on over the sea, losing height, gaining height, ready at any moment to abandon the aircraft on the water. Gerald could not seem to control the aircraft for any length of time. We would falter, waver, then flog steadily on, but just as steadily we were losing height, and as we saw the English coast knew we must either bail out or attempt a crash landing. We were going down rapidly. The aerodrome was thirty miles inland and we would never be able to make it the way the aircraft seemed unable to maintain height.

Johnny went back to the flare chute and released a flare.

Light as bright as a street lamp lit up the field below, and Gerald called to standby for a crash landing. The field appeared to be a pasture, and as we lost height I hoped, frightened, that Gerald knew what he was doing. I braced myself in the turret and everybody went back to the crash-position seats between the wings. Then I saw the dark field coming up fast, and hoped it was meadow as it appeared to be, and remembered a crew on an operational training unit who had done the same thing only to run into a stone wall on landing.

Now! Now! Now! I thought, and pushed my back hard against the doors of the turret and waited, empty, hollow, and tense.

The dark ground rushed past only a few feet below. I estimated the aircraft was travelling about one hundred and thirty miles per hour. All the ground was only a fleeting dark blur. On and on the aircraft raced. When will we strike, I kept thinking waiting seconds that were centuries. Then I knew suddenly, as the aircraft hung poised for an instant just above the earth, that here now comes the ground. Crash? I ground my teeth, my back stiffened.

Gerald's voice: 'Stand by! We're going to prang!' Oh, God, down-rushing to smash to nothing!

And then the aircraft struck the ground and a bright jagged thin light jiggled crazily inside my head as my temple banged hard against the side and the roof of the turret. Then there was another smashing bang and crunch as the aircraft sloughed and skidded madly to a standstill.

Gerald, panting and relieved, sighed over the intercom: 'Christ! Here we are!'

'Everybody okay?' Pop called.

'Okay, okay,' came back our voices, weird and a little insane, hurried and urgent, as if we were calling in answer to something that had not yet happened.

We climbed out and looked at the aircraft, the collapsed undercarriage, the cracked and broken metal sides of the fuselage, the nose down-thrust almost in the ground, the tail turret now setting

66

higher than the nose. We walked around looking at it, exhilarated by our luck, our stomachs still queer and empty, our hands shaking.

'Dear God . . . our life . . . so this is it?' And I felt exuberant and terrified to have gained admittance to it.

Overhead the stars shone clear and cold, for ever the same, looking down, while somewhere in the night it seemed secret, unreal voices laughed and mocked at us.

CHAPTER TWELVE

That winter and spring, after several months on operational flying, the crew I was in felt they wanted and needed a rest. One morning I went to see Hill, the Wing Commander, and told him the crew was tired and wanted to get away for a while.

In the Wing Commander's office I saw on the wall near the door a chart, a long rectangular list of all the crews and the position of each member. 'Matter of fact, old boy,' he said shyly, as if regretting what he had to say, 'I rather need you chaps now. For example,' he went on, 'say a gunner is sick today and you're a gunner,' he said, gesticulating with both hands. 'Say your crew is standing down. Well, you, or whoever is standing down, are the only substitute crew I have. Understand?'

'We've got to get away from here a while,' I said.

'I would like to let your crew go,' he said. 'But it wouldn't be fair to others. You're not due for leave just yet.'

'It's not that we're nervous,' I lied. 'It's just that we're fed-up, you know. We've seen so many fellows killed and missing that we hate flying. If we could get away for a while – '

'It would only relieve you temporarily, then as soon as you had another shaky trip you would be the same again. It's best to stay on. I know.'

'All right. But how about forty-eight hours?' I asked.

'Forty-eight hours?' The Wing Commander leaned forward in his chair. 'Why, surely.'

Then he frowned, looked thoughtful. 'But I think there's a call on tonight,' he said. 'You'll be working.'

'Couldn't we stand down? Put on that new crew. Give us a rest tonight. Maybe it will be an easy target.'

He laughed. 'Where might that be?' He looked at me and smiled faintly. It was as if we both had a secret joke.

I smiled, shrugged my shoulders. 'Oh, St-Nazaire, or maybe Lorient. I don't know.'

The Wing Commander laughed.

'Do you honestly believe we'll go there again after the past five trips? Why should we go there any more?'

'There's plenty probably we could still work on.'

'Ridiculous.' He laughed. 'Both places are flattened. You'd better run around to the gunnery office. It's half-past nine.' He glanced at his wrist watch, fumbled among some papers on his desk.

'When do you think we could get some leave?'

'As soon as your turn comes up.'

'But we haven't had any for three months.'

He grinned. 'That's right. Once every three months. Price you pay for being an experienced crew,' he smiled. 'Actually, I'm quite busy.' He glanced down at the papers on his desk.

I went outside and looked down the empty concrete road, past the armoury and administrative buildings, to the highway at the edge of the aerodrome. Then, from the highway, groups of two and three airmen appeared, some walking, some pedalling slowly on bicycles. They came closer and I saw my crew among them, and Harry, the other gunner, come up.

'Where the hell you been?' he asked. He looked tired, unshaven, eyes red-rimmed and bloodshot from the night before. He stood with his hands in his battle-dress pockets. 'There was a roll-call at crew conference, I told 'em you'd be along in a minute. Where the hell you been, Mack?' He took out a cigarette.

'Seeing the Wing Co about some leave.'

'Any luck?'

'Same old guff. Maybe next week. Got a forty-eight though.'

'Hell,' he said, 'I'll go nuts if we don't get out of here soon.' then he laughed harshly.

'What was the weather forecast? Think there'll be a call on tonight?'

'Probably. Cold frost coming down from Scotland. If we're lucky it might shut down here just about take-off time.'

'Hope we're lucky.'

'Brother,' he said, 'you're not kidding. After last night I want no part of the Ruhr for a while.'

'Maybe we'll get a nice mine-laying stooge.'

'Fat chance of that,' he said. 'Not a cloud over the Continent tonight.'

'Nice,' I said. 'I'm just in the mood for Happy Valley again tonight.'

'Who you kidding, Mack?'

Now what would come tonight, I thought. If there was a raid tonight, what would happen? Stop thinking about it. Maybe there wouldn't be any. Since the night before, and the night before that, with waiting outside the target area at Duisburg while they conned our aircraft ahead, and the night before that at Essen, caught in the searchlights. I did not care about anything. In the mornings there was no worry. I was back safely, and now back with all the strain gone, it all seemed so easy. It had been like that on the past two mornings; but now, waking after Duisburg last night, I kept seeing the aircraft caught in the searchlight ahead, minute and silver, diving, twisting; the flak-bursts, tiny and white, high up above me, following the aircraft, while my own aircraft hung in a kind of terrific suspension, where all movement seemed to cease, with the sky light as day from the fires far below, and then on out over the fires, with the bombs gone, and looking back at the conned aircraft making one last desperate struggle to escape, turning slowly over on its back, one engine smoking, falling, falling, falling, spinning down into the lights. But in the mess in the morning all that seemed unreal, far away, and with my crew safe once more it did not seem as if that could ever happen to me. But it can, I thought now, it can happen to us. We are experienced, but it can happen to us as easily as anybody. No, nothing was going to happen to us. Nothing.

But I had seen other crews with the same sure feeling of invincibility and it did not help them when luck went against them. Well, if I was due to go there was nothing I could do about it. I did care. I only lied to myself that I didn't care. Once I was in the aircraft, if there was a call tonight, all this thinking would stop. Maybe. Once I had something to busy myself with. What the hell was the good of worrying anyway? Sure, just try not worrying.

I remembered before worry began, before the squadron began to lose crews. When it seemed to be impossible for anyone to be missing and it was all a rather pleasant, exciting adventure. But it was no longer an adventure, the night after a low-level attack. And I knew I was a fool even to expect anything but despair or exhilaration. I remembered afterwards coming in to the interrogation officer, with all the empty tables in the briefing-room, and sitting down, drinking hot tea, exhausted and numb, explaining the trip. And how empty the room was, and then in the mess at five o'clock in the morning, waiting for the others to come in for breakfast. But they never came back. And when it was light in the morning I knew they were all either dead, prisoners, or in the North Sea.

They were crews I ate and drank and laughed and talked with. And I waited weeks to hear any word of them, expecting each morning in crew conference that a message had arrived from the German Red Cross. But it never arrived, and no one ever heard of them again. Deeply regret to inform you that your son, lover, husband, brother, failed to return last night from operations. . . . Gentlemen, our target for tonight is Düsseldorf . . . New crews will please remain behind for special instructions. And so the days passed.

How long since I had been to London on leave. Three months. And I thought of those mornings of going on leave, of the crew walking out along the road to the bus, everybody gay and a little mad with happiness, suitcases piled in the bus, and then the train steaming plumes of smoke in the winter-afternoon air under the glassless roof of the York station. 'So long, fellow! See you, chaps! Have a good leave!' And a wonderful feeling of relief with the spires of York Minster fading across the afternoon sky, and the first beer in London in a pub up the street from King's Cross, the lights bright in a theatre that night, and sleeping late in the mornings in a warm room: and worry and cold and fish-and-chips and exhaustion and standing in the dark in the rain waiting to take off lifted from my life by all the light, weightless hours of looking down Piccadilly or walking in the Park in the mornings knowing the day was all mine.

Walking along the road to the sergeants' mess I thought of the single letter from Diana two months ago, saying she would meet me in London. And now, in the months between, the months when caring about anything did not matter, there had always been many women, for tomorrow was not tomorrow. Tomorrow was nothing; death in the North Sea, blowing up over the target, a stalled engine on take-off, a night fighter. So tomorrow was made today. It must not escape. Tomorrow was perhaps the end, only your mind did not give in to that completely. There was always hope, or you could not go on. But *today* I wanted to live my life. So on nights off duty in the dark with someone I did not know it made no difference, it took away loneliness and made everything all right. Let another raid come, and relieved and tired I did not care then what happened flying. So many things could happen. But now, with whoever she was, always a different one, I had taken away nights alone, and as long as that was gone it mattered little who killed the loneliness that came of too much despair and exultation.

When the letter came I knew I was no longer alone, only a page of Diana's script and I was back again beside her on that night of the raid, and the feeling to see her was so strong I was all new again, to me she was the most desirable person in the world, caring and loving again, and everything was all only wanting to see her. London was going to be all seeing Diana. Whatever it was I had lost, seeing her would bring it back again. And then came waiting for her that evening in Waterloo Station. 'Arriving seven o'clock,' her telegram read. The train came in and I stood outside the gates and watched for her in the crowd coming past the ticket puncher. But she was not there. And then the platform was empty. God, had there been some mistake? But there was no mistake. The train timetable showed the time was correct. And then, sick and empty with anxiety, calling all the hotels, looking all over London for her, and another night of leave, of bars and talk and dancing, of trying to forget I would not see her, and later another letter from her saying she had arrived on the train but somehow we had missed each other.

The next night I was on the train returning to Yorkshire, and the next night over Berlin, wondering if I'd get back through a cold front, trying to climb above the icing clouds, then finally on the way home falling, iced-up, over the North Sea, with two engines suddenly stalled and Johnny, the radio operator, sending an SOS, until finally the engines started again and I came back low over the sea with two engines missing and popping.

And the nights when someone did not come back I remember, and how at first it bothered me, and how the smoking wreckage of a crash bothered me. Not many, but I had seen enough aircraft running smoothly and fast along runways and I had seen them rise and something happen, a wing go down, a stall, a propeller dropping off, and then explosion and smoke and flame, and running across the field and stopping beside the wreckage while they pulled scorched, crumbling bodies out on long hooks attached to poles. But now, when I had seen enough of it, it was all the same. I did not want to think of it but it did not bother me any more.

I remembered now all the faces, laughs, and parties in the mess, and when they were gone their faces were forgotten in a week. So what did it avail to die, I often thought, but as many went on I went on. Anyway I had felt myself change from wanting many things to wanting almost nothing, and I could look back on myself, on how I was at different times, when I left home, when I saw Gloria, when I was in New York. I was afraid of many things in those days, but now I knew how ridiculous those fears were, how ridiculous so many things were, and how ridiculous I had always been with people – my mother, Gloria, my sister. How ridiculous I would always be, following my immediate desires.

'How long before running up the engines?' Gerald said.

The crew stood now around the aircraft.

'Ten minutes,' Pop looked at his watch.

'Chaps, want your caffeine now?' Gerald reached in his pants pocket.

'I don't want any,' Harry said. He shook his head.

'It's a long trip.'

'I can stay awake,' Harry said. 'Besides, it goes through my kidneys too quickly.'

'Okay, you're your own boss,' Gerald said. He passed the caffeine around.

Then it was time to run up the engines. I sat in the mid upper turret and watched the green twilight die across the field and the air turn dark away off on the bottom of the sky.

Then Gerald: 'Starboard outer okay, Eddie?'

Eddie, the flight engineer: 'Okay, skipper. Run 'er up.'

Then taxi-ing slowly away from the dispersal point. There were so many places I would like to be right now, I thought.

There was in the days at the beginning of 'ops' coming into London on a leave, walking out of King's Cross in the early morning air, catching a taxi to the Green Park Hotel. Before even the pleasure of a leave was killed by the thought that lay at the back of my mind each day of those early leaves. I will be returning to 'ops' soon. Returning to 'ops'. But before I lived only from raid to raid, thinking only of the next one after one was over, there was a London I could enjoy on leave, a London I learned to love, a London of sunlight in Trafalgar Square, and the first afternoon I wandered into the old smallness of Shepherd's Market, and the *Daily Telegraph* after breakfast while walking through Green Park; all those sunny mornings and days of different leaves; sun on the tar along Piccadilly, and the crowds going to work, and dinners up in Soho, and then later the Ritz

Hotel bulking clear and dark in the moonlight as I walked along at midnight with the last taxi moving fast along Piccadilly towards home.

And from the American Eagle Club I could look across the rooftops of Leicester Square. There was the Café Anglais, with its doors open on sunny days. The chorus girls in the slacks and heavy make-up waiting for the matinées, and the air crew on leave standing at the bar; and their voices. 'Bloody hell, they had us conned. I thought sure we'd had it.' There was Berkeley Square and the moonlight in the cool leafy darkness of spring, and the square empty after midnight, and coming along Curzon Street in the dark with the guns pounding far away across the City.

'There's the green light now, isn't it?' Gerald asked from the cockpit, now looking out into the dusk along the length of the runway.

'No, not yet,' Eddie said from the astral dome.

'Give me the word when.'

'Righto.'

'All set, chaps?'

'Okay, boy, take it away,' said Reg, the bomb aimer.

'Okay, Gerald,' the voices came in from each position.

'There's a green,' Eddie yelled. Engines roared.

Well, here we go, I thought. What will happen tonight? Will we get through? A fighter off the Dutch coast? Flak over the target? A wonky compass? What tonight? I braced myself in the turret and watched the trees blur that made the skyline in the west. The green light blinked again and was gone. The aircraft bounced, lifted.

Yes, I would like to be in London tonight. London with Diana. The things we would do. Where would we go?

Riding or walking with her through the traffic up past Hyde Park Corner, cars and buses and taxis honking and rushing past in the twilight. Or maybe in a taxi with Buckingham Palace beyond the driver's cap, sitting close to her, while the Palace came up and then went past on one side, and then Sloane Square just as it was getting dark. Then the driver paid and walking through the vacant square along the street to the Antelope pub. And just as we went in, on the stillness of the spring air, the round clear shapes of the barrage balloons beyond the rooftops, and then later walking back through Eaton and Grosvenor Squares, the buildings clear in the moonlight.

But those were only some of the places at certain times I would like to have Diana with me. I knew many more places. Chelsea

73

and the Blue Cockatoo. The Strand swarming with people just before dinner. But now I could be in none of those places. I thought of sitting down to hot dinners in fashionable restaurants. That was one of the confusing things about the war. The ones who were fighting ate so badly. Well, perhaps it was only because so many of them were not around long enough even to digest a fashionable meal. Oh, to hell with it. Why die crying? The world lay below in vague dissolving patterns in the fading light.

'Pop, you got a course?' Gerald asked.

'What time do you have?' Pop asked him.

'Eleven past ten.'

'Two eight zero magnetic. Set course in five minutes.'

'Righto.'

Gerald was a good pilot. He was a pre-war officer, inclined to be regimental and slightly stuffy on the ground, very competent, and always eager to be top man in whatever he did. I remembered the first day I met him and how he was like so many English, whom, if you did not understand them, and what had shaped them, you would dislike. They made a fetish of modesty and reserve and many of them could only express themselves by forever using the same expressions over and over again.

They had disliked me at first and I them. But I changed and they changed. And I saw that, carrying their handkerchiefs in their sleeves, and rolling their r's, and treating the war like a rugger match, they brought as much courage to a desperate situation as the ones who made a fetish of explaining loudly their experiences.

But I saw that some still respected the way in which the words honour and glory and war were still used.

It was the way they thought and felt. And I could not change it; war was a part of their life. All right. But war was pain and misery for too many, and pain and death were never honour and glory. War was dog eating dog. Savage against savage. I fought in it now because I knew I must devour or be devoured. But the words honour and glory were being debased again, the process of war was being honoured; war was not worthy of the adjective honour. The process of war was only a symbol of man's stupidity and blindness, but now, as before, in press and pictures, the process was being praised. Why couldn't it be explained in terms of what it truly was, and then explained as absolutely necessary only because men were too much animal to become truly men?

'There's the coast,' said Reg over the intercom.

'Where are we? Can you get me a pin-point?' Pop asked.

'Anything you bloody want, darling.'

I cocked the guns and leaned back in the turret and thought of Reg. He often said, when everybody was sitting around talking in someone's room, that he had joined only because everybody else had and he didn't want to be left at home, and besides he was tired of Toronto. I saw the dark line of the coast far below and a single light winking on the long dark arm of a headland and then we were out over the sea.

'About five miles south of track,' Reg said. 'But we're all right.'

'Can you see any water?' Pop asked.

'Little. Want a drift reading before it's too dark?'

'Please,' Pop told him.

'Hardly any white caps. Very little wind.'

'What's the drift? God damn it!' Pop said. 'Get me a drift!'

I felt the strain closing down on each member of the crew.

It moved there into everybody, into the silence, an invisible emanation, a portent, impalpable as smoke, an emptiness of stomach, a dryness in the mouth, a waiting, looking out into the dark, watching the stars wink and the sky turn darker, and then the moon hanging high and naked in a cold, empty, and remote world of waiting and hoping.

It was very dark now and the moon had been shining for some time and I saw ahead all over the sky the first small flashes of bursting flak. Just quick, jagged winks of light, and then to the left a searchlight beam probing, sabreing the darkness, and Gerald slid the aircraft from side to side, and then dived and climbed so as not to lose any height crossing the Dutch coast, and the sudden round puffs of flak-smoke burst below with a yellow-red flash in the centre, and then I saw the scattered balls of smoke dissolve and thin and drift away in the searchlight beams, for now more beams arched across the sky ahead, and then suddenly coming out of nowhere was the thin black shape of a fighter, exhausts glowing, thick-nosed and thin-winged, coming on fast out of the dark side of the sky. I sat tight inside, ready and watching furiously on all sides.

'Get ready to turn starboard!' Harry yelled to Gerald. 'There's something coming in!'

'Mack!' Harry called to me. 'Can you see him? I think he's underneath to starboard!'

'I see him. He's not coming in. He doesn't see us.'

With the fighter rushing past underneath, my heart feeling almost stopped with excitement, holding hard to the gun-control handle, watching the shape of the fighter steadily, through the red glow of the ring sight.

'He's going the other way!' Reg called from the nose. 'There he goes!'

My mouth dry, my stomach empty, I relaxed. I had seen them before. But now this one after me, or at least it appeared he had been going to attack. They always looked dangerous as hell no matter how many times you saw them. Flak didn't bother me. Detached, I could watch it bursting. But now I felt shaky and tight inside. I took a deep breath of oxygen. The tension was destroyed. I felt pleasantly drowsy, as if I would like to close my eyes and sleep.

Gerald put in the supercharger and crossing the Dutch coast the aircraft climbed steadily. I looked at the guns, they were not freezing up, and at the dark side of the sky, and the Zuyder Zee passed below in its old familiar shape. The aircraft flew on with Gerald weaving it gently from side to side above the depthless dark, seeing now and then below a white night fighter flare lighting the whole sky, while time passed interminably, and then looking out I saw a German beacon flashing, a new one I had never seen before. And ahead the clouds coming up unexpectedly, great motionless piles of cumulus taking light from the moon, and a star winking, seeming to move and follow the aircraft until I felt almost certain it was a night fighter with a light on it signalling; sitting, heart pounding, watching it, then checking it stationary against the movement of the aircraft; and the star did not really move, and then on and on, darkness and stars all around, and to the rear the twin dark shapes of the rudders. Then I was passing Bremen to the left, with its flak and searchlights working as a positioning point for Pop, and then I was past Bremen and looking ahead in the darkness for the first signs of a single searchlight beam straight up and down, or a cone and an intermittent burst of flak among the beams, and the first red flare that would designate the target. Then suddenly ahead there was the first far faint wink of light on the ground and one searchlight beam. Then ten more minutes and the aircraft turned to starboard, Reg calling, 'Seven more minutes to target. Anybody see any flares yet?' And looking ahead I saw red flares at different heights slowly falling into a cone of searchlights, and suddenly in the air among the searchlights more falling flares, like a Fourth of July celebration long ago at home, and I knew the pathfinders were in over the target. Then the aircraft turned and made a circle and I knew I was running in directly from the west, and then I was diving and in over the barrage, the flak bursting all around so thick it seemed I could not pass between the bursts, and then over the fires, really burning now, a monstrous layer of white sparkling glare, as even as cake frosting, and then bombs gone and out of the light into the darkness again, and Gerald calling jeeringly that the German Home Guard must be working the flak and searchlights tonight, and looking back I could see only the great white sparkling round lake of glare, round and as wide as long, the centre of Hamburg. And then the wonderful sense of relief of having it finished, like coming out off an operating table and knowing I was all right.

It was quiet in the aircraft and no one said anything. Lonely and remote I flew on in the dark, again watching, hoping, waiting.

Over the sea on the way home a light winked an SOS on the water, but all I could do was take its approximate position. Someone had gone down. That was the way all the nights were now.

CHAPTER THIRTEEN

It was dawn when I left the briefing-room after interrogation. Outside the air was cold and damp. Chill moisture blew in the cold wind off the bare dirt fields as I walked slowly along the road from the sergeants' mess to the Nissen huts. I opened the door of my room and went in. Sitting on the edge of the bed I undressed. Craven was in his bed, the covers pulled over his head. I was exhausted. I heard Craven move and sit up in bed. I looked over at him. He was smiling faintly, sitting up, a grease-stained outline of his oxygen mask still on his face.

'Have a good trip?' he asked. He reached over on to the table near his bed and got a cigarette and his lighter.

'Not bad. Usual stuff, you know. Hot enough.'

He put the cigarette in his lips and looked suddenly at me as if to see if I were watching him. I noticed his hand was shaking as he held the flame of the lighter to the end of the cigarette.

'I'm really in the soup!' he said. 'Turned back again.'

'What's the trouble?'

He shrugged his shoulders. 'I don't know. Oil pressure dropped down and I said to hell with it, we'll go back.' He didn't sound too sure about what he was saying. Still, it was none of my business.

'Glad you're back,' he said. 'I suppose you know we lost two crews.' He seemed to be watching me as if he were waiting for me to say something. I couldn't tell what he was getting at. He smoked the cigarette in a hurry and lit another.

'Yes,' I said, and got into bed. 'New crews, weren't they? Hell of a place to send fresher crews.'

'You know, Mack – I had a feeling you weren't coming back tonight.'

'They're not going to get me now, brother. Only five trips to go.'

'I know this must sound silly,' he said. 'Look,' he pointed to an old tin candy box on his table. 'I've just got an itching feeling I'm going to cop it one of these nights. I've got some letters in there. Wonder if you'd mail them for me. You know, just in case.'

I lay in bed, unable to relax, and listened to him sitting up moving in bed. I heard him pick up a book and the click-click of his cigarette lighter and the blowing sound he made exhaling smoke. I could not seem to relax. Perhaps because it was cold in the room. Some mornings after a trip I went to sleep almost immediately. This was not one of those mornings. I heard him turning the pages of the book, then he said, 'Hell, you're not sleeping either, Mack. Don't try to fool me.' He laughed.

I sat up in bed.

'Who's trying to fool you?'

'Want something to read?' he asked.

'No.'

He held a book out towards me and I looked at his eyes. There was something wrong all right. But was it my business to ask? No one on the squadron ever questioned another's feelings. There were enough complications in this life without intruding on someone's privacy. But he kept looking as if he wanted to tell me something. I could sense it.

'What's the matter, Dickie? Something's really got you.'

'Guess I've lost my nerve.' He did not look at me. He looked away.

'Hooey. You just think you have.'

'No. There really wasn't anything wrong with the engine tonight. I just panicked and turned back.'

78

'You'll be all right.'

'No. I'm finished. I know it.'

'I know how you feel,' I said.

'No,' he said, shaking his head. 'You don't know what it's really like. Each trip I get worse.'

'Have you told the CO?'

'Sure. He thinks I'm trying to pull a fast one. This is the tenth time in twenty-five trips that I've turned back.'

'Don't quit. Can't you just force yourself to go on? You're close to finishing a tour.'

Craven dinched out his cigarette. There was an abstracted look in his eyes.

'No. I just think up excuses, or take any little thing that comes along and use it for a reason to turn back.'

'You'll come out of it.'

'You've never seen anybody with it bad.'

'Maybe I'm seeing one now?' I said.

'You are, brother. If only we hadn't been shot up so damn badly on those first trips.'

'That's what started it?' I asked.

'Yes, but I'm hopeless now.'

'What about your crew? What do they think?'

'They think I'm all right.'

'You are up a tree,' I said.

He sat there chewing his lips.

'You know I'm not pulling a fast one, don't you?'

'Sure, Dickie, sure. I believe you.'

'You don't just think I'm trying to duck out, do you, Mack?' He kept watching me closely as if hoping I would say only what he wanted to hear.

'No, Dickie, I know how you feel.'

'No, no,' he said insistently. 'I know how you feel. But you don't know what it's really like to be so damn scared your legs get paralysed just from thinking about crossing the Dutch coast.'

'Well,' I said, 'I worry a lot if that's what you mean.'

'But you feel you're ready to do the right thing if an emergency comes along, don't you?' His voice was anxious, as if he needed my answer as proof to himself that he was more afraid than anyone else.

'Yes, sure,' I said. I was not lying.

'That's just it,' he said. 'I've reached the stage where that least little thing throws me off.'

'Uh-huh,' I said. What more was there to say to him? He was a good friend but I could not help him. Nerves were a personal matter.

'I'll see the MO,' he said.

'Yes, that's the ticket all right.' I was impatient to get to sleep now. I had started to relax.

'You don't think I'm just packing, do you?' he went on, his voice jerky.

'I've got to get some sleep, Dickie,' I said. 'You see the MO. He'll fix you up. Everything will be okay.' I slid under the covers and pulled them over my head to keep my face from getting cold when I was asleep.

'Good night, Dickie,' I said. I heard the click of his cigarette lighter.

'Good night, Mack,' he said.

But even under the covers it was still cold in the room, but I did not get up to put on another sweater or Dickie would start talking again. I was too tired for talk. Too tired for anything. Two crews were missing. Ellsworth and Price they had said, in interrogation. At six in the morning still no word from them. Their names scrubbed off the board. What sweethearts, wives, fathers, mothers, would get a telegram in what parts of the world today? I tried to remember who were in the two crews. I could not even remember their names. Well, none of them were my friends. But did it matter much now even if friends did not come back? I did not think it would. Death now was no more astonishing than catching a train. After a while I went to sleep. The next day the MO sent Craven away to a rest home, and Harry, my closest friend in the crew, moved in on Craven's side of the room.

CHAPTER FOURTEEN

On the nights when flying was cancelled by bad weather, or on nights that we were free, seven of us always went to the near-by town, and we went always together. There was Reg, Harry, Kit, Bus, Moe, Casey, and myself.

How can anyone ever tell of love among us, of nights together in an aircraft, yet of each man more alone than he had ever been in his life, of hours of darkness, waiting, watching, thinking, not knowing what was coming out of the night? Of long hours thinking, Oh, God! What's that dark streak over there in the sky? Suddenly fear coiling in my stomach; and of those nights like hunted animals, sitting in turrets, at navigation tables, behind control columns. How can one tell of the love and loss of self born out of fear and strain; and tension, and the magic of returning turned to exultation and exhilaration when we rode back, seven together in a truck, across the aerodrome, in the dark cold air of winter and early spring dawn, exhausted and jubilant, faces bearded, white and grey and tired, against dark sweated hair, and voices in the dim-lit smoky air of that bouncing truck, 'Oh, I say, it was a prang, wasn't it? . . . Keeeerist! was that you in that cone? . . . Ho! Ho! Ho! I say, I thought you'd had it . . . We stooged right past you! Damn good show, I'd say . . . Everybody back?' And somewhere in the dark beyond the North Sea and the Zuyder Zee fires still glowing. And somewhere, someone not coming back. And so in the exhilaration of one's own safety each man became a brother. And to each other all were wonderful people.

There were days when we hated flying, and were glad there was none, and then, on those afternoons, happy with the prospect of having an evening in town together, we stood on the side of the road that ran through the aerodrome and waited for the bus to carry us to the nearest town. The bus was always crowded and gay and noisy. It went on across the moors and came into town in the dark.

In the evenings before we went out in a crowd we all walked from the bus through the town to a young curate's apartment, where we ate and washed and changed clothes. That winter and spring it was a strange life for all of us. We were over the Ruhr one night, and watching a Bob Hope picture the next, warm and comfortable in a theatre instead of being cold, worried, and careful, eyes smarting and almost blind with strain and fatigue. I can remember all the times walking from the bus to the apartment. We always took the same route. On the way we passed the main theatre, and if we liked the picture we knew we would go there that night. We went along in the dark through the market square, to pass down narrow streets under the old town wall, and along to the curate's flat, where he would be waiting for us. There was always the odour of warm food cooking, the black-outs drawn, a fire in the grate, the radio playing, and dinner plates on the table. The war was a long way off during those hours, and it seemed all a dream. We sat in front of the fire warming our hands, listening to the evening news. 'Last night our home-based aircraft attacked targets in the Ruhr.' It was all unbelievable that the words were connected with us in any way. We felt only the warm fire and smelled only the food cooking, and listened for the dance music to play. The flat was small, but there were two big bedrooms upstairs and we slept there, many nights, away from cold damp billets where you slept wearing your flying sweater and used your overcoat and leather flying jacket as extra blankets, and hoped the fire in the stove would not burn too low during the night. Across from the apartment was a park, and in the mornings, with the black-out down, we looked out at the sky and guessed at the weather, hoping some mornings if it were foggy that it would hold, while we stayed in the apartment warm and comfortable, talking, reading, writing.

One night the curate sat down on the lounge beside Johnny Casey, the radio operator, and said, 'Did you write home this week?'

Johnny, who was eighteen, said, 'Yes, I wrote home yesterday.'

'I just wondered,' said the curate. 'You really ought to write home often, you know.'

Johnny was shy and introspective, and though he was always with us he was never really one of us in the way we were loud and boisterous together. Nor was he as strong as he looked. He often sat and just stared abstractedly at the fire in the hearth; and at the aircraft often before take-off, though we felt glum and worried we tried in loud joking not to show any uneasiness, and in this Johnny was not with us. The corners of his lips would droop and he would look no one in the eye. He wanted no one to see how he felt. He did not look well after fifteen trips, and he was always tired and sleepy. The curate said now, 'You're not going out tonight, are you? You want to get some rest, Johnny.' He spoke in a tender voice, as though he felt Johnny were only a child. He cared a great deal for Johnny because he was so young, and because Johnny was alone with himself and his worry of not coming back. It was a worry we all had, but we did not think of it when we were away from flying.

On the floor by the fire was Kit Conway, an American from Columbus, Ohio, who was big and heavy-set, and lumbered from side to side when he walked. He enjoyed teasing the curate when the curate was particularly solicitous of Johnny's feelings. He winked at me now. 'Come, now,' he grinned, addressing the curate. 'Johnny doesn't want to sleep. He'll be dead next week anyway.' Laughing loudly. 'Let him come out for the dancing girls and sin. Hey-ho! Johnny?' Johnny smiled poorly. He sat there thinking of something else. The curate smiled. He understood us, and did not care what we said. Or if he cared he did not say anything. Kit looked at his wrist watch. 'And what time do you think it is, brothers?' he asked.

'Time for you young goats to go out, I suppose,' the curate said.

'Ah, yes, gentlemen,' said Kit, raising one finger, affecting a deep ministerial voice. 'Come, it is time for sin and beer.' He looked at the curate to see if he were annoyed. He enjoyed annoying him, though the curate would never show he was annoyed. We all stood up and put on our overcoats.

'What time will you be in?' the curate asked. Johnny sat beside him on the couch. We stood at the hall door, ready to go out.

'Ah-ha!' said Kit, again raising one finger. 'Who knows?' Then in another voice, 'In fact, my friend, who the hell cares?'

The curate was used to this. He did not say anything.

'Good night,' we chorused.

'I'll leave some tea out for you,' we heard him call down the hall as we went out. It was always the same. We came back at night to hot tea and cakes. His bed was the couch in that room. Sometimes he stayed up for us, but he was always very tired, for he worked all day in the Church Canteen, so sometimes we did not wake him to talk if it were after midnight when we came in.

Moe, Kit, and myself were Americans. Eddie was English. Bus, Harry, Johnny and Reg were Canadians. I was more close to Kit, Reg, and Harry than to the others. Harry was from Vancouver, and he had worked as a clerk for a trucking firm. Bus was from Ottawa and was to be a dentist. Kit had been bored by a job as a furniture salesman and hurt by a wife who had divorced him. Moe had been unemployed in the States, and Reg had worked in Toronto in a department store, and on nights we were in town we always stopped at the Half Moon pub.

It does not seem now that any of us were very good patriots. We fought but we did not believe in politicians, nor any of the empty abstract speeches which were used to explain the cause and what we were doing it for. Bus, the tall dark boy who was to be a dentist, was a rear gunner, and had shot down five night fighters. We all joked about dying because if we did not put dying on an absurd plane the thought could easily destroy our confidence. We were frightened by the idea of dying but we did not think about it seriously until we had to, and we were all proud of the squadron for which we flew. When we were together the bond between us was an inexpressible feeling about what we had been through together. If I had not flown with the others, I would not have the feeling. I did not know for certain if it were love because, as many things go, even that feeling went finally under strain, and towards the end there was nothing left except emptiness and an irritability, and a savage hope you did not believe in that you would all come through alive. Sometimes I prayed. It helped some, but all did not come through alive.

Anyway, at night I went to the movies or to the Half Moon, often to both if there was time. The Half Moon was small and always crowded with air crew; and smoky and noisy, and full of people talking. It took about a year for a crew to complete thirty operations and in the years that air crew filled the Half Moon the girls, mostly civil servants, who came there were never without friends. And the girls could always give the target and exact date when some crew had gone down, and air speeds, and bomb loads, and which were the most difficult targets in Europe. As a standing joke the Half Moon was termed the 'briefing-room', for, as the girls graduated from one tour of crews to the next, the talk was always of the missing, the dead, dates, and the names of targets.

When our crew first met we were all shy towards each other and asked questions that had very little to do with what we really wanted to know. Then gradually, each in his turn, told what he had done before the war.

We went drinking and talking and then in those days it was something because there was such a bond among us. When we went after girls it was because we were lonely, and because, though we did not believe we would die, at the same time we never doubted that we might die, so those who say it was wrong have never been young and going to die, because in the days of many dying around you, wrong is a difficult thing to understand. And dying can be a very lonely process, especially if there are nights when you can see the possibility of it coming a long way off.

The curate felt as we felt, that the war was an evil of the worst odour, but that it was necessary. He never said anything about our personal lives, but tried to show us in every way his idea of a personal life. But then we were not as he, but it did not come between us, and in many ways he was as much one of us as anyone could be. There were always arguments about God, but the curate had a feeling for God which he never had had to realize by any other process than the feeling itself, while we had given up depending on feeling for telling the heart what was true. We felt we could run our lives on truth being only what we saw. So nights we argued that, and soon we all became so involved that we could not solve anything, and I think we would have been convinced of how true the curate's feeling was if only the pubs had not closed so early. When we came in later, after a dance or closing time, we were all always too tired, or often too drunk, to do anything better than sleep.

The curate always telephoned the aerodrome after a raid on Germany. At night he would hear us setting course over the city, and in the morning he would hear us coming back in the dark. He always telephoned the sergeants' mess to learn if we had all returned safely. When we were broke he loaned us money. One night we came into town and Kit was not with us. Kit was in another crew on 'ops' that night, and the crew in which Harry, Johnny, Reg, and Eddie and I flew were standing down, as the saying goes, because we had been on operations three nights consecutively, while Kit's crew had been standing down. It was too bad he was not here, the curate said; he had found a butcher shop eager to sell several large venison steaks and we would have them for dinner tonight. The curate was thirty years old, a large well-built young man, a former college athlete, but by no means addicted to athletics in any sense, and the next morning his eyes, which were round and pale blue as a child's, darted slightly in a worried look while he asked of Kit and leaned over the frying pan in the kitchen, poking a fork into the frying bacon.

'Where do you think they went last night?' he asked me the next morning at breakfast. 'I heard them coming back about five o'clock this morning.'

'Five o'clock!' It was winter. 'Probably southern Germany if they got back that late,' I told him.

'Wonder how Kit is,' he asked apprehensively. I did not say anything. I smiled. Harry smiled. I could see Kit tired and bleary-eyed right now, as I could see myself in the same position. It seemed funny thinking of Kit out there at the aerodrome, and me here in the apartment.

'Hope he's all right,' said the curate mildly.

'Kit's all right,' I said. 'What the hell!'

'Do you think it would be too early to telephone the drome?' He spoke quietly, as if apologizing for even hinting he felt anything were wrong.

'Oh, why worry?' said Harry, irritated, still sleepy and tired from too much beer the night before.

'Well, I just think I will anyway,' the curate said shyly. I heard him take the frying fork out of the skillet and the skillet off the stove. He came out of the small kitchen into the room where we were seated at the table by the window, that overlooked the street and park across the way. 'I know it must sound ridiculous,' he said, 'but I simply must telephone.' There was no telephone in the apartment. He rolled down his sleeves and put on his coat while he said there was some bacon cooked in the kitchen.

We watched him go out in the hall and heard him get his hat off the hook and put it on. We did not say anything. We went on eating. Then we heard him go downstairs and close the door. When we finished breakfast it was time to catch the bus to the aerodrome to be there in time for the morning conference of all air crews. We were walking along the street passing the cathedral when we saw the curate returning. He came towards us fast and stopped in front of us.

'Well, he's gone,' he said. He stood there looking at us. 'He didn't come back. I called the mess.' He stood there in front of us, his face white, and he could have cried if he had let himself go. He stood there holding on to himself, looking at us as if he expected something we might say or do would help.

The words 'he's gone' did not mean anything to us.

'Yes,' someone said, 'that is tough.' Then, 'Oh, well, Kit'll turn up.' Then, laughing, 'They won't get old Kit. He's probably setting up an egg-stand right now wherever he is.' Kit had a reputation as a salesman because of his enthusiasm for planning ways to make money after the war.

But we had been too long with death to be anything but detached about it. Too long with guarding ourselves against caring, because a caring man was apt to be a nervous man, so in guarding against feeling we were that much better and stronger on a raid. It was later, perhaps, when we were alone that the caring came, but the first impact of a friend's death was neither a shock nor a hurt. Only the sounds of words coming out of someone's mouth. And two weeks later when Johnny was killed we learned again how easy it was to forget. But then it was necessary to forget. Later we could never forget. For when it was all finished the detachment left us, we could forget none of the dead, but think only of how in seeing the actions and deeds of others in the world, at home and in England, the ones safe and sound, away from the fighting, in seeing that we could think only of how easily others forgot.

But that morning we were already in danger of being late for the bus and we could not afford to get in trouble at the aerodrome by not being on time, so we said good-bye to the curate in a hurry, told him if we were not flying that night we would be in town and went away, running along the street to catch the bus.

CHAPTER FIFTEEN

That night and for several nights after we did not fly, but we stood by to fly.

Some of the fresher crews went to Italy, but not the crew I was in. Italy was a long trip, though it was never considered difficult because the opposition at Turin and Genoa was never comparable to a German target, and at that time we were being used only on heavily defended targets because of our experience.

Mornings it was foggy and rainy and cold, and two mornings after Kit was missing I woke in the Nissen hut from a dream of falling in flames, unable to bail out, with my harness caught in the turret and fire coming back along the inside of the fuselage; I woke and heard Harry calling in his sleep from the bed across the room, 'Weave! For Chrissake, Gerald! Hell, Gerald! Weave! For God's sake!' I sat up in bed and snapped on the light. 'Hey, Harry! Harry!' I yelled. His voice ceased and he rolled over in his bed.

I looked at my watch. It was eight o'clock. On the table by my bed was an old snapshot of Gloria. Yes, I had wanted her then. I had wanted all the things she was, comfort and security and money. I wanted them without working too hard, but now none of it seemed very vital to me. Perhaps it would later. I was happy here among friends. I hoped all would be safe from now on. I had lied to myself many times but it did no good to lie now. I did not want the things I had once been too confused to know I wanted.

'Harry,' I called. I got out of bed and put on my flying boots. The floor was of stone and cold to walk on. 'Harry.' I went over to his bed and shook him by the shoulders. He lay still.

'Harry! Come on! It's eight o'clock.'

He moaned, said irritably, 'Ah, bugger off. I don't want any stinking breakfast.'

I knew he wanted breakfast. He just didn't want to get up in the cold room. I pulled back the blackout curtains and started to dress.

'You coming, Harry?' I asked, pulling on my trousers.

'Okay, Okay,' he said, sitting up in bed, yawning, shivering, rubbing his eyes. He pushed the blankets down and swung his legs over the side of the bed and picked up his socks.

'How do you feel?' he asked.

'Lousy.'

I had been drinking beer until late in the mess the night before and now with the room cold it was not so good.

Harry pulled off his pyjamas and flying sweater, and bending over, shivering, his teeth chattering, he struggled into his underwear, standing first on one leg and then on the other. He sat down on the bed and began to button his shirt.

'Remember when we were nice young men and didn't drink?' he said, grinning, his head back while he tried to insert a collar stud in the front of his collar.

'Come on, brother, rise and shine.'

'Rise and shine, hell. I'll rise, but I'm damned if I'll shine on these mornings.'

'The evils of drink, my boy.'

'Say,' he said suddenly, his hands coming away from his collar. 'You know what day it is? I wondered what made me get up.' He started to button his collar again. 'It's pay day, you dope,' he said.

'My God! if it isn't!'

'You know something? Remember last month when someone stole my bike?'

'Yes.'

'You know I have to pay the squadron for it. Well,' he smiled to himself. He paused; he was standing by his bed looking at me. He was standing there grinning. 'You know,' he said, beginning to laugh, 'after they take out of my pay for the bike each month – you know what I'm getting per night to go to these god-damned German targets.' He began to laugh harder. 'Ho! Ho! Ho!' – throwing his head back while he fastened his tie. 'Sixpence a trip until I get the bike paid for. I'd like to find the sonofabitch who stole it. My God! Sixpence a trip to Essen. I must join a new union.'

'You won't find your bike. No one ever does around here.'

'I know it.' He went on laughing, fixing his tie.

I got up and went to the mirror on the wall by the door and began to comb my hair.

'You know,' Harry said, 'maybe it will rain to beat hell today.'

'Maybe you wouldn't like a nice night over the Third Reich?'

'My friend,' he said, 'I'm not in the mood for war today. Today is pay day.'

'Today we join F.D.R. and Eleanor.'

'My friend,' said Harry to himself in the mirror, 'Ah hate work.'

'Young man, there are medals for those who will go to Berlin tonight.'

'Suh,' said Harry, affecting a Southern accent, 'make mine a nut-brown ale. Ah thank you, suh.' He knotted his tie.

'Today for the crap game,' I said.

'How you done lately?' Harry asked.

'Broke even.'

'Maybe today is your day,' he said. 'Ho! Ho!'

'Ho! Ho!' I laughed bitterly. Harry had won most of my money in the crap game the previous pay day.

We finished dressing and discussed whether we should change underwear today. If we changed we would have to take a bath, and in the ablutions building, that stood in the centre of the moors, with the doors open most of the time, it was too cold to bathe. We decided against bathing until we got to the curate's flat again.

We went outside in the morning air that was cold and full of fog.

Walking, Harry shook his head from side to side.

'God,' he said, 'I must have been blind last night.'

'Hell, yes. We all were.'

'Fun, wasn't it?'

'With us, it is,' I said. 'Because we like each other. It might be a bore with someone else.'

'It's getting to be a bore even among us,' Harry said disconsolately. 'What do we do? We fly. We eat. We drink. We make love. Then we fly some more. I don't even appreciate the part other than flying any more.'

'You've just got a hangover.'

'A kind you don't know about. Not alcoholic,' he said. 'Just hangover from living.'

'Boy, you are in nice shape.'

'I don't know why you feel so cheery,' said Harry. 'You're in the same boat as I am.'

'You're just tired.'

'Oh, sure,' he said bitterly. 'You know all about it, don't you?'

'Thinking about Kit?'

'No, hell, no. He's gone. That's all there is to it. I'm not going to mope around about anybody who's dead.'

'You've got it figured out then,' I said. 'I don't know why I should have to reassure about anything so you'll feel better.'

'You don't have to. I'm just in the dumps.'

I walked along the road to the mess keeping my head down against the wind. There was water lying in the muddy fields on both sides of the road, and among the trees on the far side of the field the ground was thick with fog and we knew we would not have to fly today.

Ahead was the sergeants' mess, a squat, low, long, greenish cement building. To the right of it was the officers' mess, a similar building.

'Did you go over to the WAAF dance for a while last night?' I asked Harry.

'Yes. Deadly. You didn't miss anything.'

'Think maybe I'll stay in tonight and write home.'

'Tuppence-ha'penny you're on the bus to York,' he said, smiling.

'It's a bet.'

Harry was looking thoughtful for a moment.

'I wonder what keeps us going,' he said. 'Go into town. Pick up a girl. Get tight.'

'I wouldn't worry about it. I used to worry about things like that.'

'Let the future come, eh?'

'I don't know,' I said. 'I don't know a thing any more.'

Harry laughed. 'Did you ever?'

'Nope.'

'Okay, let's eat.'

'Here, Rex! Here, boy!' Harry called, and the mongrel that slept in the mess came out of the mess hallway and jumped on our legs. 'Hello, boy!' We stood and petted him. 'Good dog,' Harry said, patting his head.

In the mess it smelled sourly damp of our breakfast cooking and the telephone was ringing. We went into the dining hall, to the long wooden tables that stretched the length of the room, and ate our breakfast of beans-on-toast and hot tea. We were eating at the table.

'And this morning,' Harry announced, grinning over a cup of hot tea, his mouth full of beans. 'This morning, our delightful friend Air Vice-Marshal Harris is rolling over in bed selecting his silver dart with which to select tonight's target on the map by his bed. "Hawkins!" he calls.' Harry brandished his fork in a peremptory manner, pointing the fork at my chest. ' "Hawkins my man, bring my morning spoon of champagne and two poached eggs".' Harry touched my chest with the pointed end of the fork. ' "Quick, my man. I must be up and away to my office. My bomber boys stand stamping their feet in the cold, praying for the fog to clear. Aha!" ' Harry would roll his eyes, gesture with his fork. ' "My bomber boys are even now crying to get at the Hun".'

Just then Edith, one of the WAAF waitresses, came up to the table and leaned over Harry's shoulder.

'You know where Johnny is?' she asked. She was a homely girl, with glasses and buck teeth. This was a week before Johnny died. She was a hard worker in the mess but inclined to sleep with any number of people, either with the hopes of getting married or, as most of us suspected, because she liked lovemaking. We never understood why she did not like Harry enough to sleep with him, for there were very few men on the station with whom Edith did not sleep.

'No, I don't know!' Harry said angrily. 'Probably in bed! Why?'

Edith looked reproached and shy.

'There's some mail for him. I just wanted to give it to him.'

For a moment Harry forgot his unsuccessful attempts with Edith, and wanted now to annoy her. He looked dead-panned at her. 'Johnny who?' he asked, looking puzzled. Then, 'My dear young woman, someone's misinformed you.

'Oh, go to hell!' Edith said to him, and walked away.

Harry laughed. 'Poor Edith. You know, Mack, I think she's in love with Johnny. This is the second morning I've seen her looking for him with his mail.'

'She's got a tough racket here,' I said. 'About five shillings a week for working like a horse. Mopping and cooking ten hours a day. What the hell, if she wants to be nice to Johnny, leave her alone.'

'My, my, aren't we sympathetic! Come on, let's see if there's any mail.'

We went into the lounge and over to the brick fireplace, first to see if there was any heat. It was cold in the mess. I could see my breath vaporizing on the air. A crowd sat in the chairs around the fireplace, but there wasn't any fire. If there was not any work to be done on the squadron, no guns to harmonize, no test flights, the idea was to keep up the appearance of work anyway, and to do this a fire was not lit in the sergeants' mess until noon, the only sure way of keeping the sergeants out of the mess if they were not flying, for I soon learned that one of the important ways of life in the Royal Air Force was always to appear busy, and if that were impossible one must hide, so no one would have to complain that someone was not working, though work might be already finished. It was all part of the game and many were experts at it.

When Edith came in with the mail the crowd moved out of the chairs and over to the mail rack on the wall by the door. Harry and I were pressed tight in the crowd around the mail rack. Hands were reaching and grabbing for letters, and Edith was shouting names and putting letters in the rack when no one responded to the call of a name. We got our mail. There was a letter from my sister and a Sunday newspaper from home.

I went back to one of the big chairs by the fireplace and sat down. Just then Eddie, our flight engineer, came in. He was older than the rest, about thirty-five, with iron-grey hair, an Englishman, with a pipe clenched between his teeth. He came over smiling, his eyes red-rimmed; he looked tired. He had just returned from a raid on Turin. We had not wanted him to go with a green crew, but as we were standing down that night, and a green crew lacked an engineer, Eddie had had to go. It was the crew's first operation.

'Whew!' Eddie shook his head now, smiling. Bus and Reg and Moe came over to ask him about the trip. 'Shaky do last night,' Eddie said. He took the pipe out of his mouth and tamped down the tobacco with one finger. Laughing. He shook his head again thoughtfully. 'Only pay parade could have kept me from going directly to bed this morning.'

Harry asked, 'Good trip?'

Remembering it and now safe, Eddie smiled, 'Bloody awful. What a navigator! I'll never go with a green crew again as long as I live.'

'Hell of a break making us work with crews other than our own,' Harry said.

'Nothing you can do about it,' Eddie smiled.

It seemed so many members of crews were missing as soon as they were asked to work as spares with other crews. We did not think it fair to send out a man with, say, fifteen trips to his credit to work with a crew on their first trip, but it was the way things worked.

Harry asked, 'What happened?'

Eddie took the pipe out of his mouth and poked at the air with the stem of the pipe. 'You know just before you cross there' – poking the pipe-stem in the air at the imaginary jagged crests of the Alps – 'right there,' holding the pipe still while he looked at Harry. We stood listening. 'Right there,' Eddie went on. 'You know, just to one side on Mont Blanc where you cross – the bloody port engine cut at sixteen thou.'

Harry said, 'Owah!' and clapped his hand to his cheek. We knew the dangers of that route if an engine failed.

Reg smiled. 'You're a lucky boy, Eddie!' He clapped Eddie on the shoulder. 'What'd you do?'

'Jettisoned our load,' said Eddie. He put the pipe back in his mouth. 'Jettisoned our load,' he smiled, 'and got the hell out of there.' Then he looked serious for a moment, 'We were losing height all over the place. Couldn't climb at all.'

Bus looked at the clock above the door. 'Damn near nine,' he said.

Crew conference was at nine.

'See you chaps in town tonight, eh?' said Eddie, and winked, not wanting us to think he had been bragging about the difficulties of his trip. He went over to the rack for his mail.

I sat in one of the chairs by the fireplace and opened my mail, my sister wanted to know if I had everything I wanted – food, razor blades; also had I heard the news, many of the gay ones the lovers of parties, of life, laughter and their own egotistical selves, were gone, dead, missing, captured. Names, vague. Almost unreal. The rest of the letter was about home and the baby she was going to have. I put the letter away and opened the paper from home and began to read.

CHAPTER SIXTEEN

The next night and the night after we still didn't fly. Each day and night the weather was good and on those two days more new crews joined the squadron, and more new aircraft arrived. So we knew a big raid was coming. We expected it in a few days. We had only two more raids to complete a tour of thirty.

Two nights after Eddie returned from the raid on Turin I was in town standing on a street corner wondering whether to go to a movie first or directly to the Half Moon. Everybody would be there drinking and talking, and laughing all night. Just as I was about to go into the Half Moon I saw a New Zealand airman walk past on the other side of the street. He was tall and stoop-shouldered. He was walking slowly, with his hands in his pockets and his cap slouted far over on the back and side of his head. He looked like one of the members of my gunnery course back in Canada. I walked over behind him. I remembered his name, Lofty Dowman. He turned when I called and came back and stood by me.

'My God!' I said, pleased to see an old friend. 'How're you, Lofty?'

'How're you, Mack?' He smiled and we shook hands. His smile was slow and his hand felt soft and peculiar. He seemed to be abstracted.

'Good enough,' I said. 'And you?'

'Fair, boy, just fair.'

'What's new?'

'Suppose you heard about Bijur?' he asked. 'Went down at Bremen last month.' Lofty had a funny little wistful smile, as if he were explaining Bijur's death in terms of, Well, so what, eh? Here we are, aren't we?

'What're you on?' he asked. 'Done many trips?'

The subject of Bijur was gone.

'Halifax. Two more trips and we're finished. How have you been doing?'

Lofty grinned.

'Pathfinders,' he said. 'Lancasters. Good kites, eh?' He

winked. There was great rivalry between Halifax and Lancaster crews as to which were the better aircraft.

'How do you like the town?' he asked.

'It's a place to go at night.'

'Now you're being complimentary,' he said, and laughed.

'Let's get a drink, if you're not doing anything,' I said.

'Righto, boy. I'm just passing through. Going back to the squadron.'

'Where you been? On leave?'

'Yup.'

'Lucky boy.'

Lofty grinned, feeling his advantage of just having had leave. 'Too true,' he smiled and patted me on the back.

The White Horse Tavern was just across the street. We went in. It was crowded, full of troops. When the beer came it was weak as usual. We drank and stood at the bar and talked about the old class of gunners. It seemed he had checked on all of them and he and I were the only ones left now of the original class. The rest were dead. Lofty looked quietly thoughtful across the bar at his face in the mirror behind the bar.

'You look cheerful as hell,' I said.

He turned and grinned. He looked much older than when I had known him in Canada. But then that was nothing new. Most people did after two years. We had another beer and went outside and walked up the street past Market Square.

'Where we going?' he asked.

'The local dive.'

'Okay by me,' he said. 'Doesn't matter.'

We walked out of the square and into the narrowness of Coney Street and along Coney Street to the first turning on the right. The Half Moon was on the next corner. Lofty kept walking along looking down at the pavement. He did not seem anxious to talk. The minute I started talking he seemed to be thinking of something else. Maybe I was boring him. I looked at him. He turned, feeling me looking at him.

'Forget it,' he smiled poorly.

'What's the matter?' I asked.

'Hell, I don't know,' he said, shaking his head.

'What's the trouble? Get shot up badly or something?'

He nodded, not saying anything. We went into the Half Moon and up to the bar.

'Think I'll have a whisky,' he said.

'You want to take it easy.'

95

'Don't worry about me,' he said. 'I'll have a double whisky.'

'Two doubles,' I told the bartender.

He went away. We leaned against the bar.

'Where'd you get shot up?'

'It wasn't once,' he said. 'Six times. You had any bad luck?'

'Not really bad, I'm still here.'

'That's all that matters, brother.' He laughed.

'Remember the cause, brother,' I said, and laughed.

He grinned. The drinks came and we tossed them off. We stood there talking.

'We haven't been properly educated politically,' he said. 'You've got to have too much or too little in order to develop a true patriot's feeling for a war. We've always had just more than enough.'

'Don't analyse it.'

'I won't,' he laughed. 'Buy you a beer instead.'

Just then Harry came in from the lounge. 'Hey, you,' he said. 'I missed you at the curate's. What bus did you come in town on?'

'Four o'clock.'

'Oh, that's it. I came in on the six.' Then, 'Hello, who's this?' He pointed a thumb at Lofty. 'Who's your friend?' Lofty grinned and put out his hand. Harry and he shook hands. I told them each other's name.

'Come on in the lounge,' Harry said. 'All the lads are in there.'

It was the same every night in town. A big table packed with beer glasses. Harry, Reg, Moe, Bus, and others from the squadron sitting around talking. There lay our youth; the smeared, wet, ring-shaped stains of beer glasses.

'You going to De Grey Rooms?' Bus asked.

'Again?' I asked. It was a dance hall. The same girls every night. Sure, why not, I thought.

'Got any tickets?' I asked.

'No, I know two girls we can get some off though,' said Bus.

'It stinks,' Harry said. 'Same girls. Same line. Same faces. No thanks. I think I will stay here and live a quiet alcoholic life.'

'Care to go to the dance?' I asked Lofty.

'What is it like? Any good?'

'Oh, you can have fun. If you don't go too often.'

'Okay, sure, try anything tonight,' Lofty said.

We had another round of scotch. Double.

'What's the matter with you?' Harry asked Lofty in a kind of belligerent manner. Harry was getting tight.

Lofty did not say anything.

'What the hell you looking so grousy about?' Harry asked insistently, looking at Lofty. 'Nothing's wrong with you. No one's shooting at you, are they? What the hell's wrong with you?'

'None of your goddam business,' said Lofty. He turned to me. 'What's wrong with him?'

'Not a goddam thing wrong with me,' said Harry, sitting up in his chair suddenly. 'We just don't like long-faced bastards sitting around here, that's all.' He leaned forward. He was more drunk now than I thought.

'Oh, take it easy, Harry,' Reg said in a disgusted voice.

'Come on,' Bus said. 'I'm going to the dance.'

'Come on, Harry,' I said. 'Aren't you coming?' Everybody stood up. Harry sat in his chair looking sullen, staring at all the empty beer glasses on the table.

'Oh, go to hell, all of you,' he said, not looking up. 'I don't give a goddam for any of you.' He stared dully straight ahead.

We all looked at him for a moment and then went out. We walked up the street to the De Grey Rooms. It was a big square hotel with a ballroom on the second floor. We went inside and upstairs. The band was playing and it was crowded and hot, and now, like many dances that once were good and became no good when you went to them too often, this one might be good tonight or might not. I didn't know. Often I wondered why I came. Dancing bored me, but it was better here than staying alone in my room on the squadron. I couldn't concentrate on reading any more.

I stood in the stag line and watched the dancers moving past. If I danced I knew exactly what my partner would say. The same old conversations with different variations. I was just leaving when I saw some American officers come in at the door. They were noisy and talking loud, and in the centre of them I saw Diana. I felt all faint inside. I wanted to see her and still I did not move. She was smiling and laughing and talking to an American officer. The crowd around me pressed me in.

I didn't know what to do. She hadn't written since that day we had missed seeing each other in London. I stood and watched her dancing past with a big dark American captain. What was she doing here?

I went downstairs and had some coffee and sandwiches in the dining-room. I was sitting there when one of the Americans came in and sat down at my table. He was a big young pilot. I asked him what he was doing around York.

'Just looking at the stupid English,' he said, and laughed. 'Why, what're you doing?'

I didn't say anything. I saw him looking at the USA flashers on the shoulder of my uniform.

'You ought to be fighting with your own people,' he said.

'Yes, I suppose so.'

'What do you think of the English?'

'I think they're all right.'

'They're terribly behind the times though, don't you feel?'

I had met other Americans in England before, and when I did I was often embarrassed for my country. There were always a few Americans who wanted to cause friction, entered an English pub, or any gathering, seeming always to feel that because their uniform was a different colour they were something more than blood and bone, and that as a reward for their beaming presence all English within the vicinity must respond to them like filings to a magnet. Somehow they always made me disgusted. They are my own people, and I should understand them, but I did not find that tendency among the English, for the Englishman may feel just as superior but he never intrudes his superior composure on anyone's feelings. It's difficult to explain, and perhaps the disgust I felt was only brought on by my not being seen by Diana. Then why don't I go up to her, I thought; don't sit here.

'Sure,' I said absentmindedly to the American. 'Yes, they're quite behind the times.'

I got up and went upstairs to the ballroom. Bus was just coming out. 'I'm going up to the curate's,' he said. 'This place stinks.'

'You used to like it,' I said.

'My boy,' he grinned, 'that was before I made all the women in here. The weary victor goes home.' He went on downstairs.

Reg came up to me in the ballroom. 'Say, have you seen the ATS officer that came in with the Americans?' he asked. 'She's all right.' He made a circle with his thumb and moved his arm back and forth. It meant he was interested in her.

'Yes,' I said, looking over the floor for her now. Reg did not know I knew her.

'Oh no, you don't,' he said, laughing. He saw me scanning the crowded floor.

'I saw her first, my friend,' he said.

'You think you did.'

Lofty came over. 'How're you doing?' he asked. 'You know,' he said. 'I don't care a damn about dancing any more.'

I patted him on the back. 'You must be in a bad way. You haven't looked as if you were enjoying yourself since I met you tonight. What's the trouble?'

'The whole crew's dead. I was the only one got out. Got shot up on the way back over the French coast. Three weeks ago.'

'Oh, you'll be all right in a week.'

'I'm the only one left, Mack.'

What the hell did he want sympathy for, I wondered. Sympathy didn't help anyone nowadays.

I saw Diana coming through the crowd. She saw me.

'Mack!'

'Diana!' I said. She hurried over. 'What are you doing here?' she asked.

'Stationed here. You know that. You knew I was around here. You wired me here once, didn't you? If you remember.' I was angry at her.

She saw it.

'Why haven't you answered my letters?' she asked.

'Your letters? Hell,' I said, 'I never got any.'

'I've written, Mack.'

'Are you lying?'

'Mack, don't be silly. I've written, worried, written, and never an answer. I thought you were dead.'

'You never wrote when I was down south,' I said.

'Darling, how could I? You know why.'

'I always told you you'd get over anything. What's the word on John?'

'Don't worry, I haven't gotten over anything. I've just put away the feeling for him. He's gone, Mack.'

'Hell, I'm sorry.'

'No, it's all right. I've wanted to see you.'

'Couldn't find anyone else?'

'You know you don't have to talk like that to me, Mack. You never did. I could have fallen in love with you easily.'

'I never knew it.'

She laughed. 'You don't think I'd let you know, do you? I couldn't then. My feelings were so mixed up, I didn't know what I was doing.'

We were standing in the ballroom doorway. The crowd brushed against us as it passed. I heard the music stop and knew it was time for an intermission. I was happier than I had been in a long time.

'What are you doing here?' I asked.

99

'I'm on leave. My grandmother lives near here in the country. I'm going out there in the morning.' Then, 'Darling, let's get out of here, please. I've been up in bloody Edinburgh instructing in an ATS school for six months. Come on.'

'What about your American friends?' I asked.

'Oh, those people? They aren't anything. One sat at my table at dinner and then asked me over here.'

'I bet.'

'Darling, don't be jealous,' she laughed.

'I'm not.'

She laughed again. 'Oh yes, you are. You are sweet. Come on, we'll go back to the hotel and talk. Darling, it's been such a long time.'

'It's been more than that. You don't know. I've thought of you all the time.'

'Darling, I've missed you so much.'

We went downstairs and got her coat and walked back in the dark to her hotel.

We went upstairs to her room. I kissed her at the door. 'Darling,' I said, laughing, 'you are funny.' I turned and looked at her. I wanted her more than anything in the world.

'Don't you understand?' she said. 'I couldn't tell you what I felt in Bournemouth. Everything was too involved.' She opened the door behind her and leaned forward and took my hand. I went into the room and she closed the door, then she turned and put her arms around my shoulders and kissed me. She was tall and I felt all of her against me.

'Darling,' she said. 'I've needed someone like you so much. Do you know how much I've missed you? No one has been anything to me.'

'Do you know how much I've missed you?'

We stood there laughing. Suddenly I put my arms around her and held her for a long time.

'I have to go in the morning,' she said.

'That is hell.'

She saw what I was thinking.

'No,' she said, 'you can't stay here. These people who run the place know my grandmother.'

'Dear old England.'

'Dear old England,' she laughed. 'I'm sorry.' Then, 'Darling, I love you so much.'

'I love you, darling.'

'No, you can't stay here.'

'All right.'

'No, darling, you can't. Oh, please.'

'Please, darling,' I said. 'I have to leave in the morning too. There'll be a call on tomorrow night, I know.'

'Oh, my darling, I'm sorry.'

Her hands held my head tightly and I was kissing her throat. 'Darling,' she said. 'To hell with dear old England!' I looked up at her and she was laughing a little. She held my face between her hands and kissed me.

Maybe I was not in love. Maybe I was only lonely. Maybe I was both only more lonely than I knew. But I lay there and did not care whether it was all only because of loneliness or what it was. I knew only that I was happy, that I was not happy like this with anyone else.

In the night I woke and she was beside me and I woke with the feeling it was morning, feeling with all the regret and disappointment in the world that there would be a call on in the morning for a raid. I heard her wake. I started having the old feeling that I would be late to the squadron for something important and that I would be in trouble. Love was stronger than duty, but duty had more authority over me.

'Darling,' she asked in the dark of the blacked-out room, 'are you asleep? You've been talking in your sleep.'

'I'm all right. What time is it?'

'I don't know. I don't care.'

'I don't either, but if it's morning I have to go.'

'Don't go.'

'Darling,' I told her, 'I'll have to. I want you to know I hate to go on this trip tonight, and I love you, and I would rather be with you than anywhere in the world.'

'Oh, darling.'

'Darling,' I said, 'I wish we were married.'

'Where do you think you'll be going tonight?' she asked.

'The damned Ruhr.'

'Are you scared?'

'Not now. I will be. Too true. I wish we were married and all this were all over and we were away some place together.'

Very slowly she said, 'We aren't the only ones who feel that way.'

'I know, darling; you give me the best reasons for fighting this war. That's a pretty good one, isn't it, for the ones who feel like us? Sounds good.'

'It'll have to do, darling, until I think of some new ones,' she said.

'What time is it?' I asked.

She snapped on the bed-lamp and looked at her watch on the table by her elbow.

'Half-past five.'

'I'll have to go at six.'

'Darling,' she said, her voice catching, 'you'll take care of yourself if there's a call on tonight, won't you?'

'Sure,' I said. There was little else I could say in answer to a question like that.

CHAPTER SEVENTEEN

The next morning at crew conference the report came through from Met that the weather was perfect over the Continent, and at eleven o'clock that morning in the gunnery office we heard there was a call on, overload petrol tanks, a long trip. We checked and harmonized our guns and went back to the warmth of the mess, the *Daily Mirror*, the ceaseless dice and card games, the fire in the hearth holding out the damp cold air of the Yorkshire moors. And so after lunch we were again seated around the fire, dozing, talking, listening to the radio. The bar was open, and Harry and I drank two beers, listening to another air gunner playing the piano in one corner of the lounge. After a while I looked at the clock over the doorway. Two o'clock. Two hours until briefing. Where were we going? Overload tanks. A long trip. Where?

At three o'clock I went down to my room and wrote two letters home, changed into my flying boots and slipped my flying sweater on. I felt no apprehension. It was my twenty-ninth trip; an unreal world of fire, smoke, death, and fatigue was now almost as ordinary as the old world of going to work in a news-paper office. I sealed the letters; there was nothing in them; only that I was all right and hoped everyone at home was all right. I couldn't think of anything to write. I went out and along the road to the briefing-room, thinking of Diana, wishing I was going to be with her tonight.

And here again was the inside of the briefing-room, the raised dais, the Wing Commander standing there; the air filled with the murmur of voices. Wing Commander Hill was a dark-haired young man, well liked because, though he was compelled by the Air Ministry to do only one raid a month, he went on all the raids, never missing the most dangerous ones.

He was twenty-six years old, and he did not come back that night and no one ever heard of him again.

Now, raising his voice above the murmur of voices, he spoke to the room: 'You all know the target tonight. I'll give you the latest gen.' He looked slowly round the room and began to smile. 'Gentlemen,' he said, quietly smiling, 'it's low-level tonight.' He stood there grinning. A sighing *Phew*! went up from the crowded room. The target was Stuttgart. Great God!

We climbed over the aerodrome, then turned south; far behind winked the circular lights of the aerodrome. The moon hung naked and high overhead, lighting all the clouds below in a smooth field of white, peaceful as sleep. Here we go again, I thought, resigned, hating it.

And down across England, over the dark land, familiar aerodrome lights winking signals, searchlights already on, awaiting the enemy. How damn tired I am of it all, I thought, and cocked my guns. How tired I am of strain, and the mere wear and tear of trying to stay alive.

There were lights in the Thames Estuary. Over there is London, down there somewhere, I thought. How wonderful it would be to be there with Diana tonight.

Then the last winking signal light that masked the edge of England. We were dead on track. How far we have come in experience, I thought. Pop with his navigation, Gerald in flying, Harry and me on the guns. How much more confidence we now have. Then I looked ahead and saw the searchlight beams and gun flashes high over the coast of France and forgot all about confidence, feeling once more only my empty hollow stomach, my practised hands now ready on the guns.

We flew on, crossed the coast, joking and talking intermittently; Pop occasionally giving a new course; all our voices as easy and sure as though we were back in the mess.

We saw all the familiar gun flashes and estimated just about where we were, each man picking up an old familiar navigational pin-point here and there. 'That's Paris over there,' a voice would say. Or, 'Here comes that old German beacon we picked up for the first time on the way to Munich.'

We went on in the moonlight and began to descend.

After a while Pop's voice: 'Ten minutes to target.'

Gerald's voice: 'Right, Can see it now, old man. All set, Reg?'

Reg's voice: 'Give me a wind, will you, Pop?'

Pop gave him a wind.

Reg's voice: 'All set, Gerald.'

Ten minutes, I thought. I felt cold and tense, yet confident nothing could happen. I wish it were over, I thought, I wish we were out past the target. I looked ahead at the target, a great bowl of light in the dark sky. Reg began to tell Gerald which way to run in so as to avoid the searchlight cones. Then we were in over the fires, swinging and diving, the sky filled with anti-aircraft fire. Gerald was singing over the intercom and Reg was calling out instructions. 'Left . . . left . . .'

Then the upward heave and I heard Reg say, 'Bombs gone! Let's get the hell out of here!' The anti-aircraft fire was bursting just above on both sides, sudden white balls of smoke with a yellow flash in the centre. I swung the turret back and forth, watching directly overhead for circular vapour trails that would mark a night fighter circling high over the target area.

Reg's voice: 'Hold 'er steady, Gerald. I'll get another picture.'

The aircraft bounded suddenly and rocked crazily as three black balls of smoke drifted past underneath. It looked too close. Still, with so many aircraft over here, I thought, it's only luck when they hit one. There are too many for them to predict one directly over the target. Anyway, it was a reassuring thought. I went on searching the sky for the fighters.

Then we were beyond the target, and looking back I saw, on the rim of lighted area, horizontal lines of tracer, then a sudden glow of fire and the multi-coloured burst of flame of an aircraft exploding.

Harry's voice: 'See that guy go down, Mack? There's slews of night fighters around. Keep watching, boy.' Then we saw two twin-engined fighters, with lights in their noses, signalling each other, as they came towards us. They came on flying level towards our tail. As they began to open fire, little winks of orange light flashing from their wings, we began to climb and dive. In the darkness, the lines of tracer were like long threads of fire.

'Don't fire until they get in close,' said Harry. Lines of tracer raced past just above the port wing. Then one fighter flew out on to our port beam.

Harry's voice: 'Watch the one on the beam, Mack?'

Me. 'Okay: Okay.' Stomach tight and cold with excitement.

Then I saw the tracer from Harry's turret stream back in a long arc and into the nose of one fighter. Then a pennant of flame jerked suddenly out from the nose of the fighter, then more flames enveloped the wings, and it dived suddenly down through the cloud, an orange glow showing momentarily through the cloud.

'There's one bastard,' called Reg.

Then Harry excitedly, 'I got him, Mack! I got him!'

'Here comes the one on the beam,' I called. I saw tracer going into our port wing, then part of an engine-cowling whipped past. I held my guns on the fighter, firing steadily. God, why doesn't he go down, I thought, why doesn't he fall? He came steadily firing. I was terribly frightened now, my body covered with sweat, a rotten, dry, copperish taste in my mouth, my stomach tight and cold.

I kept firing and the fighter broke away, diving underneath. We were diving now, then racing along just above the ground. If only the damn moon weren't out, I thought, but there it hung big and naked, all the land and sky drenched in light. Again the fighter attacked, firing, pulling away out of range. Reg called up to say he was hit in the head by something but not to bother because he felt all right. Pop went into the nose with the first-aid kit.

Then suddenly the top of the turret burst off, and cold air and splintered glass struck my face. I could see a jab of flame jumping from one of the port engines. I felt faint and tired, and continued firing, watching the fighter coming on again winking long curves of tracer. Then suddenly I felt I could no longer hold the gun-control column; I felt too weak and tired even to press the firing button. Oh, God, let it come, and all tightness and hollowness seemed suddenly lifted from my body. There was a blinding flash of light in the back of my head and I felt myself fall backwards, and feebly strain to climb out of the turret.

From far away Gerald's voice: 'Parachute! Parachute! Bail out!'

If only I could sleep, I thought, just sleep. And another blinding flash of light filled my mind, and everything seemed to wilt hazily and beautifully into a kind of pleasant, easy, relaxed dream.

And suddenly to my surprise I was home. There was the house, big and rambling under the leafy coolness of old elms. I'm home, I thought; the war is over, home in my own room again. And I looked out the window of my bedroom into the sunny stillness of the garden. Home, I thought, I'm home. It's all over.

Then there was another blinding flash of light and in my mind I had fallen suddenly out of my bedroom window.

CHAPTER EIGHTEEN

I woke in the dark, felt cold air on my face, and knew I was falling, and pulled the ripcord and felt my legs jerk wildly apart. Then I was floating easily, swinging from side to side. Then the swinging ceased, and looking down in the dark it was impossible to see anything. My head throbbed. I floated a long time, and when I struck the ground I did not see it coming. I fell on my back, but there was very little wind and the chute did not drag, though I lay there with my breath gone. After a while I sat up and felt the ground under me and saw I was in a ploughed field. Then I noticed one of my flying boots was gone. I got up and unfastened my chute harness and gathered in the chute, which was beginning to inflate. I carried it rolled in a bunched mass under one arm and set off walking across the field. After a while I began to sweat. I wondered if I were close to the sea. If I was, and had to sleep out at night, I would need my fur-lined flying suit, but then I remembered the best time to escape was to walk at night, and I decided to leave the flying pants and the chute here. I came out of the field on to a dirt road and climbed a fence on the other side and found a patch of bushes. I took off the flying pants and hid the chute and pants in the bushes. I had no flying helmet. It must have been jerked off as I jumped, or I must have unconsciously pulled it off myself to keep from choking on it. I wondered which way the road travelled.

All that night until dawn I walked along the road and saw no one. When it was light I went off into a field and sat down and ate a breakfast of three malted-milk tablets from my emergency-ration kit which I always carried inside my flying jacket.

When I finished eating, sucking each tablet slowly, it was bright daylight, warm, and the sun was up. I took off my flying jacket, looked about me and then realized that I was in a kind of rolling valley. There was no one around. I estimated I must have been some place north of Paris when I bailed out. If I went south I might be able to get to Gibraltar, but the route would take weeks. I decided to try for the French coast. I started across the field and the bootless foot began to hurt. I had foolishly walked on a stone road and now the sole of the sock was worn through. I took the boot off my right foot and put it on my left foot. It was difficult walking, but if there was a long walk ahead I wanted to protect each foot as much as possible.

I went straight across the fields, towards a long row of trees about ten miles away. It was warm that morning and I thought several times of discarding the flying jacket. About noon I crossed what appeared to be a pasture. Ahead was a high dirt road. On top of the road, silhouetted against the sky, was a German sentry. To my right was a wood. I lay on my stomach behind the only tree in the open field and watched him and wondered how I could get in the woods without being seen. I lay behind the tree all afternoon and he did not see me. About four o'clock I watched him walk up the road out of sight around a corrie. I crawled over to the woods and lay on my flying jacket on the edge of the woods. I was afraid to cross the road in daylight. I could not see all the way along it because of a bend in it from which I could be seen if I tried to cross and there was somebody in that bend. When the sun started going down I ate three more malted-milk tablets and looked out across the fields. A new sentry had appeared up on the road, and there I saw, a long way off, across the fields in the direction from which I had come, a line of men at spaced intervals. The guard on the road stopped walking back and forth and looked at them. When they were closer I saw they were soldiers, bayonets on their guns, and they were searching the fields. I looked around and tore up as much long grass as I could rip up quickly and lying on my stomach covered myself with dead leaves, grass, and as many branches as I could quickly break off the bushes alongside me. I lay and waited and heard them coming across the field and then I heard their voices. I made a small hole in a leaf and looked out. They were spaced about twenty feet apart, poking their bayonets into any high grass. I didn't know what to do, then I saw a soldier coming towards where I lay. His legs, coming straight at me, came on closer until I could see the creases in his leather boots. Just as it looked as if he were going to stick his bayonet into my pile of grass and leaves, with the bayonet and gun already pointed in my direction, and just as I was about to stand up, the soldier on his left called to him and he moved across and away, and I could hear them talking and kicking at a dead log. He came back but he did not come as far over as he had been, so when he started prodding forward again he passed only a few feet to my right.

But he was past. I lay as still as possible, and when I no longer could hear them in the woods it was dark. I stood up and stretched, and started towards the road. I thought only of getting back to Diana. When it was dark I crossed the road while the guard was at the far end of his beat. I walked across a meadow in the direction of the long line of trees. I felt it must be, according to my calculations, the trees that marked the course of the Somme river. If I could get north of the Somme, then walk west, I could arrive at a place where the French coast was quite near enough to England to risk a crossing in a small boat. If I could locate a small boat. And the Somme river was heavily defended. I went on in the dark, and changed the boot twice from one foot to the other. Both feet were sore when I saw, against the dark sky, the still darker jagged crests of a long line of trees.

CHAPTER NINETEEN

That night I swam the Somme and lost my one boot and flying jacket. Then during the night I walked west, and in the morning I was standing on the edge of a big field looking at a small white farmhouse on the other side of the field. It was dawn and there was no one around. After a while a fat dark man came out of the house, and I walked across the field and found him chopping wood behind the house. He looked up surprised. Then he looked down again and went on chopping. 'What you want?' he asked, not looking up. He spoke English but it was very broken.

'Can you help me?' I explained who I was.

'How I know?' he asked. He put down the axe and looked at me. 'How I know you tell.' He shrugged his shoulders and picked up the axe.

'English,' I told him. 'I won't tell anybody. I just want help to get out of here.'

108

'Quick,' he said suddenly, and gave me a push towards the house. 'In,' he said. I saw him look anxiously towards the field from which I had come. Two German soldiers were coming towards the house. They were walking, looking at each other, both very busy talking. Their rifles were slung across their backs. 'Get in,' he said. 'Pass here every morning.'

I went in the back door and stood in the corner behind the door and waited. After a while the farmer came in.

'Where you come down?' he asked. These are not the words he used to say it but they are what he meant.

I gave him a rough estimate of where I figured the aircraft had crashed. He nodded his head, watching me closely.

'Tell me,' he said. 'Where you from in England?'

I told him where.

'I knew you were in the field this morning. I saw you from the house.'

'We got shot down night before last.'

He smiled. He shrugged. 'Yes, but how I know?'

'Take my word.'

He shook his head.

'Know you people before,' he said. 'You no fool us again. Find out about you today.'

'My God! I've got to get out of here.'

'Hide in barn. I will see about you.'

'Look,' I said, and remembered suddenly I had a packet of safety matches which I always carried on each trip. I took out the packet.

He took it and looked at it and smiled.

'Keep it,' I said.

'I will. It is necessary.'

He took hold of my arm by the elbow.

'Stay in barn,' he said. 'Come along. I will go and see about you.'

I went outside across the yard and into the barn.

'Stay here until tonight,' he pointed up at the hayloft.

I climbed up the ladder into the loft. I leaned down out of the loft-hole in the floor and said, 'How far is it to the coast from here?'

He grinned, held up two fingers, in a Victory sign. 'Deux,' he said.

'Okay,' I said. 'See what you can do about it. I'll need a boat.'

'Ho, ho,' he laughed, holding his stomach. 'A boat?' he said. Then, 'We will see.'

109

'Okay,' I said. 'Hurry back.' I was terribly tired. I noticed my hands were trembling. I was so tired I didn't even care if I ate. I fell back in the hay and slept in my wet clothes.

When I woke I heard someone in the barn below. I burrowed down in the hay and heard someone coming up the ladder. It was Pop. His head appeared through the square hole in the floor. His face was white and there was a long gash on one of his cheeks. He did not look surprised when I stuck my head out. He only looked tired and expressionless.

'So you got here too,' he said.

'This morning. Where are the others?'

'Did you see anybody bail out?' he asked. 'I didn't.'

'I was tossed out unconscious,' I said. 'I don't know what happened.'

'Gerald and Reg were dead when I jumped. God, where is something to eat? Doesn't this damn farmer feed anybody? I didn't see any other chutes open.'

'How'd you run into this spot?' I asked.

'Some farmers about a mile away brought me over,' he said. 'God, I wish I had a cigarette. What time is it?'

'I don't know,' I said. 'How are we going to get out of here?'

'Who the hell cares? I don't,' Pop said.

'I'm going to take a crack at it in a boat,' I said.

'Are you nuts? You'll never get a boat around here.'

'The farmer hinted he might be able to get one.'

'Sure. But I doubt it. Jerry's got this neck of the woods combed of anything like that.'

'I want to get back.'

'You're mad. I'm fed up. I'm going to give up.'

'Well, how about giving it a go?' I asked. 'I don't know damn all about navigation but I can sail a small boat. How about it Pop?'

'They'll only make you fly again if you go back.'

'Only one more trip. It couldn't be much worse than a prison camp. How about it?'

'To hell with it now,' he said. 'I'm going to get some sleep. Seems I've been walking and swimming the best part of my life.' He lay back on the hay. I asked him which way he had come. The same as my route, he told me. Had he seen the guard on the road? Hell, had he not, Pop said.

'How do you think I got this gash?' he said, pointing to his cheek. 'The sonofabitch jumped me when I crossed the road.

Knocked me down, started kicking hell out of me. Thought I was knocked out and started away. Pulled the sonofabitch down by one leg and choked the bastard in a ditch.' Pop started to laugh. It was not a natural laugh. A little goofy. I looked at him and he stopped.

'Hell,' he said, rubbing his hands. 'I'm finished,' Then: 'You know, I choked the bastard, held his face in some water by the road and killed the bastard. You know that, Mack?'

'Sure, sure,' I said.

He sat there rubbing his hands nervously and licking his lips. After a while he went to sleep. I sat there looking at him. He was a little bald man with two small children some place in Alberta.

CHAPTER TWENTY

In the night I woke and heard someone below in the barn. Pop lay beside me asleep. I crawled carefully to the edge of the square opening in the floor, and as I looked down in the dark someone put a flashlight beam in my face. I jumped back, shook Pop, and heard someone coming up the ladder. Pop stirred and moaned and rolled over on his stomach, but didn't wake up. I got set, kneeling, ready to swing at whoever was coming.

Then, 'It's all right,' an English voice said, and the flashlight went out. Then it went on again. A slight blond man stepped up off the ladder and turned his flashlight on me. He stood there smiling, wearing an old trench coat, and an old felt hat pulled low and slanted over one side of his face. He chuckled. I stood up.

'I knew what you were going to do,' he said. He had a little blond moustache.

'Who are you?' I asked.

'That doesn't matter. What matters is you two have got to get out of here fast, old boy.'

I looked at him. Where was the farmer?

'What's the matter?' I asked. 'Where's the farmer?'

'Don't worry, old boy, everything's all right. But you have got to get out of here quickly. Wake your friend.'

111

'Where is the farmer?'

'Look here, old boy. They found your parachute and they're searching every house.'

He bent down and prodded Pop with his flashlight.

'How do we know who you are?'

He laughed. 'Don't you worry who I am. Wake your friend.'

I wondered a moment.

'Where are we going?'

'Time enough for that. Get cracking, old boy.'

'Farmer tell you what we wanted?'

'Look, old boy. I've been doing this work for two years. I know what you want all right.'

'What?'

'A boat.' He laughed, wiggling his little moustache.

'Can you get it?' I asked.

'No, but the next best thing. A dinghy with a sail.'

'Can you get us down to the beach?'

'My boy, I wouldn't be here if I couldn't. Wake your friend. Meet me downstairs in a few minutes.'

He went down the ladder and I heard him go away. I shook Pop again and he woke and sat up, squinting his eyes to get the sleep out of them.

'What the hell do you want?'

'Come on,' I said. 'You're going to navigate a dinghy across the Channel.' I could not keep from laughing at Pop looking disturbed out of his sleep.

'Don't be damn dumb. I'm going to sleep.'

'Like hell you are,' I said. I shook him. 'Come on Pop, please. Hell, I want to get back. Please.' He was tired and exhausted, he did not care. He lay back. I grabbed him by both shoulders and pulled him up.

'They're searching every house around here. Please, Pop.' He looked sleepily at me, a smear of dried blood covering one side of his face. After a moment he rubbed his eyes, seemed to think about something; then, looking at me, he pushed my hands away from his shoulders and stood up.

We stood there shaking the hay off, then we crept down the ladder. In the yard between the barn and house it was raining. We looked out. No one around. We ran across the yard and knocked on the door. The Englishman opened it and came out.

He pulled down his hat and turned up his coat collar against the rain.

'All set?' he said.

112 .

'Let's go,' I said. 'It's a hell of a night to go any place in a dinghy. Where'd you get the dinghy?'

He only smiled. He was more than proud and secret about his work.

'Come on! Come on!' Pop said. 'Let's not stand here in the goddam rain asking questions.' We walked straight out of the farmyard, through the field which I had crossed over before, and along a lane that passed the woods to the west of the field. We walked for an hour along the edge of the woods. After some time it stopped raining and the moon came out, and then I smelled the sea and saw the moonlight on it. We walked down a path on a cliff and through an opening in the barbed wire by the beach. All the sea was clear in the moonlight. We went along the beach a little way, and back in among some rocks was a dinghy with a small improvised sail.

'It's not a hell of a lot,' the Englishman said.

'Where'd you get it?' I asked.

'Bomber crashed near here. Not in bad shape. Farmer got it out.'

'Thanks a hell of a lot,' I said.

We got in the dinghy, Pop sitting in the stern. Our clothes were soaked. Pop was coughing. The Englishman stood looking at us.

'Have you a compass?' he asked.

'Yes,' I told him.

'Well, all the best,' he said.

'We'll need it,' Pop said. 'Hey, give me the compass, will you, Mack?'

We pushed away from the rocks and poled our way out into the surf. Then we were out in the sea. The waves were so high we did not even have time to turn and wave good-bye to the Englishman. When we were a long way out and sailing with the wind we heard shots on the shore, and saw some lights that went on and then quickly off. But we could tell by the sound that the shots were not aimed in our direction.

CHAPTER TWENTY-ONE

We sailed against the waves, then after some time, when we judged we were about five miles from shore, the moon went behind a cloud and it was dark, and it began to rain again. We tried to lie flat in the dinghy to keep the cold spray from blowing against us, but it was no use. We lay side by side and I could hear Pop coughing. The wind blew us along, and we tried to hold the dinghy on a rough compass course that Pop had computed by the stars, but then after a while even the stars were invisible behind the clouds, so we were not certain just where we were headed, though we tried to maintain a north-westerly course by using only the compass. The dinghy rolled and tossed between the waves, and Pop held the tiller in one hand while he bent down watching the compass. We took turns at the tiller, but the rudder was very small, and out of the water most of the time because the dinghy rolled so much.

After two hours we knew only that we did not know in what direction we were heading, and the wind changed and began to blow towards the south. We pulled down the sail and wrapped it around our shoulders.

Then we did not bother to steer. It did not seem any use. We lay in the bottom of the dinghy, close together, and tried to keep warm, with the sail over us.

'I think we've had it,' I said to Pop.

'What time do you figure it is?' He lay very still, his eyes closed, his hands over his head.

'About midnight,' I said.

'How do you feel?' I asked.

'I don't know.'

'God, I wish I had something hot to drink,' he said.

'Are you sure you're all right?'

'Sure I'm all right.'

'Put your back against mine.'

'Okay,' he said.

We lay back to back and shivered. I got up and slapped my hands and chest. Pop sat up, and we started to slap each other's

114

shoulders, but we were too weak to keep at it, so we lay down again, back to back.

'Jesus, poor Gerald and the boys,' Pop said, and laughed ironically. Then, 'They're better off than we are.'

'Hell, we'll get out of this somehow,' I said. 'They can't kill us now.'

'Ho, ho,' Pop laughed. 'Who can't?'

'Not if you don't let them.'

'Brother,' Pop said, 'don't go bombastic on me. I'm not in the mood.'

We lay there for what seemed hours. I could feel nothing after a while in either my legs or arms, and my hands were so cold I could not close them. I called to Pop and he did not say anything. He lay on his stomach with his hands over his head, and after a while when he did not speak I rolled him over and saw his face was blue and his eyes closed. He looked almost dead. I felt his pulse; it was still beating. The waves were high now and I was afraid to move very much for fear of tipping over. It was still raining and I lifted Pop's head and slapped his cheeks. After a while he opened his eyes. After a moment I didn't feel even strong enough to hold up his head. He closed his eyes again.

I dropped his head and lay down, and reached over and slapped his face once and stopped. I saw him open his eyes. It was as if when he opened his eyes I felt I had done all I was capable of doing, and now if he wanted to live it was his own situation to handle. Or maybe I was only imagining he was bad off. I did not know.

We did not seem to be moving in any definite direction. The wind was still blowing south and we seemed to be drifting that way. My stomach was empty and the ration kit had been washed overboard. The French evidently hadn't had any food to spare, or they had not had time to prepare any. Anyway, they had not given us any. Probably the news the Germans were searching for us had forced them to play their hand with us too quickly. Now I was hungry and cold and too weak to move. It is difficult to describe how one weakens so quickly in the water under cold wind and rain, but it comes more quickly than you can imagine. We were quite strong when we set sail and now in the dark at about midnight we could hardly move. Perhaps some of it was from the shock of being shot down. We lay there and tried to sleep. Towards dawn Pop opened his eyes.

'Try and put the sail up again,' he said. 'I think the wind is shifting.' He had pulled himself together and was hanging on to himself by sheer determination. He was not a young man. At the beginning of his flying career he had tired easily in the air on high-altitude flight, and now near the end of his tour of operations he tired even more easily, as all of us did, as none of us now was as strong as we were on our first trips.

'I don't think I can,' I said.

'Try it. I know *I* can't,' he said. 'The wind's shifting north. It's our only chance.'

He held my leg by one ankle and I got a hold on the mast with one hand and pulled myself up, holding one end of the sail in the other hand. The sail hung wet in folds stuck together. I tried to throw it up so it would top the mast but I could not throw hard enough. The sail fell back and out of my hands. It lay on the floor of the dinghy in a piled wet lump. The dinghy rocked in the trough of a wave.

'Oh, what the hell,' I said and sat down.

'Try it again.'

'Hell, I can't. You can see that.'

I didn't seem to have any legs and I felt sick and faint even from standing.

'Christ, I'm cold,' said Pop.

'Come here,' I said. 'Put your arms around me.'

Pop smiled feebly, laughed a little.

'So now we'll make love,' he said. Then he laughed. 'God,' he smiled, 'I wind up making love to you, what an end.' Grinning he rolled over close to me. We lay there facing each other for a moment, then Pop put his arms around me and I put my arms around him. He held me pressed tightly against the length of his body. He was cold and wet, and there was no heat between us, only his wetness and coldness against mine, and in a little while I felt him shivering, and then soon we were both shivering against each other.

'What a hell of a husband you'd make,' Pop grinned. His face was white and blue.

'You'll never get any testimonials from me,' I told him.

But we knew we were only fooling each other. He knew what I was truly thinking and I knew what he was thinking.

Then I felt the rain cease and the wind die down. It was dawn, but there was no light. In a little while it was lighter and I saw the sea was calm, and the dinghy rocked gently on smooth water with fog all around. Ahead and on all sides there was water for about a hundred yards. Beyond there was only fog. I looked around at the fog and then at Pop.

'How would you like a nice steak?' he said, grinning.

I tried to smile, to keep the atmosphere all right. I smiled, but did not say anything. What the hell's the use, I thought. I knew of plenty of airmen who had died out here after ten hours. They would never even attempt to locate anyone by air in this weather. Still, perhaps they would be searching the Channel after the raid three nights before. Perhaps there had been a raid last night. They would be looking for crews that might have ditched. Still, I hadn't heard any aircraft going over last night. Maybe the raid had been on Bremen, or some place in North Germany. No, they wouldn't be looking for anyone this far south.

'Where do you figure we are?' I asked Pop.

'Some place in the Bay of Biscay. Keep quiet. Save your strength. For God's sake!'

I started to think about Diana, but I had to stop that. Thinking about her, and how I might not see her again, took more strength out of me than anything. It is marvellous, I told myself, what I can stop thinking about if not thinking will some way help me to stay alive. I lay there and looked at the fog and made my mind a blank, by rolling my eyes around and concentrating on that.

But not for long. Where was Diana? What was she doing? I started thinking. She would be in Edinburgh now. Only on a forty-eight-hours leave. Yes, she would be back in Edinburgh. What was Churchill doing this morning? And Shirley Temple and my mother and my sister? And Gloria? Back at the aerodrome I was already listed as missing. Already someone was probably living in my room. What the hell. Turn it off. It would not go off. Pop's arms around my back were cold as two dead eels. He needed a shave. His eyes were closed and the side of his cheek scratched against my neck. My cheek against Diana's throat. Diana. Oh, what the hell. I closed my eyes and dozed, then later slept.

I woke and the fog was gone. Pop was still sleeping. My arm and leg joints were so stiff I could not sit up. Overhead the sun was shining. I felt dry, and looking at the sun I decided it must be about three o'clock in the afternoon.

There was a light breeze, and while Pop slept I tried to put up the sail but I could not stand. I lay down and put my arms around Pop. He felt warmer, and I lay close against him.

Later, when Pop was awake, we heard an aircraft high overhead. We lay on our backs, and though we could hear only the high far-faint sound of the engine we waved our arms. The sound came closer, then we saw high, high against the empty blue sky, a

117

small silver flick of light and heard the high thin whine of a Spitfire. The sound died away.

We lay back and put our arms around each other. Though the sunlight had dried us, the air was thin and cold.

'I think we've got a chance,' I said.

'Just keep on thinking it,' Pop said bitterly.

'Don't give up.'

'Who the hell's giving up?' Pop said. 'What're you after – a medal for saving my life? You sound like you're trying to talk me into giving up.'

'What a hell of a good delirium you could work up with a little yellow fever.'

Pop laughed, his face was only a few inches from mine. We looked into each other's eyes. His eyes were smiling about whatever he was thinking.

'Let's not quarrel, Tootsie, now that we're lovers,' he said.

We lay there and laughed a little. It was a great help.

Later, when the sun began to set, there were clouds in the sky again and a light rain began to fall. By this time we had given up all hope. We only wanted to sleep and maybe die while we were asleep. We did not think we could live through another night. Just then Pop said, 'Hey, listen!' In the sound of the rising wind I could not hear anything.

Then very faintly the sound of an aeroplane somewhere overhead in the rain. We looked up but did not see anything. The rain was now falling hard and driving, and it is always difficult to tell the direction of sound in rain, especially the sound of an aircraft.

Then Pop saw it, low and dark, coming over the water. I was looking the other way and Pop called to me. The sound came closer then, passing about a hundred feet above the dinghy. I saw the awkward-looking wings and cigar-shaped bottom of a Walrus. It banked in the rain and flew back over the dinghy. Pop waved. I waved. I saw the flaps come down on the wings and knew it had seen us and was coming down for a landing.

'Oh, God!' said Pop, as if he were in pain. I was too weak even to be happy with excitement. I knew I ought to feel goofy, cock-eyed with happiness, but there was no feeling at all. I heard the sound of the engines throttling back, and closed my eyes. I started to think of Diana but it all stopped! I did not even feel anxious to see her.

CHAPTER TWENTY-TWO

But a week later after I came out of the hospital I was as anxious as ever to see her. And later I was in Edinburgh, and outside the hotel room the Edinburgh street was filled with cold bright sunlight. A tram clattered past. In the room it was quiet. Suddenly, the night before, a strange empty feeling had come over me. I sat now on the edge of the bed, looking down at my shoes, wondering what had happened to the expectant, exhilarating feeling of going on leave to see Diana.

On the opposite side of the room Diana stood in front of the dressing-table combing her hair.

Why did I really come, I thought. A strange lost empty feeling possessed me. I felt the corners of my mouth stiff and the muscles in my cheeks unable to draw back my mouth in a smile. Everything seemed senseless, to no purpose. I could get up and walk around the block and come back and read a magazine, I thought. I could do that. Why? Then what? I could do a million things and I know them all, and some of them are good. Why not? But what good would it do, whether to sit here or move? Finally I said, 'Let's go and eat, I'm hungry as hell.'

'Just a moment, darling,' Diana said.

I looked at her long dark hair and khaki uniform, the comb moving in her hand in her hair.

I got up from the bed and walked across the room, then sat down again. Breakfast, I thought, breakfast and I'll feel good again, and we'll have the whole day ahead of us. The whole day, and I can get up when I like, and do what I like, and no flying, no worry.

Outside it was sunny, and walking in the cool air and seeing the grass and the trees green, and holding her arm, I felt all right again.

I must be mad, I thought; there are thousands of wonderful things to do. Here is a wonderful beautiful girl with me I've wanted to see for a long time. I wonder what could have been the matter with me back there in the room. I looked at her face and saw her smooth skin and wide clear blue eyes and full red lips, and in the morning there I felt I wanted her all my life. I held her hand tightly.

'I was going away last night.' I laughed, squeezing her hand, looking at her, wondering why I had wanted to leave her. It was all silly now. Of course, this leave was wonderful.

Her look told me she thought I was only teasing, starting some aimless banter for the fun of it.

And it's true now, I thought. It is only for fun I say it now, but last night I would have gone. Where? For what?

In the café, alone with her, too early for luncheon trade, and too late for breakfasters, I felt safe, as if I did not mind sitting here for a long time reading the papers, eating, and looking at her. There was not the feeling of wanting to hurry off or wanting to escape a nameless sense of urgency, and I ate quietly, and when I went outside it was noon. And I knew now what we could do. We would go to a moving picture sit quietly and be lost in it, and content when we came out, relieved. Relieved of what? Living?

And in the movie I held her hand and wondered why I had ever been bored with a movie. It's all going to be a good leave, I thought, just as I felt it would be.

That evening we sat in a pub, with a low-beamed roof, because she liked that kind of a place. And we drank and talked, and none of what we said seemed pointless and boring. The lost empty feeling had passed, and I smiled and thought of a long time ago when first I had met her and all the things we had said then. If said by someone else they would have seemed ridiculous and absurd, but because I had needed her then, I remembered how I had seemed clever and purposeful, and how I had first felt I was in love with her.

'Remember,' I said now, 'I hardly knew what I was doing the first time I told you I loved you?'

She laughed. 'You were oppressive, darling,' she said. 'You were too damn lonely to be interesting.'

'And now I'm not lonely?'

'And now you're not lonely. Period. Satisfied?'

'Hmm, let's have another drink.'

We were sitting like that when I had the queer feeling again of wondering why I was sitting here; of suddenly feeling nothing towards her, of wanting to be alone, of knowing that would be no good either after a while. You were alone for a while and then you were tired of being alone and empty. I was tired of a good many things.

'Come on. Let's get out of here.'

'But, darling,' she said, 'I'm having a wonderful time. Why do you want to go?'

'I don't know,' I said angrily, regretting it, for I knew I was angry only at myself. Why can't I just sit here and be happy, and have a nice girl and feel towards her as I always had. I did not move.

She just looked at me quietly.

'I'm going,' I knew I was only saying it to torture her because she was content and I felt aimless and upset.

'Don't be such a childish fool, Mack.' I could almost have taken her hand and sat down, I wished that I could.

But what for, I wondered. What can I find in holding her hand, in loving her? No, I thought, I don't love her, I don't love anything. I just keep feeling I want to do something, go some place, and know at the same time that wouldn't work either. Hell, nothing works any more.

'Darling,' I sat down. 'Look,' I said, 'I don't know what it is. Only try to understand.'

'Oh, yes,' she said bitterly. 'Lovely. Try to understand.'

But what more can I tell her when I can't understand it myself, I thought, when now I am always wanting to do something other than I'm doing, and then when I'm doing it, wondering why I am doing it? What the hell's the matter with me?

'Good-bye,' I stood up.

'Where are you going?'

'London. What the hell for I don't know. I just can't stay here, that's all.'

Maybe, I thought, maybe it will be different there, maybe it will be different always in a lot of places.

But on the train to London I felt I should not have left her. I knew that for me there was no one like her in London. Maybe there is no one any place any more, I thought. Maybe there is nothing any place. No, no, that's wrong, I told myself in a queer panic.

'King's Cross! King's Cross!' shouted a voice across the noisy air, and the station platform swarmed with people.

London, I thought, London! This is going to be good, and I remembered the exhilaration of returning to London on other leaves a long time ago, glad to be away from flying.

'Bitter,' I told the bartender in the pub down the street, and with my suitcase against my leg, and back in London again I was happy for a moment.

I'll keep this feeling, I thought. What the hell was I ever bored about? And I came out into the soft twilight air and looked up in the air at the barrage balloons in the still evening sky.

I feel pretty damn good, I thought, and got a room and looked at myself in the mirror over the washbasin and shaved. I'll go to a bar and find someone to talk to, I thought, coming out into the street later.

And I went into a bar and found someone, a soldier and an airman, and I talked and they talked, and for a long time that evening everything was all right. They all seemed friendly. This is wonderful, I thought. All the people smiling at each other, talking, laughing. A wonderful fine leave.

Then suddenly sitting there I wondered, What am I saying? What am I doing here? What are these people saying? Why the hell do we sit here being so damned friendly? It gags me spewing out words to each other.

'Oh, it's a marvellous show. You simply must see it,' said a female voice somewhere in the room.

I'll go someplace else, I thought; I'll go someplace else and there will be different people. No, I thought, I can't do that. We'll all say the same things again. It won't be different, and someone will smile and someone will be friendly, and someone will be amusing. And someone will be this, and someone will be that.

'God's teeth,' said a female voice beside me, 'this is awful liquor.'

And now I knew I could not be in a new place all the time before an old place depressed me, before all the thinking started, saying to myself, Why? What for? Am I alive? Am I dead and don't know it? Wanting always now to go on to something else. But to what? For what reason? There did not seem any reason for anything any more. I had lived too long on sensation and exhilaration.

Walking home that night I felt I knew for an instant an answer to whatever was upon me. I've explored every form of hate and friendliness, I thought, and there's nothing ahead but seeing, hearing, smelling, countless, endless repetitions of human relationships, identical even in repetitive variations from the few fundamental patterns.

'I'm being called up next week,' a passing voice said. And I walked on through other voices. Voices, foolish, endless, aimless, full of empty words. Empty as my own.

'Darling, I love you.'

122

'Taxi!'

'So I told him . . .'

'For God's sake don't wake me until noon,' I said to the night clerk at the desk.

But I did not sleep late that morning. I woke early, sitting up in bed, feeling suddenly how good and wonderful it was to find a day all new ahead of me, a day for living differently than I had lived other days.

And I sat in bed thinking, if I just stay like this, just sit here quietly, it will all come to me, an understanding of what drives me on to trying anything, seeking in anything, and all things, a nameless end and meaning.

But nothing happened, and I could neither think nor feel my way through to an end, a meaning; and after a while I got up and dressed and went downstairs and ate breakfast, as I had done many mornings in many places, thinking of myself going through the performances of washing, eating, sleeping, as if I were really only a part of myself standing to one side watching my body go past in a robot-like process of arm and leg movements, as if I were really only a sawdust-stuffed doll of myself moving towards nothing.

And now I'll read the morning paper, I thought, while eating breakfast, and then I'll go out and walk along Piccadilly in the sunlight. Nothing to do. Wonderful. Just walk in the sunlight and no one to tell me I'm on Ops tonight. Then what will I do, I wondered, and wiping my chin with my napkin I got up and went out.

I enjoyed going to a movie that day, enjoyed anticipating the unused time ahead of me, but in the movie began to have the feeling again I could not stay there. And I was bored.

The action in the movie and the actors that were once funny to me were no longer funny. I heard the lines being said, and sitting quite still I felt as if a part of me another person who looked and dressed like me, was seated in the next seat, laughing and enjoying each comical line.

What the hell is so funny, I wanted to say to the imaginary yet almost perceptible presence of myself sitting next to me. What the hell is so funny about this movie? It's not funny. It's dead, it stinks. I'm dead. We are all dead.

I left before the movie finished, and outside felt relieved to be away from it, as if I had escaped myself, or a part of myself I no longer wanted and hated yet wished for vaguely.

I went into a bar and there were people, and standing against

123

the bar, drinking scotch, which I did not taste, I wondered, what I would say if someone spoke to me. But why should any of us speak to each other, I thought, we never say anything anyway; and I paid for the drink and went out, again glad to be some place else.

That night I lay in bed and thought, I'll go back to Edinburgh. If I go back there everything will be all right. But I knew in my heart everything would not be all right.

We only go around in circles, I thought; if I go back there it will only be the start of another circle.

So in the mornings I walked the streets, reading papers, wondering what to do, to drink? To go to a show? To find someone and talk? But what is there really to talk about, I asked myself. All of us are only repeating. On and on and on. The same words, different mouths, worn out with repeating.

I considered going to the country, and basking in the sun, but once there I knew how it would be; wondering what was going on in some other place, knowing too that nothing probably was going on, but bored there even in the sun.

So soon there were only a few days left before I returned to the aerodrome. I began to count them, asking myself, why don't I return early? There is nothing here, and the aerodrome life that not so long ago had been very real, and something to get away from, now in some peculiar way became attractive. It will be good to be back, I thought. There will be friends, and whatever I say will seem all right, no matter what, not without point, meaning and feeling.

Then there were hours I regretted I was not with Diana in Edinburgh, hours I wondered if she was not my life. No, I thought, there is nothing that is really our lives. It is all of us, all of it, and there is no complete single meaning or purpose.

And the day came to return, and I was relieved, as I had been the day I was told I was going on leave.

On the train I thought, maybe I've been near death too long. Maybe that's it. Maybe when it comes every week and friends go and you feel nothing about them, neither regret, pity, nor sorrow, maybe then you are dead too. And in fighting for life maybe I have lost it myself. Maybe there is no meaning in the saying that life is only meaningful in how you live it and for what you die, for in being near death you learn that words will never truly explain any meaning. And meaning becomes nothing, and life becomes an endless process of waking and sleeping.

But the next day when I sat high in the turret again, the gun-control column in my hand, and I heard the four throttled engines roaring hard forward, and looking out beyond the tail of the bomber into the windless sunny afternoon, sitting in the sound of engines, I felt again there was a meaning to life and I was no longer restless, sitting now in the object I knew I would soon hate, soon again bringing with it a world of darkness and of stars, strain and tension, hope and fear. But now strain and fear were not on me, they were as vague as the feelings were now becoming which I had been subject to on leave, and I knew now only that I was back, that I felt all right again, and that I would write Diana and tell her I loved her more than ever.

CHAPTER TWENTY-THREE

A few mornings later I heard that Craven had returned to the squadron from a rest home. That morning the gunnery officer told me that I was to fly my last trip with Craven. I objected, but there was nothing I could do about it. I was just leaving the gunnery office when I saw Craven standing in the hall outside the Wing Commander's office, looking as though he were wondering whether he should knock and go in or wait and have the administrative sergeant clerk announce him.

It was hard to tell about a new commanding officer. The old Wing Commander had gone down on the last Op. This new one might be as regimental as hell, and then he might not. After a long moment I saw Craven knock, then gingerly open the door and go in. I ran outside and stood to one side of the open office window and looked in.

'Good morning, sir,' Craven was saying to the officer behind the desk on the far side of the small room. The officer did not look up.

A nice domineering type, the old head-down, long-pause-before-speaking technique, I thought, giving him the business.

'Morning, sir,' Craven repeated, and stood rigidly at attention.

'Well?' still the head did not rise.

'Flight Sergeant Craven reporting, sir,' Craven said.

'And just what is that supposed to mean to me, Flight?' asked the Wing Commander, lifting his head.

'Thought you knew I was back, sir,' Craven said. 'You phoned the mess for me, didn't you?'

The Wing Commander picked up a pencil and drummed on the desk. Craven looked at him, not knowing what to say. The Wing Commander looked back, saying nothing.

Craven looked at the Wing Commander, a tall, handsome man of thirty-five, with a long, straight, wedge-shaped nose.

The Wing Commander tapped his pencil once more on the table, and looked thoughtful.

'You're the one's been in a rest home, aren't you?' he asked. Craven nodded. The Wing Commander pursed his lips thoughtfully and slowly tapped the desktop several times with the pointed end of the pencil, looking at the pencil.

'How many turn-backs was it you did?' the Wing Commander asked.

'Twelve,' Craven answered.

'Mm, twelve?' The Wing Commander asked. 'I thought it was thirteen?'

'No, only twelve. I didn't get off the deck once. Magneto drops.'

'Yes, I must have been thinking of that. Mm, twelve,' the Wing Commander said. He raised his head and rubbed the bottom of his chin.

I studied the new Wing Commander. I wondered who he was. He had not been in command when Craven had gone away. Also this one wore no medal ribbons. Not that that was too unusual. Yet they usually have some by the time they reach this rank, I thought. It must seem strange to Craven to find the old Wing Commander gone. But in three months a lot of people could go, and they usually did.

The Wing Commander was watching Craven staring dreamily out of the window, his gaze now abstracted, though Craven still remained stiffly at attention.

'You're probably thinking things are different since you were here,' the Wing Commander said. 'Well, they are. I've made them different. I suppose you've heard?'

'No,' said Craven, 'I've heard nothing.'

'Well, they are,' the Wing Commander said; 'and they're going to stay that way.'

He tapped the desk with his pencil, watching Craven's face.

'Flight Sergeant,' he said, 'the top button of your tunic is open.'

Craven looked down at his chest. Yes, the button was open all right. How the hell had he missed that, I thought; he slipped it

126

carefully into place. I wished he could sit down. Queer the way he kept chewing on his lower lip.

'You know,' the Wing Commander said, 'I don't think I'd like you flying in my aircraft if I were in your crew.'

'It's all a matter of taste, sir,' Craven said.

The sonofabitch, I thought, what's he trying to put Dickie through?

'I hope you're all right now,' the Wing Commander said. He was smiling. It was a smile all right, only no one would like it.

'Yes,' said Craven, 'I'm okay now.'

Suddenly the Wing Commander ceased smiling, and his gaze made a slow, careful, measured tour of Craven's body.

'Your buttons, Flight,' he said.

'Yes, sir?'

Craven cast his eyes down at his chest, holding his neck straight and stiff.

'Well, sir,' he began, raising his eyes.

'Craven,' the Wing Commander's face was hard, 'I'm accustomed to having my airmen smart, whether they're on ground or in the air, at all times. Their uniforms pressed and their buttons polished.'

The Wing Commander ceased. The room was very quiet. He sat there now, his elbows on top of the desk, while he rubbed his hands back and forth together and looked at Craven.

'When do you think you'll be ready for Ops?' he said.

'I'm ready now,' Craven said. 'I told you I'm well and rested.'

'A lot of people here – your flight commander says in his report you were only "slinging lead" after that crash. That you were all right after you came out of the hospital, that your turn-backs were intentional.'

'I'm only human,' Craven said.

'We haven't room for that type here,' the Wing Commander said.

Craven only looked at him, saying nothing.

The Wing Commander appeared to be studying a spot on the wall somewhere just behind and above Craven's head. After a moment he said, 'You'll be on tomorrow night, if there's a call.'

'Tomorrow?' Craven said, surprised.

'You heard me, Craven.'

'But hell, sir, I haven't even got a crew,' Craven said. My God, he might put him on with some fresher crew. That was a sure way to get it in the neck, a sure way. He licked his lips, and put his teeth together hard.

'We're short of pilots at present,' the Wing Commander said, his voice was cold, inflectionless.

'Couldn't I get in a few circuits and bumps first? After all, sir, I haven't flown for three months.'

'If there's aircraft serviceable,' the Wing Commander said. 'But I can't risk wrecking aircraft on training. You're supposed to be trained already, Craven. I have a certain number of aircraft to get into the air on every operation. I intend to meet Group's orders, no matter. Do you understand?'

'Well, I might get knocked off taking off on the Op just because I lacked a spot of freshening up,' Craven said, watching him closely now.

'I'm willing to take that chance, Craven. Better you went that way than trying to freshen yourself up on circuits and bumps. I'm sorry, but I have neither aircraft nor pilots to spare.'

'You are cheerful, sir,' Craven said.

'I'm not being paid to be cheerful,' the Wing Commander said, 'nor is it your place to be interested in attitudes. Your crew will be Flying Officer Dawes' old crew and Mack Norton. He has one more trip to complete his tour.'

'Dawes' crew?'

'He was killed in a flying accident. They're just waiting here for a new skipper.'

'I never heard of them,' Craven said.

'Well, it's your new crew,' the Wing Commander said. He opened the drawer in his desk and took out a package of cigarettes and laid them on the papers by his elbow.

I knew what he was thinking. It is always difficult to make these kids understand the war isn't something they were trying to keep anybody alive in. We are only interested in using you, realizing our training investment. You weren't anybody. Craven, you are only a pilot in an endless procession of pilots. I wondered if Craven's nerve were truly gone. Maybe all this talking was only Craven's method of putting off returning to operational flying. All this request for freshening up. Only a stall. Maybe he was finished.

'How many trips have Dawes' crew done?' Craven asked.

Craven, I thought, there's no way out of it for you. There are ways out, but they'll break you if you try to use them.

'Two trips,' the Wing Commander said.

Both mine-laying trips, I knew; hell, they've never even seen a major target. Well, no need to tell Craven. He would find out soon enough.

'That's hardly fair, sir, expecting me to take on a crew as fresh as that,' Craven said.

'Fair? What do you think this war is — a cricket field, Flight Sergeant?' the Wing Commander said.

'Well, hardly. I didn't mean that, sir,' Craven said.

'You ought to know by now this is not a business in which you fulfil your wants,' the Wing Commander said.

'Yes, I know,' said Craven. He got ready to salute and leave. 'Only I thought . . .' he began.

'You thought,' the Wing Commander repeated after him, and picked up his cigarettes and waited for Craven to speak, knowing there was really nothing Craven could say.

'Couldn't I wait until next week, sir?' Craven asked suddenly.

'No,' said the Wing Commander. He lowered his head and waited for Craven to leave.

Craven swallowed hard and cleared his throat.

'But the other gunner, sir?' he said.

'He's quite ready,' the Wing Commander said. 'He knows his way around. He's been on the squadron two months.'

'And the navigator has done only two trips?' Craven asked.

'He was top man in his class at Observers' School,' the Wing Commander said.

'That loesn't mean a hell of a lot when you're trying to find Bremen with somebody who's never been there before,' Craven said.

'I am sorry, Craven,' the Wing Commander said. 'Things are that way, that's all.'

The Wing Commander avoided Craven's eyes, and picked a cigarette from the packet.

'You know what'll happen to me if I refuse to fly, don't you?' Craven said.

The Wing Commander shrugged his shoulders and lit the cigarette in his mouth.

'Jesus Christ!' Craven said.

'I'm sorry,' the Wing Commander said.

'Oh, sure,' Craven said. 'A lot of help that is.'

The Wing Commander slowly exhaled a long puff of smoke. He looked bored. Craven looked hurt, morose, evidently wondering how he would leave without losing any more face.

'I think it's a damn dirty deal,' Craven offered as a parting shot. 'I might just as well go out and shoot myself.'

The Wing Commander nodded, laughed sympathetically, blew out a puff of smoke, then smiled his implacable smile, and put the cigarette back in his mouth.

'Thanks,' Craven said. He was angry now. It was as if the Wing Commander, in some secret reserve of laughter showing faintly in his eyes, were enjoying Craven's poor luck. 'Thanks a lot, sir,' Craven said dryly.

'Not at all, Flight,' the Wing Commander replied, imitating Craven's tone of voice. He was smiling faintly now, smoke wreathing his face, while he watched Craven. He almost seemed to be grinning.

'Well, guess I'll check into the mess,' Craven said.

It's strange, I thought, the Wing Commander instead of dismissing him is making it awkward, so that he feels like a guest taking leave, feeling a kind of nameless guilt for leaving. But, in his heart, I knew that Craven knew the feeling of guilt wasn't nameless, and he did not want to stay with the Wing Commander looking through him, as if he were going to say, 'Craven, you've lost your guts. You've had no reason to lose your nerve outside of your own imagination like any of us, but you've let it get you.' All the same, the Wing Commander was a prime sonofabitch for torturing him this way, I felt.

'Yes, you had better check in, Craven,' the Wing Commander said, in a flat voice that was mocking.

Craven saluted and started out.

'Don't forget to polish your buttons while you're on this squadron,' the Wing Commander said, just as Craven put his hand on the doorknob.

Craven turned his head, nodded a silent yes. The Wing Commander looked at him quietly through the plume of cigarette smoke wreathing across his face. Craven turned and opened the door and went out. I followed him.

Outside it was a rather cold, grey afternoon with a slight drizzle of rain. Craven pulled up his coat collar and set off along the road through the potato fields to the long, low, green cement building that was the sergeants' mess. It really was raining now, and he carried his head pulled down inside his high overcoat collar. At the door of the mess a dog knelt in the rain, pushing his nose against the door. Craven pushed open the door and let him in.

Inside the telephone was ringing and the hall smelled damply of steamy cooked food.

He went into the lounge. In one corner there was a crowd shooting dice on a card table. In the big chairs pulled in close to the red-brick fireplace a lot of people were reading the daily papers, others were just dozing. Craven went over to the mail rack on the wall. There were no letters for him. He found a vacant chair near the fireplace and sat down.

To Craven all the faces in the mess must have been new. He looked like a new arrival. That vaguely shy, vaguely hesitant expression.

After a while, a little more confidently, he asked the sergeant in the chair next to him, 'Is Pop Parry still around?'

'Sorry,' answered the sergeant, 'I don't know him. I've only been here a week myself.'

'May I borrow your paper when you've finished?' Craven said.

The sergeant handed him a wrinkled copy of the *Daily Mail*, and then slumped down in his chair and closed his eyes, leaning his head to one side, supporting it on one hand. There was no news in the paper. I looked over his shoulder at the headlines and wondered what they were doing at home, and wished I had a *New York Times*. Probably all the women back in the Savoy-Plaza bar were smiling at all the nice young men in uniforms. It was about all there ever was in the papers now.

After a while it was two o'clock and everybody began to leave to get down to Flight Offices to their sections. Craven looked at the sergeant in the chair beside him. The sergeant turned and opened his eyes, yawned, stretched, and looked at Craven.

'You new here too?' he asked, yawning, covering his open mouth with one hand.

'No,' Craven said; 'I've just been away.'

The sergeant sat there looking at Craven. 'Whose crew you in?'

Craven laughed bitterly. 'Nobody's. Just making one up for me.'

'I suppose you know things are getting pretty shaky around here?' the sergeant said.

'Yeah. There are a lot of new faces.'

'That isn't all. Wait'll you run into the new Wing Commander.'

'Where's Hill?'

'Hill? Think he went down on Stuttgart last month.'

'Jees. You sure?'

'Yeah. Sixty-second trip. Nice – huh?'

'Lovely.'

'Mack,' the sergeant said to me. 'They heard any thing on Wing Co. Hill?'

I shook my head. 'No. No word.'

Craven took out his cigarettes and lit one. He took a deep breath and, inhaling a long drag, held it. He smoked one cigarette quickly and took another. I noticed his hand was shaking a little.

'Sorry,' he said to the sergeant just as he started to put the cigarettes back in his pocket, 'meant to offer you one.' He held out the package.

The sergeant took one, snicked a match in his thumbnail, and lit his cigarette.

Someone turned on the radio and a dance band started playing.

'You met the new Wing Co. yet?' the sergeant asked.

'Yeah,' Craven said. 'Nice cheerful sonofabitch, isn't he?'

Then he said to me, 'Well, Mack!' Then, laughing, 'Hear you're my gunner.'

'Yes, how're you, fella?'

'Wing Co.'s a bloody butcher,' the sergeant air-gunner named Steve put in. He was leaning over the arm of his chair towards Craven, his chair was on the other side of the first sergeant's chair.

'He doesn't care how he gets kites into the air. Just so long as he keeps his good name at Group,' the sergeant air-gunner said. 'If there's something wrong with your kite just before take-off and you get it working and you're twenty mintues or half an hour late taking off, he'll still tell you to go. Just so he gets his quota into the air.

'He's a yellow bastard too,' the sergeant said. 'He only goes on easy trips, like Lorient and St-Nazaire. Takes all the gravy. Never catch him on a Ruhr show.'

'Remember Bruno? He practically murdered Bruno?'

'You mean Bruno's whole crew!' the sergeant said. 'Whole damn crew! Sent 'em on a Turin do when they were all tired out! They'd operated five nights out of eight and the night before were shot up over Duisburg. They should have been rested. Bruno was shaky as hell. He crashed into the Alps. Whole crew went for a Burton.'

'Oh, he's a prime bastard all right.'

'Say,' the sergeant said, suddenly addressing all of us as if he were going to be very confidential with a secret, 'I hear Craven's back. You know, the bloke that packed up after doing about a dozen turn-backs.'

'Care for a cigarette?' Craven asked, and passed the packet around. I did not say anything, nor look at Craven. He seemed to be taking it all right.

132

The clock on the wall showed two-thirty. The lounge was almost empty now. Crumpled newspapers filled the empty chairs.

Craven smoked another cigarette. He said he wished he had a drink. He hadn't had a drink since before going away to the rest home. He felt droopy, he said. Maybe if he had a really good night in town, a girl, a good dinner, and a good show, he would snap out of it, at least for a day or two. In the old days it sometimes used to work wonders, he said. For a day or two. He wished he could find Parry now. Maybe if he went down to the Navigation section Parry would be there. No, he guessed he had better straighten his billet. He'd locate Parry at tea. We put on our coats and went outside in the cold rain to our billet, the familiar small room in a Nissen hut in a potato field about a quarter of a mile from the mess. When we finished sweeping his room, we lay on the bunks reading old copies of *Punch* and *Flight Magazine*.

Craven was still lying on the bed when I heard someone come along the narrow hall of the Nissen hut and stop outside the door and then open it, and then he looked up at a round-faced, partly bald-headed man about thirty-five, smiling, standing just inside the door. He closed the door and, smiling, looked down at Craven on the bed. Craven put down the magazine he was reading and sat up suddenly, swinging his legs off the bed.

Craven rubbed his hands together and grinned. 'Jees, how are you, Pop?' he said.

'How you doin'?' the bald-headed man said. Then to me, 'How're you, Mack?'

'Okay, boy.'

'Jees; it's good to see an old face,' smiling. Craven looked up at Pop. 'For Chrissake, take the weight off your feet and sit down, pal.'

'So you're back?'

'Sure, sure, waddiaya know? What's new?'

'Same old gaff,' said Pop. 'New boys. New Wing Commander. How you feeling?'

'Okay, boy, all set.'

We were old friends, all very fond of each other. We were quietly smiling at each other now. Suddenly, as if he remembered why he was here, Craven stopped smiling.

'Hope to hell you're not flying with anybody,' Craven said.

Pop shrugged his shoulders but said nothing. He came over and sat on the foot of the bed. 'Cigarette?' he said.

'Here, try mine. Camels. Got 'em from home,' said Craven.

They smoked and Craven tended the fire in the stove for a moment. He knelt in front of the stove poking at the coals with a stick, saying nothing. Then he came back and sat on the edge of the bed.

'Well, what's cooking with you?' Pop blew a cloud of cigarette smoke.

'I was wondering if you'd do a trip with me. I gotta do a trip if there's a call on tomorrow,' Craven said, looking down at his feet. 'Mack's coming.'

'I'd like to,' said Pop. 'Only I'm screened. I finished on Berlin while you were away.'

Craven looked at him quickly and smiled. Lucky devil, I thought. Still, maybe if Parry hadn't done thirty trips, if he wanted to do another trip, they'd let him, if he asked to go.

'You know how it is, Dickie. I'd only be forcing my good luck.' Pop shrugged his shoulders.

'Yeah, I know,' Craven said.

'I don't want to go for a Burton any more than anybody else does. I've finished for a while. I'm no hero,' Pop said.

'Sure, sure, I understand,' Craven said.

'You feel ready for a trip? You know you've been off for a long time.'

'Sure, it wouldn't bother me. Well I mean if I can only get one trip under my belt I'll be okay again, you know?'

'Whose crew you taking?'

'Some sprogs and Mack for his last trip.'

'Jesus, that would be pushing my luck.'

'What the hell, Pop,' Craven said, pleading; 'I know how you feel, but I gotta get a good navigator.'

'Are you sure you're ready?' Pop asked. 'You know, if it bothered me the way I think it bothers you, I'd just pack up. Call it quits.'

'Oh, sure,' said Craven bitterly. Then, snapping his fingers, 'Just like that, I suppose? I told 'em once my nerve was gone. They don't believe me. Think I'm kidding. Trying to pull a fast one. Think I'm trying to work my ticket.'

'You ought to pack up all right,' Pop said. 'You're really in a bad way.'

'No,' Craven said, 'I figure I can get over it. One trip without any trouble and I figure I'll be okay.'

'Well, it's up to you. I know I'd quit.'

'Nope. I might as well see it through.'

Pop watched him closely now.

134

'You're only risking the lives of six other chaps, you know,' he said.

'Tell that to the Wing Co.'

'That bloody twerp,' said Pop. 'From what I hear, every time he hears there's a call on to go to Essen he scrubs himself, or gets out of it some way.'

'I know I'll be all right,' Craven said. 'I only need one trip to be all right again.'

'Sure, they all say that,' Pop said.

'Well,' said Craven, 'there's always a chance somebody'll prove the statement correct.'

'Only you might not be the one, brother. I've seen 'em come and go too easily to believe experience or anything else but luck is any help over there, and you've always been damned short on luck.'

'Well, maybe it'll change,' Craven said. 'Waddya say, Pop? How about it?'

Pop said nothing. He only looked thoughtful.

'It never used to bother me,' Craven said. 'Not until I had that run of bad luck getting shot up and those crash-landings.

'No kidding, Pop,' Craven said, insisting on his soundness. 'All I need is a good navigator.'

'Well,' Pop started to say, then ceased, musing for a moment. Then, 'Hell, Dickie, I've only one more trip to do to make it thirty. They've screened me on twenty-nine.'

'Nothing'll happen, Pop. I just feel it. Not after all the luck I've had. Come on.'

'I'm a damned fool if I do.'

'And I'll be a dead cookie if you don't. You know what it's like going with some of these sprog navigators. You're lost the minute you cross the French coast. You gotta do it, Pop.'

'Okay. Only one thing. You feel panicky at the coast and back we turn. Okay?'

'Okay. It's a deal.'

'And you pack up here then? Tell them you've finished. No matter what rank they threaten to reduce you to?'

'I won't have to.' Craven was grinning. 'Not after a trip with you, pal.' He felt better now.

'I'm not that good,' said Pop. 'Don't ever be too sure about anybody or anything in this business.'

Smiling to himself, and not looking at Pop, Craven pulled out a package of cigarettes and stuck one in his lips. It's going to be okay now, he was thinking. Everything one hundred per cent better now that he had Pop, best navigator on the squadron. All a pilot really needs is a good navigator, he was thinking. He passed the cigarettes to Pop, and snicked a match on his thumbnail.

'Let's go down to the mess and have a drink,' Pop said.

'Swell,' Craven stood up.

We went out smiling, smoking.

The next afternoon we sat at the table designated for Craven and crew in the briefing-room. The navigator's and bomb aimer's briefing was finished. Craven and Pop sat at the table alone, waiting for the rest of the crew to come in for the general briefing. A band of sunlight fell across their table from the open window above their heads. On the map of Europe in front, on the wall of the long, table-filled room, I looked at the white ribbon tacked down at one end on England and then, stretching out across the North Sea to the coast of France, slipped nicely between two red-marked defended areas and on across Northern Germany to the big red-marked patch that was Berlin. Craven sat there looking at the tape. Great God, I knew he was thinking, what a target to get for a first trip after laying off. From the back of the room I heard people talking, coming in, sitting down at the tables.

'Know anything about these guys going with us?' Craven asked, trying not to show in his eyes what he did not want to think about.

'Don't worry, they're all right. They've made a trip or two,' I said, and grinned and laughed.

'Yeah, I know. I just found that out this morning,' Craven said. But he did not smile, and his gaze returned to the tape on the board.

And then the room was full of everybody, navigators moving up and down the aisles between the tables, green canvas bags full of maps and instruments heavy against their legs, gunners, pilots, wireless operators, bomb aimers, talking over their white turtleneck flying sweaters, loose about their throats, each crew getting seated at their table.

The door clashed and closed at the back of the room.

Just then the wireless operator, gunner, and bomb aimer came up and slid in on the benches by the table.

The gunner I had talked to that morning, a young Canadian with a black moustache and a nice smile, caught Craven's eye and grinned.

'Well, here's the ropey lot,' he said, and, smiling nicely, gestured round the table at the others. 'Kershaw, Brookbank, and yours truly, Fred Schmidt, two generations removed from tonight's target.'

Craven smiled and nodded hello round the table.

'Hardly a bit of gravy tonight, eh?' Schmidt said, with a little laugh.

'It won't be too bad,' Craven said, hoping his voice sounded confident. Mustn't worry, I knew he was thinking.

'Helluva nice spot to come back to Ops on,' Schmidt said.

'Oh, I don't know,' Craven said. 'Lots of worse places. Better than Essen. Besides, it ought to make all the people happy who read the *Daily Mirror*. Really a *Daily Mirror* raid, isn't it?'

'Maybe you'd rather go to Essen instead? Just so you'll be doing some real war work,' Schmidt grinned.

'All the same to me,' Craven said. 'I don't give a damn where we go. Long as you get back is what counts.'

'You're not kidding, brother,' Schmidt said. He had been shot up twice out of two trips. In the beginning, before he had seen a target, he had been very keen. Now he was not so keen, I knew, but he was probably more careful.'

'Guns okay?' Craven asked.

'Everything jake. Harmonized and tested them this morning,' Schmidt said, still smiling his nice easy smile.

The Intelligence Officer, holding a wooden pointer in one hand, a sheaf of papers in the other, came along between the tables and stood up on the stage in front of the map.

He began to speak on the importance of the target, the last time it was bombed, where the defences were heaviest, where the searchlights were thickest.

After that the weather man stood on the stage, and with a pointer explained on a tacked-up meteorological map of Europe the weather situation. The room was quiet and everybody looked intently at the wall with the map on it. Everybody was listening carefully, and in a few moments the weather man finished and left the stage. The weather is not too bad, I thought. A cold frost over the French coast, but we can climb over it easily.

'I notice the Wing Co. isn't on tonight,' the bomb aimer said.

'Hell, you can't blame him. If you could pick your targets, and scrub yourself when you wanted to, you'd do it,' Schmidt said.

'It's hardly fair, though, being exempt from danger when someone else in the same job isn't,' the bomb aimer said.

'This isn't love we're playing at, brother.'

'You're not kidding. But I'll settle for the Victory medal and long-service ribbon,' the bomb aimer grinned.

I looked at the target map of the city between my hands on the table, while in front, on the stage, the bomb leader was giving a few last-minute instructions to the bomb aimers. Pop had been to Berlin before. He would remember it as a long hectic trip because there had been so many variations of course to make, so many new winds to find. Still I knew he was not worried. He had been through too much to worry. I hoped Craven would be all right. In the old days Craven had been a good pilot. Anybody would have flown with him. But not now, after all those turn-backs and then later just blankly refusing to fly without any apparent reason. Pop, I knew, had only told Craven to quit out of sympathy, hoping that somehow his sympathy would in some way help to restore Craven's confidence. No one, I felt, had a right to quit unless their nerve was really gone. And I did not believe Craven had ever been like that. I could tell when someone was really finished. Craven, I felt, had quit. Still he might be wrong. Many would like to quit, I thought, many; and we're all scared but we go on. I sat looking at the map of Berlin. I had been scared so many times, but I had gone on. Yes, maybe if Craven got through this one okay a little of his old confidence would return.

And now, when briefing was finished, everyone came out and got on his bicycle. I saw Craven standing alone, looking as if he were remembering being alone like this before, and the worry had not started yet. Sometimes it started before briefing. Some-times after. You never knew when. But Craven might still feel all right. Maybe, I thought, he might go all the way through the trip not worrying. Maybe he was all right again now. But I knew he wasn't sure, and I walked back along the road to my billet and changed my shoes and put on two pairs of warm woollen socks and my flying boots, and stuck a flashlight in between my socks and boot so that one boot bulged on the outside. Then I went back to the mess and sat in one of the chairs around the fireplace and waited for the operational tea to start. I looked into the fire-place and there beside me was Craven, looking as if he wished he did not have to wait so long between briefing and being in the air-craft ready to take off. Everything might just go all of a sudden with this waiting and then he would be thinking again of dying, of perhaps not coming back, and it would be all up with him.

Finally operational tea was finished, the plates of eggs-and-bacon and cups of hot tea, and everybody talking and joking or not talking and joking, and the bus ride out past the farmhouse by the potato field, and the locker-room crowded with everybody pulling his gear out of his locker. Finally all that was behind, and

Craven looked confident and happy standing by the aircraft, four-engined, rearing big on clean black tyres on the concrete dispersal point, with the windmill in the field behind silhouetted against a fading western sky.

We stood talking in the still evening air, waiting for the sound of the first aircraft across the field to start up its engines. Craven divided the flying rations, and when he came to the bomb aimer, a dark curly-haired boy of nineteen, with an officer's flat hat raked on one side of his head, he stopped. He wanted to make sure of one thing.

'Ever do second dicky?' he asked the bomb aimer.

'Sure,' the bomb aimer said.

'Okay. Then right through the gate with the throttles tonight.'

The bomb aimer nodded, not smiling now. He looked serious.

'I'm not taking any chances. Not a hell of a lot of wind to help us off tonight. Full throttle, thirty degree flap. Okay?' Craven said.

'Righto,' the bomb aimer said.

From across the field came the sound of the first engine starting up.

'Okay, let's go,' Craven addressed the crew.

'Cheerio,' said one of the ground crew as they passed him. He was under the wing sliding a chock against one wheel.

Then the belly door closed, the black-out curtains on the small side-windows drawn, the compass turned on, ticking over quietly in the darkened fuselage, the navigator, bomb aimer, and wireless operator seated in the crash position midway back in the fuselage, the sound of the starboard outer engine spluttering, roaring, catching, missing, catching, filled the intercom wire, and the aircraft trembled under the power of the other three engines starting. In the rear turret I switched on the ring sight. Roaring, rising, falling in crescendo, the engines warming strained the aircraft against the wheel chocks.

The aircraft taxied out slowly on to the perimeter path of rolled asphalt that led around the aerodrome to the take-off runway, and looking out over the nose, working the throttle slowly on one side to turn the aircraft, I knew what Craven was experiencing, seeing all the remembered familiar features of long ago evenings: the moon over the dark crests of the trees across the 'drome, and dusk changing the world into a kind of soft green lake of light. An aircraft ahead, with its slow blurs of four propellers, braked and stopped. Craven braked. I felt all the weight of the aircraft lunge forward and stop. I looked at my watch, seven minutes before take-off. And now on the perimeter track, one behind the other, propellers turning slowly, twelve aircraft loomed big in the thickening twilight, waiting to turn on the runway. In the dark clotting of the people beside the runway a light flashed green, and I watched the first aircraft ahead swing big and dark and pause there for a moment, and then tail up, sky appearing under the tail, run smoothly forward, faster and faster, and then at last only a climbing silhouette of wing against dying sunlight still in the western sky.

Now in my mind I saw all the crew in their positions, knew what they were feeling. Now in my mind I saw Craven looking at his rev and boost gauges, his hands damp inside his gloves and his stomach hollow and empty with fear.

'Engineer,' Craven called over the intercom, 'the starboard outer revs are fluctuating to beat hell.' He sounded worried, the tone of his voice revealed it. It was hell if an engine should cut on take-off. Eight thousand pounds of bombs on board. I had seen too many hit the deck and blow up on take-off. No, Craven mustn't let it bother him. Maybe he was okay now, sure. Oh, sure.

'Come on, let's go,' the bomb aimer yelled.

'How about that starboard outer, Engineer?' Craven asked over the intercom. God, I hoped nothing would go wrong now. I still had a horror of crashing on take-off because of engines cutting.

'Okay. Okay,' said the engineer. 'She's okay.'

Pop sat rigidly in the seat in the crash position, bracing himself with his back hard against the fuselage, his heels jammed against the side of the opposite seat. He felt the tail lift, the engines gathering power, and then going fast along the runway. He wondered too if they'd make it. Sure they would. Of course, silly to think otherwise. Still, they might not. Any number of things could happen on a take-off. Twenty tons of metal and explosives moving at one hundred and twenty miles an hour. He was remembering the night taking off for Lorient when somebody had left the front turret unlocked in the dark; moving one hundred miles an hour along an icy runway with a full load of bombs they'd swing off and over across the field. And that night if we hadn't cut the engines we'd have had it sure. Pop now and again felt the sudden floating lifting sensation of bouncing air borne off the runway. Then suddenly he felt the right wing drop a little, and God, he was probably thinking, we're not high, a quick sickening feeling in his stomach for an instant until he felt the wing come up and they were climbing again. He went forward to his desk and compartment under Craven's feet.

Craven called to him on the intercom, 'How long before we set course, Pop?'

'About seven minutes,' Pop said. 'I'll tell you when.'

'Want to set course right over base?' Craven asked.

'No, that's okay,' Pop said. 'I'll get us a fix. Just take it easy.'

'Okay,' said Craven. 'You're the boss.'

Pop sat at his table, a small target of light on his map, a pencil in one hand, his eyes squinting at the figures on the paper held down by his left hand. He felt as steady and secure now as if he were in an office on the ground. He began to figure rapidly on the paper.

The hand on the starboard-outer rev's dial in the panel in front of the flight engineer, standing in the astral hatch just behind Craven, flickered and jumped back and forth. Suddenly one of the glowing exhausts began to fade black.

'Engineer! Engineer!' Craven called, staring wildly at his instrument panel. 'Starboard outers cutting.' Craven felt the wing going down on the starboard side. 'For God's sake!' he yelled. 'Engineer!' Just then the engine caught again and Craven felt the elevator-sinking sensation leave his stomach. He held tight to the control column and over-corrected, bringing the wing level again. There were small beads of perspiration on his forehead.

Quietly, from where the curtains were drawn, where light and space were shut out, where he could not tell if he were in trouble save for frantic voices over the intercom wire, Parry gave Craven the course to fly.

'Course is zero eight two magnetic.'

'Okay, Pop, turning on.'

Craven holding the control wheel in both hands, watching the compass arrow move on the dial, put a little pressure on the right rudder pedal against the sole of his flying boot, and wondered should he turn back. He glanced at the rev and boost gauge. God, if only he could get a credible reason for turning back. Revs and boost gauges seemed all right now. He couldn't very well turn back only because one of his engines had cut and caught again. How could you prove that was dangerous, or that it had happened? He was glad it had not cut completely. He knew he never would have been able to maintain height at the altitude he was now at with a full bomb-load on. He took the pressure off the rudder pedal, turned the control wheel to port, and watched the turn and bank indicator line come back level in its round dial.

'On course, Pop?'

'Okay.'

Craven remembered the afternoon coming into the mess just after he had flatly refused to fly, after a night over Calais caught in the searchlight, the rear gunner yelling: 'Weave! weave! For Chrissake weave! The stuff's coming up right behind us!' He remembered that and all the terror and fear he had gone through to get out of the searchlights, climbing and diving, the beams following, the rear gunner yelling, 'Weave! For Chrissake weave!' And he remembered all of it clearly when he told the Wing Commander he was packing up. And then later in the mess no one saying anything, not really unfriendly or hostile, oh, pleasant enough. Yet the glance of an eye, a certain tone of voice, that told him they were finished with him, too. And then he had gone away to a rest home, remembering there all the turn-backs he had made before being caught in the lights that night over Calais. Yes, it was that which had finished him. Calais. He hated the thought of the place.

Now far below, the ground was dark. Rivers were silver twists of light caught, held and gone, clouds floated by underneath, fat as whipped cream. Up here, it was still light, and looking out Craven remarked the dying sun and western clouds turning soft and pink and gold, the world vacant, profound, and tranquil. He held the control column steadily and reaching down behind his left leg tripped the switch turning on the automatic pilot, felt a gentle lurch on the controls, then everything steady again, the control wheel jittering free of his hand. Rubbing his hands together he felt better. There was still sweat in his gloves.

Pop sat, bent over his table, wondering whether to alter course now, or wait until the bomb aimer saw a pin-point on the English coast. Pop estimated they were now approximately five miles south of course. As he checked his wind and drift, he decided to hold to the present course until crossing the English coast. He called me, asking for a drift reading from the rear turret.

I told him there was too much cloud underneath now to take a drift reading through the gun sight, and went on cocking my guns.

Then over the coast, the bomb aimer in the nose looking down at the sea breaking dark against the cliffs, the long line of foam collaring white against the beach, and far over to the port the dark triangle of headland was the last of England. Then out over the sea, and soon the sea gone below, and stars beginning to

142

blink on the dark side of the sky, and Pop wondering how far they were drifting to port, asking the bomb aimer where they had crossed the coast.

'I think we're just south of track,' I called.

'Headland was right near us, about five miles to port, Pop,' Craven said.

'If there are any more navigators in this crew they can come up here,' Pop said sarcastically.

'We were only two miles south of track when we crossed the coast,' the bomb aimer said.

'I'll alter course two degrees. Okay?' Craven said.

'Okay,' said Pop, and started working on the course for the next leg of the trip, while, comfortable with a pillow against his back, Craven sat back, watching his instruments, telling himself everything was going to run nicely from now on. Little bit of trouble with the engines. Hell, nothing more. No more trouble. Share of trouble already had for this trip. And sitting there he watched the sky turn dark and the stars come out, sitting quietly with his hands on his knees, telling himself everything was all right.

The bomb aimer, looking out through the perspex nose, saw slightly above and to starboard, seeming to hang motionless, an aircraft, and felt happy, because we're in the main stream, he thought. In the main stream we always crossed the enemy coast with many aircraft, and it was considered safer that way, for so many aircraft confused the radio location station, whose job it was to direct night fighters on to our tail.

When far ahead Craven saw the first faint burst of heavy flak, that winked small as distant fireflies, the rear gunner was moving his turret back and forth, certain he had seen a dark object cross the sky to the rear.

Pop heard it all as he started to tell Craven a new course to fly; me yelling that an aircraft had passed from starboard to port in the rear. Could anyone else in the crew see? For God's sake, what was it? And if anybody could see it, to say so, and the engineer's voice interrupted both Pop's and mine. Yes, he could see something down there. For God's sake! 'Down where?' I bellowed, 'down where? You stupid bastards! Learn to call the sides of the aircraft! Where? Where? What do you mean, down there? Port or starboard? Up or down?' And then I saw the craft, the single rudder, the nose, engines, all in line, passing overhead, twin circles of flame from the exhausts outlining the head-on view of the engines, the long narrow fuselage vanishing past. Junkers

88, with three airmen, scared like us, looking for us. 'It's going away to port,' I called.

Might be heading for another kite, I thought. Perhaps he doesn't even see us. Maybe he doesn't want a scrap. Just up here doing his patrol until its time to go down.

Craven turned the aircraft hard to port, and felt the pressure holding him down on the seat as the aircraft went down in a long diving turn. But there it was silent, exhausts glowing, long dark fuselage hovering just over his head now. Craven pulled the aircraft level, and bending over, adjusted the supercharger knobs.

The Junkers was still overhead. It couldn't be going to attack from that position. No one ever did that. Still, he might be trying something new.

Suddenly Craven pushed the control column forward and to starboard; it was going to attack; Craven held the aircraft in a dive and I saw the Junkers overhead lift one wing and pull up its nose to do a stall turn. He's going to dive straight down on top of us, give a burst as he goes past too fast for us to bring our guns to bear on him. Must be an old-experienced deflection shot. I called Craven. Yes, he saw it.

Craven pulled the control column back into his stomach. He saw twin threads of red fire pass just in front of the port wing; he held the control column back hard in his stomach. Geeze! Too damned near. Get out of here fast. This guy is good.

I felt the aircraft stalling, the controls ineffectual in Craven's hands. Then he pushed the nose down and opened the throttles. 'Here he comes again!' I called. 'Port quarter 'bout eight hundred yards. Get ready to dive-turn port.'

Then, watching the wing-span grow in the ring sight, holding tightly to gun-control column, my thumb on the firing button, the Ju. 88 climbed winking, firing flashes; the Ju. 88 came steadily up, firing.

'Turn!' I yelled. 'Hard over!' And leaning forward, right eye just behind ring sight, I pressed the firing button. Missing, I moved the gun-control column gently, and swung the guns until I saw the trace passing just in front of the Ju. 88. It was in close now, still firing. All a big shapeless black blob, full of gun flashes, but it was over-shooting. I held down the firing button, while I watched the long, dark, slim belly pass through the ring sight absorbing the red, streaks of tracer.

And then it was gone, and we were diving into the dark side of the sky.

'Jesus!' I breathed heavily.

Craven, pulling back on the control column, noticed by the altimeter that they had lost five thousand feet.

'Are we much off course?' Pop called.

Craven looked at his compass.

'Only ten degrees,' he said.

'Good,' Pop said. 'Get her back on.'

Craven licked his lips. Soon they would be crossing the Dutch coast. Another few minutes. Well, he had just turned at the right moment. Now to get some altitude back. He couldn't risk crossing the coast at this height. In his mind, like a dark heavy shadow, he saw all the distance across Europe that lay ahead. Now he did not care. When they came close to us, and we almost got it, I did not care. Neither hope nor despair. I was just tired, feeling drained and still keyed up in a queer way. He checked his revs and boost gauges, and noticed the oil temperature was high on the starboard outer. Well, no matter. They could blow him to hell now and he did not care.

Climbing steadily, trying to cut down the glow of his exhausts by reducing revs, but knowing it was no use, Craven saw ahead the dark curve of the Dutch coast.

A searchlight went on, its white beam dead ahead.

Craven turned the control column hard over to port and back to starboard, weaving from side to side.

The searchlight slid under the wing. It swept back, looking for us, and again it was ahead, only to one side. A flash of light glared on the windscreen in front of Craven.

They're firing. Heavy flak. Only one gun, I thought, and Craven put the aircraft into a steady gentle weave. Then the searchlight was far behind, I reported. We had crossed the coast. We were now over enemy territory. Below the world was a bottomless darkness. We droned on, lonely, remote as a gull.

After half an hour Craven told Pop there was flak and searchlights ahead and to port. Pop decided they were on track. The searchlights and flak were there according to schedule.

Craven was probably thinking of his next leave, probably dreaming, when the flight engineer called to say the temperature on the starboard outer engine was up to one hundred and twenty-five.

'Better feather it,' Pop said.

Craven looked at the oil-temperature gauge. He wondered if he dare keep it running at that temperature. Still, he'd have to if he were going to maintain height.

'Are you going to turn back?' I asked. My voice sounded shaky.

'Like hell,' Craven said.

'Don't be a bloody fool!' Pop yelled.

'We're going on,' Craven said.

'The engine'll go all to cock in a minute if you don't feather it,' the engineer said.

I guessed from then on what Craven was thinking.

So now they all want to go home, Craven was thinking. Well, they bloody well won't. Now he was this far, past the enemy coast the first time in thirteen attempts, he was elated. He felt a kind of exhilaration, a release from worry. No, they wouldn't get him tonight. They had scared him, and now suddenly all that was finished. By God! they'd never get him now.

'Okay, Engineer, feather it,' he said. 'We can make it on three.' Outside, the engine-exhaust glow slowly died.

'Three!' Pop yelled. 'Are you nuts?'

Craven said nothing. He was staring straight ahead.

So, they thought he had lost his nerve. So, they had all been wrong with their little feelings of having been brave because they had gone on when he hadn't. He's show them now. They were all fools. But he'd show them.

When he felt and heard the other starboard engine cutting, shouting 'Engineer!' Thinking what the hell's that man's name, while he fought with the controls to keep the starboard wing up, he was almost normal again, no longer intoxicated with courage from the elation of having conquered for a while an old fear, and he knew coolly and quickly he could not go on. Still, there are other targets, he told himself, feeling calm exhilaration return when the engine ceased to splutter and he was confident once more of maintaining, at least for a while, his height on three engines. Yes, there were other targets.

He would bomb something. Perhaps not Berlin – Duisburg, he thought suddenly.

Duisburg, he thought, probably already in his mind figured out a rough course. He would go in and the searchlights would go on and then he'd know where he was. Duisburg! He banked the aircraft hard to starboard, watched the compass-needle swing on to two-zero-three, unplugged his intercom cord and sat back.

Duisburg – he held the aircraft straight, climbing steadily.

Suddenly the aircraft rose and fell, as though it were running over a bump, and I felt the control column jump in his grip. He pushed the throttle forward as the aircraft bounced again, and he pushed the nose down, diving. He picked up his intercom cord and plugged in. Craven, pulling the control column back, waiting for someone to say something on the intercom, saw six puffs of black smoke directly ahead and a little above. Diving, weaving, another six puffs of black smoke dissolving past on the same level, only now to starboard, the aircraft bumped from the explosion, the heavy guns on the ground trying to predict his height and course. Banking hard over from side to side, panting, sweating now, Craven saw the bursts dissolving past further to starboard.

The guns ceased, and the sky was dark. Then suddenly the first searchlight beam came up, probing, stalking, searching. I was calling it was right behind and below. They were really after us now. A lone duck. Craven still diving and weaving, sweating, panting, turning the control wheel from side to side.

Craven, heart pounding, damp under his arms and on his stomach and back. Three more searchlight beams came on. I called, 'They're coming up to starboard. Weave! For f— sake!'

Craven pushed hard the right rudder pedal, swinging the control wheel to the left. The guns on the ground were silent, waiting. The searchlights swept up and past to one side of the aircraft.

Craven yelled, 'What the bloody hell! We're stalling!' And the controls went dead in his hand.

Then we were hanging motionless, suspended in the air, and I saw only stars and sky beyond his windscreen, and Craven feeling there was nothing he could do. Why should it stall? They must be hit. Craven took his hands off the control wheel, and reached down beside his seat for the elevator's trim control wheel, and the aircraft suddenly whipped downwards, diving. Maybe he could trim it out. Maybe. Oh, God, what the bloody hell was wrong? So this was it! He saw the needle on the airspeed-indicator dial pass the three hundred mark. He felt himself lifted off his seat, his head striking once against the roof. A black puff of flak burst directly ahead. He saw the white layer of clouds below resolving larger and larger. Then the control wheel was in his hands again, and he was easing it back.

'Don't pull out too quickly! Easy, boy!' Pop called, his voice cool, steady.

Craven felt himself slowly sinking back on to his seat as he saw the dark sky meeting the faint line of the horizon beyond the nose.

Craven held the aircraft straight and level for a moment, then

147

rocked it from side to side, testing both aileron and rudder, and then tried a slight climb.

The engineer called upon the intercom.

'I think our wing bomb doors are shot away,' he said. 'There's one hanging.'

The searchlight beam had come back now across the sky, and guns were firing again. It was all bursting to port above. Where the hell are we, Craven thought. The gun flashes, a glare of light with an orange centre, were closer now for a moment.

Craven dived away to starboard. He pulled up level, asked me where the searchlights were now. Still coming along behind, I told him. Below, in a straight line of black puffs, heavy flak was bursting. Craven banked the aircraft back and forth, from side to side. On the ground, the gun crew listened, plotting our course, but not firing. They were waiting for us to fly straight and level, if only for a moment.

Craven tired and angry. The bastards! Thinking they could get him. He'd dump the load on them. To hell with Duisburg. He pushed the control wheel forward and to starboard, and in a diving turn, looking out into the dark for the searchlight cone that had been after him, he told the bomb aimer to open the bomb doors. 'We're going to run through the lights and drop our stuff.' As he brought the aircraft level he saw the cone of searchlights ahead, like a many-legged octopus, reaching out for him. The guns fired and the aircraft bounced upwards.

Craven pushed the control wheel forward and then pulled it slowly back. The control felt sloppy. Are we hit? Still it did not seem possible. When we were hit I heard the dull shocking thud of the explosion.

As Craven tried the controls for lateral movement he felt someone touch his shoulder, and turning his head he saw Parry standing beside him.

'Let's get the hell out of here, you bloody fool!' Parry's voice came over the intercom, as he looked steadily over the top of his oxygen mask at Craven's face.

Craven looked at him and grinned. They couldn't touch him now. No one could touch him. He was free. He grinned.

And there ahead and below was the searchlight cone. They were flattening towards him now. Leave here now? Ho! Ho! This was going to be good. Those buggers with their searchlights and guns! This'd teach them! The saucy blighters!

He held the nose straight down, headed towards the cone of beams, and the guns again ceased firing.

Diving, Craven swung the aircraft from side to side in a gentle weave.

He pulled back the control wheel, flew straight and level, and told the bomb aimer to pick up a beam. Then he felt the shocking *boompf* of the first explosion under the tail, and then the control wheel was torn from his hand. He had held a straight and level course too long.

The next six flak puffs, all in a perfect row, like a line of small sausages, burst at the same height and to one side. Then suddenly the windscreen shattered in front of his face, and he felt the glass tear his cheek. Another six puffs, directly underneath. *Boompf boompf*, and a long red streamer of light flak came winding, sneaking upwards under the nose. He braced his back against the seat and looked at his instruments. Then the cockpit was full of the smell of cordite and the window next to his shoulder burst and vanished. Craven blinked his eyes to get the blood out of them. His forehead was gashed.

Oh, God! Oh, God! he must have been thinking, frightened and blinded for a long moment.

They were going to get him! Damn it! Damn it! He was angry, tired, and now badly frightened, but he felt steady, calm.

And there were the searchlight beams. Now they were on the aircraft, filling the cabin with light. Craven crouched. Oh, hell; so this was it! Right in his eyes now.

Craven pulled back on the control wheel. God, if they could only get out of here. He felt the aircraft climb, the beam of light still in his eyes.

He didn't feel brave now. Not now. And he wasn't exhilarated. He yelled to the bomb aimer to drop the load, and at once felt the bombs go and the aircraft lift.

The guns got his range as he tried to sideslip out of the three beams now holding him, and as he held the control wheel hard over he heard the three shocks, and in the glare of the explosions he felt something hot and shocking knock him back against his seat. He held hard to the wheel and slumped forward. The guns fired again, missed, then, diving, he was clear of the searchlights. He pushed himself off the wheel and tried to sit up straight. He couldn't feel any strength in his hands. He opened his eyes. The sky was dark. The beams were somewhere behind.

He sat there, trying to hold the wheel steady. A warm rill of blood wound sinuously down his chin from one corner of his mouth. Oh, God! Get me out of this! There was a terrible pain in his chest. Oh, God, please.

'Pop,' he called weakly. 'Pop. What's a rough course out of here?'

'Two one zero magnetic.' Pop was beside him, looking at him. 'Here, let me take over,' he said. 'You're hit and you don't know it.'

'I'm all right,' Craven said. 'Don't worry, I'm okay.' He couldn't seem to get his breath. Pop watched him. Craven held tight to the control wheel. He felt as if he would break inside if he didn't hold on to something.

Well, he was all right. Sure I'm all right, he thought. If only I would keep my eyes open. His head started to slump forward. He felt a terrible burning feeling in his chest. He squinted downwards, trying to see the face of the compass. What was the course? Oh, sure. The course. Course. Must get on course. Mm, funny feeling in his hands. Sleep. Sleep. Open eyes. He leaned forward to look at the compass and felt himself passing out against the wheel. He put his head against the dial panel and pushed, and nothing happened. He didn't move. He fell forward against the wheel. Then he felt somebody's hands under his armpits and a faint voice saying something blurred, and Pop was lifting and dragging him from behind the wheel.

The bomb aimer and I came forward, and laid him on the floor beside the pilot's seat. 'Oh, God! don't move me,' he said. 'It hurts too much.' We wanted to take him back to the rest position where there was more room. Here we could not stand beside him. It was too narrow. I knelt at Craven's feet, and the bomb aimer, kneeling at Craven's head, unbuckled Craven's parachute harness and put a parachute pack under his head.

I went and got the hypodermic needle and morphine from the first-aid box on the port side of the fuselage. I knelt over Craven and pulled a hunting knife out of the side of my boot. I always carried a knife on operations. You never knew when you might need one, escaping, if you bailed out or crashlanded in Germany. I cut a long slit in the sleeve of Craven's jacket and got one hand inside the slit and tore a big opening, and then got just the tip of the knife into Craven's sweater sleeve and shirt and snicked both open with a quick, deft, upward-jerking slash. Craven's face was the colour of grey putty. He looked so sleepy now he could not keep his eyes open. He wanted to smoke but there was a terrible pain inside his chest, and I could see he was afraid to take a deep breath. He could taste a bubble of blood in his throat. It kept trying to come up, and he wanted to cough it up like a piece of phlegm that was gagging him. He felt the needle prick the flesh of his arm. He wondered what would happen if he coughed. He was afraid. I'm not going to die, he thought, but he was afraid. He looked in my eyes.

He closed and opened his eyes. Then blinked, then evidently certain his eyes were open, yet he couldn't seem to see.

Then I heard the heavy steady rhythmic thrum sound of the engines again. Craven had gone off a long way, beyond hearing and sight. Now he was back for a moment. He looked drowsy. He looked queerly at me as if I were vague and shapeless. God, are my eyes gone, he must have been thinking. There. He blinked his eyes fast. There, he could see now. He saw me leaning over him. The pain was leaving his chest now. He felt better. He smiled.

'Have you got a – ' Craven started to speak. No, he mustn't smoke. Bring up the blood bubble. Keep the bubble down.

I looked at the bomb aimer and shook my head from side to side. Then I looked down at Craven and said nothing. We knelt there, looking at Craven. Craven kept blinking his eyes as if he were trying to keep our faces from fading and coming back, fading and coming back.

Pop was at the controls banking on to a course, trying to put in the automatic gyro-pilot. Finally it was on course and he came down from the pilot's seat and knelt just behind Craven's head.

Pop's face was sweaty. There was a black greasy line over the bridge of his nose and down along both cheeks, showing where the oxygen mask had been. It hung loose now from its chin-strap.

He leaned his face over Craven. Craven squinted upwards as if trying to see who it was. He felt someone in the dark above him.

Pop motioned with his head to me. I shrugged my shoulders and held up the empty hypodermic and morphine phial. Pop looked down at Craven to see if he were watching. Craven's eyes were closed. He felt terribly sleepy, as if he were going slowly bodily out of himself. It felt nice to have the pain in his chest gone. He felt drowsily pleasant. 'I'm all right,' he said, and smiled lazily.

And now it's all over, I thought. We're going home. Now they could never make Craven fly again. They never did after a bad wound like this, and it is bad too, I thought; but maybe he'll be all right. Nothing's going to happen. Pop knew enough about flying to get the kite home. Of course, if we have to bail Craven out . . . war's over for him . . . wound not really bad . . . no pain now for him . . . my mind became vague, empty.

Craven opened his eyes. It was a great effort. He seemed to want to thank Pop if he could. Even if he could only give Pop a smile, Pop would understand that he was grateful.

Where was Pop? He couldn't seem to see him.

'Oh, God! I am blind!' he yelled. 'Oh, God, I've been hit in the eyes!'

Craven raised his right hand to touch his eyes. Pop pushed his arm down gently. 'God, where is everybody? Touching me, and I can't see you,' he whimpered.

'You're okay. Just take it easy, boy.' It was Pop's voice, very faint and faraway.

Pop pulled Craven's legs out straight. It didn't seem to hurt him. Well, he was all right there.

'Easy,' somebody was saying. The voice faded.

'I'm not scared any more, Mack,' Craven said. He couldn't tell whom he was addressing. His eyes were open very wide now. They were round and white and rolling. His lips formed a faint smile, blood at the corners of his mouth. 'I'm okay, Mack,' he said. He rolled his eyes around looking for my face above him. 'I'm over it, Mack.' He smiled slowly, rolling his eyes looking. Then he must have felt his body going away again as if he were slowly floating outwards on air into empty space. He closed his eyes. He was weak. 'Why can't I see?' he said. 'I don't remember getting hit in the eyes.' He felt the bubble inside his chest move a little. It made a choking feeling in his throat. He looked frightened again. 'I'm okay, Mack,' repeated. 'Finish a tour now when I get over this. No more nerves.' He tried to smile. It was no use.

Pop bit his lip, and turned and looked back over his shoulder at the control wheel and instrument panel.

'You better get back in there,' the bomb aimer shouted at him.

Pop stood and looked down at Craven for a long moment.

Craven's eyelids fluttered and his lips moved weakly. His eyes closed.

'I'm not afraid any more, am I, Pop?' he asked faintly, a smile starting on his lips, only not finishing.

'No,' Pop said, 'you're not afraid any more. You're cured now.' He looked down at Craven. 'Sure,' he said, 'you're cured now all right.'

I got up from where I was kneeling and went back along the

fuselage to the tail turret, and Craven lay very still, his eyelids closed, his face ashen-grey, the parachute pack under his head.

Pop climbed back into the pilot's seat, and felt the control wheel in his hand, and looked out across the dark sky towards England.

CHAPTER TWENTY-FOUR

Some days later I went on leave. I wired Diana to meet me at the Stag and Huntsmen Inn in the country town in Bucks where Ed and I had spent our first leave in England. 'Wangled five days. Leaving tonight,' she wired. I went to the station and got on the train and came down across England to Henley.

I came along the small road from where the bus stopped on the main road just up from the little town. It was another spring again, and I looked up at the woods where me and Ed had walked a year ago. I stopped at the bridge over the stream and looked down at the water, then walked on along the dusty road that went through the town.

The road passed the stone wall and the big stone house on the hill where Ed and I had stayed. Ahead was the inn, the sign Stag and Huntsmen hanging out over the road, sunlight on the red-slate roof.

The sky was clear and blue. It was a lovely April evening.

As I came up to the inn a window opened in the second storey and Diana put her head out. Smiling, she waved. I stood at the front door looking up at her.

'Well, darling?' she said.

'Hello, hello!' I felt happy and excited.

We looked at each other. The sunlight was shining on her hair. She was looking out over the green valley beyond the town.

'It's lovely here,' I said.

'It's perfect, darling.'

'How did you get in?'

'Beat you down,' she laughed. 'Come upstairs to Mrs Norton's room.'

I went in and registered. It was a small old inn with narrow hallways and beamed ceilings. I went upstairs. Diana opened the door and I went in and she closed the door.

'Put your bags down, darling, and have a drink. I wangled this out of our mess.' She pulled a bottle of scotch out of her travelling-bag. I took the bottle and partly filled two glasses at the wash-basin. I ran water on top of the scotch until she called, 'When.'

'Do you feel like a party?' I said. 'A wonderful party?'

'Darling, do I not?'

We sat on the edge of the bed and slowly drank the scotch and water.

'God, this is wonderful,' I said, and thought of life back on the aerodrome.

'I know what you're thinking,' she said.

'I'm thinking of you.'

'No, you're not.'

'How do you know?'

'I don't know,' she laughed.

'Darling, I love you so damn much,' I told her.

'Darling, I love you.'

I kissed her and sat back. The room was quiet. We sat there looking at each other.

'Do you want to hear some music?' she said.

'Nothing could be better.'

'Just lie down. I brought a portable gramophone.'

'You think of everything.'

'Don't I though!' she said. She bent over and pulled the gramophone out from under the bed. We opened the windows and watched the sun setting across the valley.

Diana put a record on the gramophone. It was a still, calm number by Beethoven. I didn't remember the title. The sound gave me the feeling of looking at a tranquil lake in the morning. It was very restful.

'Isn't it lovely?' Diana said.

'I could lie here the rest of my life.'

I lay full length on the bed, with a pillow under my head.

'You're going to sleep,' Diana said. I opened my eyes.

'What have you been doing with yourself?'

'Working.'

'Doing what?'

'Teaching a lot of little girls how to catch German aircraft by radio-location.'

'They ought to be very good at it.'

154

'Let's forget the war,' Diana said. 'As long as we're going to be here let's never talk about it.'

'It's not that bad.'

'Darling. I can think of wonderful things to talk about,' she said. 'I can think of fifty million wonderful things.'

'Like meeting you here.'

'That will do. Let's forget all the rest. Only forty-nine million wonderful things to forget.'

She rewound the gramophone, put the record on again.

'Let's stay up all night and talk,' she said. She knelt on the floor by the gramophone.

'All night?' I smiled. 'But such a long time.'

'Oh, darling,' she laughed suddenly. 'I didn't mean that.' She took my hand. We laughed at each other. She released my hand. 'I meant it was just so good to be here, that's all,' she said.

She lifted the bottle of scotch from the floor and partly filled both glasses.

'Water?' she asked.

'No, let's toss it off.'

'We'll be tight.'

'It's better than being dead.'

'Don't talk childish nonsense,' she said. 'You're not dead.'

'I know, but a lot of people are.'

'Oh, darling. Come off it. You sound like a movie script.'

She got up on the bed and lay beside me.

'It's wonderful to be here like this, isn't it?' I said.

'It's perfect, darling.'

'It's better than anything in the world.'

'What if we had never met?'

'Now who sounds like a movie script?' I said,

'Let's just lie here and not say anything. It's better than talking.'

'You're funny, aren't you?'

'Kiss me, darling,' she said. 'I haven't wanted to kiss you since you came. No, I mean I haven't because the longer I wait the more wonderful it is.'

'Darling, I love you so much.'

'Remember the night of that air raid?'

'Stop remembering,' I said, kissing her.

She put her arms around me. I held her tightly, goofily crazy about her. She rolled away and lay on her back, her hands under her head. She lay there looking at the ceiling.

'What are you thinking?' I asked.

155

'How grand it will be when the war's over.'

'It doesn't do any good to think about that now.'

'My, aren't we the patriot,' she said. 'I thought you were just in this to develop your character.'

'I was. But there's more to it now.'

'Where do you get all this change of feeling?' she laughed.

'From the dead.'

'Don't be depressing, Mack.'

'I'm not. Remember when I first told you my reason for fighting that time at the Pavilion? They were only words thought up to cover up what I didn't know.'

'You know now?'

'I think so.'

'And I thought we were going to get away from the war?'

'We are. Come here.'

'Oh, darling,' she said. I kissed her. She kissed me hard and held me pressed tight against her. I was crazy with holding her.

'I wish you had two weeks' leave,' I said. 'We could go to London for a week.'

'Let's get wonderfully high here, darling. Right now.'

'Fine,' I agreed. How far away those nights in the aircraft were already. Dear God, had it all happened?

'I'm a little high now, darling,' she said.

'So am I.'

I leaned over the side of the bed and picked up the scotch bottle. The glasses were on a chair beside the bed.

I held the bottle above her glass.

'Very much?' I asked.

'Very much,' she smiled.

I poured half a glass into each glass.

'Darling,' she said. 'You know, we are drunkards.' She laughed and drank.

'I've known it a long time,' I said, and thought it over. Perhaps we were. Oh, well, to hell with it if we were. It did not seem very important after what I had been through. Still, I thought a lot of my health. But I felt physically all right now, except I was nervous and any loud sound made me jump.

'Said anything to your father or mother yet?' I asked.

'Darling, I don't worry about them. We get along wonderfully well.'

'Wouldn't you like to get married?' I said.

'Of course. But why worry about that now?'

'I thought maybe you were,' I said.

'I don't worry much, dear. I've never had to. I worried about John. That was all. I worried about you. But I've finished worrying. You're here.'

'You'll worry again. No one ever gets away from it.'

'Be amusing, please, dear. I can't stand third-class profundities.'

'It was only an attempt. I've been attempting them all my life.'

'You don't need them with me,' she said. 'You're all right just as you are.'

'Thanks, madam.' And I bowed mockingly.

She smiled and pushed my shoulder, and I almost spilled my drink. 'Hey, you!' I said. I gave her a push with my hand. She almost fell off the bed. She began laughing. She pushed me back and fell forward, and I grabbed her, laughing. We leaned against each other, sitting up laughing.

'Let's have more barleycorn,' Diana said.

I leaned over the side of the bed and reached for the scotch bottle on the table beside the bed.

'There isn't much left,' I said.

'Put some water in it this time for me, please,' she said.

I got up and took the glasses and half-filled them with water at the tap on the wash-basin. I got back on the bed and we looked at each other. We both looked very straight-faced at each other. Then Diana smiled and I smiled. We felt funny looking at each other. We were getting tight all right. Her eyes rolled and she was doing it on purpose. My face felt queer. I started thinking about Dickie Craven being dead and then quickly stopped thinking about him. I didn't want to spoil the evening.

We lay there slowly sipping our drinks.

'The gramophone's stopped,' I said.

'I heard it stop ages ago.'

'Well, here's to our long happy life,' I said, touching my glass to hers.

'And why shouldn't it be?'

'It will be. Did I sound as if it wouldn't?'

'You sound that way too much of the time,' she said.

'Oh, come now. You're getting high. You're imagining things.' Still, I knew she was right. I heard my voice. It didn't have any particularly gay note in it. No, maybe it was because I was getting high. I had felt happy enough coming here.

'Here's to where we are now then!' she said suddenly, smiling. 'How is that?' She sat there, her glass touching mine, looking at me.

'That's a lot better.'

'Don't I know it!' she said. 'What the hell have we to be gloomy about? Don't you make me gloomy, will you?'

'I won't. Maybe we drank too much of this stuff.'

She downed her glass. 'Or maybe not enough,' she said.

'Don't go theatrical on me.'

'I wasn't. I just started thinking of John. I didn't want to. It just came over me.'

'I know,' I said. She looked sad.

I poured her another drink, myself one. We looked at each other. I wished she did not have to sit there thinking suddenly of someone who was dead. We're a fine pair, I thought. Come here to make love and start thinking of the dead.

'Hell,' I said. 'Snap out of it.'

'I'm all right.'

She kissed my cheek as if to make me feel she was all right. We lay there looking quietly at the wall across the room.

'You are lucky, Mack,' she said.

'How?' What do you mean?'

'To be here. Alive.'

'That's silly, to talk that way.'

'No, it isn't.'

'It's no use thinking about it,' I said. 'They're gone. There's nothing else to it.'

'You think you can get away from it that way,' she said. 'But you can't. Mack, you'll never get away from it.'

'From what?' I said. 'What kind of nonsense are you talking? I'm away from any thoughts or feelings I have about anybody who is dead. Don't talk such nonsense.'

'All right,' she said confidently, as if she knew something I did not know. 'You just think you'll get away from it. But wait until you hear them going over at night and you're on the ground. You'll start thinking all over again. It'll all come back to you, every one of their faces.'

'No, it won't. I can keep them away.'

I lay there and stared at the wall. And suddenly there was Craven's face, and Diana seemed a million miles away. I was far, far away from her now. I was full of a lonely, empty feeling, and Diana had no part of me. I was sober. Thinking of Craven and all of them. Eddie, Gerald, Johnny, Kit, I wanted to cry. They were gone and I was here. It seemed now the bond of friendship we had had together was all that mattered. They were gone. Gone. The words were not possible.

'Here, finish this,' Diana said.

She handed me her glass. I drank it off, not even feeling it.

'Let's not let anything come between us,' Diana said. 'I'm sorry I started it.'

That was all right. Maybe it wasn't any good that I could become so detached that in two days I could put away, and then later forget, the feeling I had towards them. I did not know how to feel about it. Oh, hell, why had it even started? Why had anything started?

'Darling,' Diana said, 'you unpack. It's a lovely night. I'm just going out for a moment, and walk around.'

'All right.'

Yes, maybe it was better if she went out for a few minutes. Then perhaps when she came in again I would feel happy, as I had felt before I started to think about Craven.

She went out. I lay on the bed a few minutes. Already the depression began to slip away. I felt better in a few minutes. How easily a feeling like this passed. How fortunate. Everything was all right. Everything worked its way out. Nothing ever truly ended badly, you thought.

I got up and took a pair of grey flannels out of my travelling-bag. I did not want to wear them too wrinkled. I hung them up and went to the window to call Diana. She would be in the yard.

CHAPTER TWENTY-FIVE

When I started towards the window to call Diana, in the yard below, I heard the sound, before I saw anything. A steady low rhythmic *vroom, vroom.*

My God, it's not an English aircraft, I thought, listening; but there can't be a Jerry aircraft this far inland. Not this year. I leaned out of the window.

The sound came closer, lower; all the sky was dark and moonless overhead.

I looked for Diana in the yard below.

There haven't been any sirens, I thought; hell, it can't be a Jerry aircraft, Not around here.

I leaned against the window sill. Across the way the towers and the chimneys on the giant stone house on the hill stood out darker against a dark sky. Below the window was the square-shaped yard, and beyond the fields of the valley. I could not see where one field ended and the other began. I could see nothing in the yard below; it was too dark.

It can't be a Jerry aircraft. It was impossible. They were only pulling sneak raids on the coast now. Still, those engines.

'Diana!' I called. There was no answer.

I started to sweat, hearing the sound come steadily along the valley. It can't be a Jerry, I kept thinking, as if the urgency of my desire would somehow turn the sound into something else. I moved quickly from the window and into the hall.

I started downstairs, running. Downstairs the proprietor was standing in the hall in a long nightgown. He looked at me astonished.

'What's the trouble?' he asked.

Running, I passed him. 'There's a Jerry kite around.' My heart felt stopped.

'Diana! Diana!' I called in the darkness of the yard.

As I started to call again the sound came rushing in overhead.

'Mack!' Diana screamed somewhere in the dark. 'Mack! Oh!'

There's one coming, I thought, in terror. Oh, God! I fell flat on the ground. There was a high thin rushing sound, and then suddenly in the high thin rushing sound there was a flash and a roar, and I felt myself sucked bodily out of myself and then back again.

I jumped up, called 'Diana! Diana!' No answer.

Nothing can happen to her, I thought. But what if something has? What if she's hurt? Dead? No, not dead. Can't happen.

'Diana!'

God, don't let it be Diana! Anything, but don't let it be Diana. Please, please, dear God. Where is she?

'Diana!'

I heard a moan. She lay in the corner of the garden and I heard her moan again. She was lying on her back. Her dress was covered with dirt and dust. Her eyes were closed. She was breathing, but there was a widening red stain across her stomach. She lay breathing through her open mouth, crying to herself, moaning.

I knelt down. She heard me. Her eyelids fluttered and opened. Her eyes were all white and wide open, staring.

'Where are you hurt?'

160

'I don't know.' She began to cry, whimpering.

There was blood all over the front of her dress. Her face was white with shock and terror.

She started to sit up and began to cough. She lay back coughing and crying softly. The proprietor of the inn came out and helped me pick her up.

We carried her across the yard, trying not to hurry so as not to hurt her; then inside the inn. and then laid her down on a lounge in the bar.

The proprietor and his wife went to the telephone in the hall. I knelt beside her. She was breathing very slowly, her eyes closed. There was perspiration on her forehead and her face seemed to be turning grey. She began to cough and a rill of blood wormed down her chin from one side of her mouth. I yelled to the proprietor to hurry and get the doctor on the telephone.

I heard them cranking the telephone in the hall. Diana opened her eyes. I smiled at her, held her hand.

'Hello, darling,' I said, wanting her to feel that everything was going to be all right. But she did not even seem to hear me. She stared blankly up at the ceiling.

The proprietor came in and shook his head and held up his hands. He shrugged his shoulders.

'The wires are blown down,' he said.

Diana did not hear.

Dear God, what could I do. She mustn't die. Oh, dear God, please. What can I do? Dear God, please.

The proprietor stood there doing nothing. Just looking down at Diana.

No, no, this mustn't happen. It couldn't, It wasn't fair. But what could I do?

Diana turned her head and smiled weakly. The proprietor stepped forward.

'There's nothing I can do,' he said. 'Nearest doctor is in Henley. I have no car.'

Diana seemed to be listening now, watching the proprietor's face.

'Oh, darling,' she said, turning to me, 'I knew it wouldn't last. I knew something would happen. Something always happens to people like us.

The proprietor looked at me and turned to go. 'I'll try the telephone again,' he said.

Diana looked at him and shook her head.

161

'Don't,' she said. Then to me, 'Darling, it's all right.' She lifted her hand and touched my hair for a moment. 'Darling,' she said, 'I'm afraid.'

'You'll be all right,' I said, smiling, holding her other hand.

Then her smile stopped suddenly and she coughed, and her hand came away from my hand, and she turned her head away and seemed to take a sudden deep breath, and closed her eyes,

I knelt there awkwardly, watching. In a little while she was dead, without opening her eyes again.

In the morning I returned to the aerodrome. Later there was a funeral at her home, but I did not go. It would not have been any use.

And a few weeks later I was transferred to the American Air Force.

CHAPTER TWENTY-SIX

I picked up my knife, fork, and spoon which the American Army had issued me. Here I was now, after three years of war, in an American Recruit Camp in England. Oh, to be home, I thought, to be gone from bugle calls and chow lines. Oh, to be back again in my car, going to work at the newspaper office, to the Saturday-night dances at the country club, to college days with Gloria, to all the egotistical twaddle of the summer parties long ago of girls and young men, all healthy and tan, explaining themselves to each other. I stood now in a chow line in the dining hall. 'So I told this babe,' said a little private ahead, as he picked his nose. Laughter ran along the line. Smelling and sweating in the close damp odour of steaming food, the chow line slowly shuffled around the room. How dead and empty seemed the laughter of these new men just over from the States, as vapid and empty as the talk and laughter of the party the night I had left home.

The ones with whom I had enjoyed laughter were all gone. Perhaps how empty and ridiculous our simple jokes and raucous barrack-room talk had sounded to others. But now here were all strange new faces, engaging in the same talk and laughter. How stale and dead it all seemed. Here they were at the beginning of the trail, and here I was at the end.

162

Oh, to be home to a long, quiet, peaceful life, I thought, home to dull city editors, and hot lights, and long hours at night over the copy desk, and Saturdays and Sundays off to do whatever I felt like doing, without asking anyone for a pass. To be home to what had once seemed a dull, stupid life, which would probably be the same again; to the petty confusion of civilian life. Oh, to return to an old ambush.

If only I could say good-bye to overbearing officers, I thought, as I scooped up a spoonful of mashed potatoes; good-bye to hot parades and saluting and cleaning latrines and sweeping floors and raking lawns, for now that was what the American Army had done with me. They said I was a neophyte, a beginner. All my raids were done at night, they said, that is not our way. We raid by day. Here is a broom, and a rifle; drill and sweep and rake lawns until we need you. Now for two months I had done that.

Oh, be not bitter, young man. Only live and try to understand.

Now I heaped my plate with pickle and steak and fresh peas and hot rolls, thinking of the old squadron living on brussels sprouts and turnips and greasy chips, of all the long cold nights, hungry and tired, that they flew. The chow line moved on, and the laughter and talk of those who soon would be dying filled the air. They stood there, pink-cheeked and young and healthy, talking of the new experiences of being in England.

'So I told this babe,' said the young private who kept picking his nose, 'I told her, listen here, babe, this line of guff may go with these Limey finks but it don't take wid me, see.' The private belched and a sergeant air-gunner behind me passed wind. God, how one noticed the disagreeable when one was bitter and tired.

I asked the air-gunner behind me how he felt about going on operations. 'I'm going to get all these Nazis bastards,' he said savagely, then laughed at his intensity.

Ahead the private was still picking his nose, still talking. 'I got these dames all figured out. Just show 'em a little cash and you're in, buddy.'

Great God, could I ever have been like that, I wondered; yes, I knew I had been; all of it in the good spirits of what had then seemed gay companionable talk on dull squares, in barracks and bars, with friends in the beginning, and here now was the end. So this is the way it ended, everything wore out when you had been with it too long. No, I was only tired. I must go back to flying when I had rested another month. There did not seem much of anything else left. Nothing with any point. The old empty lost feeling possessed me.

Then dinner was over and I left the mess hall. There beyond the drill square were the barracks block, long and green-roofed, and it was all as it had been in the beginning, the lonely feeling of being a new man among strangers in a new camp. Around me everybody seemed light-hearted and gay. To be away, I thought, from regimentation, and forms and passes, from all reminders of army life. How little I had learned. Still, there had been many moments of happiness, and for all of them I had paid my way. It was enough. I thought now of someone who had once written that in the army there is no past, that no one is married, single, rich or poor, a brilliant young man or a fool. How wrong he was. I felt I had been a little of all of those.

A column of men swung past in full pack, outward-bound for an operational aerodrome. They were all marching hard, smiling, laughing, all their past life behind them, going on now like a tide, for ever breaking and returning. I looked at them for a moment, then went down to my room to sleep. It seemed now I was tired all the time.

CHAPTER TWENTY-SEVEN

(*And now in the dream I heard their voices again and saw them coming along the dusty road from the Nissen huts to the sergeants' mess, heavy-booted, tea-flasks under their arms, flying sweaters hanging white below their battledress jackets, and it was Craven's face and voice: 'My God, I hope we're not in the first wave again tonight.' I heard the voice in the back of my head, and saw again the ranked tables and faces in the briefing-room. The Intelligence Officer: 'Gerald, special recco tonight,' and Gerald smiling while everybody joked about his bad luck to get such a job on a target like Duisburg. Then in the dusk standing by the aircraft in the cool, spring evening air, waiting to warm up the engines, and Harry, Pop, Johnny, Reg – I heard their voices now and saw them in my mind leaning against the mess bar the night before Stuttgart – Harry, Reg, Johnny, Gerald . . .*)

I felt the warm sunlight on my face and perspiration on my fore-head and rolled over on my stomach. I opened my eyes and heard someone knocking on the door of my room. I sat up, stretched and yawned, said 'Come in,' and looked up as the door opened and saw George, a young gunner just over from the States, standing in the doorway, smiling, looking very happy. 'Well,' I said, 'you're looking damn good. What's up?'

'Jees! You know what!' George said, very excited, eyes shining. 'I think I'm posted. Isn't it swell?'

'Wonderful,' I said, and lay back on the bed. 'You'll be wearing the VC before you know it.'

'Jees, I been waiting two months for this,' George said, sitting on the edge of the bed. 'I wish you were coming with me.'

'You have wonderful ideas.' I yawned and stretched. 'I have nightmares. Did you ever wake up at night with somebody frying to death over a burnt-out fuselage right in your room.'

'Don't think about it,' George said, standing now. 'It won't do you any good.'

'What a brain!' I opened my eyes and smiled. 'Don't think about it, he says.'

'Coming in to town tonight?' he asked.

'Yeah. Maybe. I dunno. Go to town, get tight, pick up a broad. My boy, my youth is past. I leave you the local women tonight.' In my mind I was studying George. A good-looking kid. I wondered what would become of him on a squadron; another face sitting behind a set of machine-guns. He stood now in the doorway, curly-haired, young, looking very cheery. How long will he last, I wondered, and knew George was very happy about leaving this Replacement Centre. Just over from the States and full of enthusiasm. 'Well, I hope you get a good squadron,' I said.

'Oh, I know I will,' George said eagerly.

'All right, you guys!' The drill sergeant bawled from the parade ground outside. 'All right! What the hell do you think this is – a country club?'

I sat up and lit a cigarette. 'Do you know what crew you'll be flying with?' I said.

'Nope. Why?'

'Oh, nothing.' I took a drag on the cigarette. I smoked a lot now. I never had before.

'They'll be all right,' George said. 'I'm not worried.'

'Sure,' I said. 'Oh, sure. A lot of guys have said just that.'

'Don't worry about me,' George said. 'I can take care of myself.'

'Well, take care of yourself some place else for a while, will you? I want to write a letter.'

'Okay,' George said abruptly, 'if you feel that way.'

'I do,' I smiled to take a little of the curse off the curtness of my speech. 'So scram, my dearly beloved jerk.'

The door closed and I lay there listening to the sound of foot-steps dying away, picturing George in my mind. He was just a big healthy kid. What the hell was somebody George's age doing in this war? It did not seem plausible. He belonged at home, sitting in a drugstore with some nice young girl, both of them sipping a soda out of the same glass. What would become of him? Here's wishing him luck, I thought. Not that he won't need more than just luck.

I sat up and tried to write a letter home. I could not seem to think of anything to write. At home they all wanted to hear about any action I had been in. What could I tell them? I'd been scared? Or what it was like? Who can ever explain what it is like, I thought, and what good does it do talking about it? It's over, finished. I wanted to forget about it. Now in the mess on the squadron, I thought, they'll just be coming in for tea. But it wouldn't be the same there any more. I didn't know anyone there any more. All the faces had changed. I tried again to write home but it didn't seem to be any use. I felt there was nothing to say. I sat and looked at the blank sheet of paper.

'Come on! Come on!' the drill sergeant bawled beyond the window. 'Snap it up! Where'd you guys learn how to march.'

I sat and looked at the pen in my hand and listened to the heavy regular sound of marching feet going past.

'Watch the cadence! Watch it! Hup, two three, four!' the sergeant yelled. 'Come on! Pick it up!'

The marching died away and the sergeant's voice grew fainter.

Someone came along outside in the hall, opening doors of the rooms, then passed, came back, and finally opened my door. It was the bunk steward, a private.

'Hey, they're looking for you,' he said. 'You're supposed to be drilling.'

'Can't you say you couldn't find me?' I asked.

'That won't do any good,' the private said. 'They been looking for you all morning.'

'Okay.' I put the pen down. 'Okay. I'll be along.'

Then I picked up the pen again: 'No, to hell with it.'

'You'll never get along here acting like that,' said the private.

'I'm tired of getting along,' I said. 'I just want to be left alone.'

166

'You can't,' the steward said. 'No one can be that way nowa-days.'

'Yeah?' I said sarcastically. 'I thought so. You might know. You've been reading the right editorials all right.'

'You're supposed to see the company commander,' the private said. 'I forgot.'

'You forgot?'

'Yeah. Come on. I'm supposed to take you over,' the private said.

'Tell him to get stuffed.'

'They can break you.' He stood in the doorway looking at me.

'So what?' I said.

'So maybe you'd like to get broken, I'm thinking.'

He closed the door and went away. I stared at the table-top. No, it wouldn't do any good to buck the system. They'd get you in the end. Three years of war. And now in this army a raw recruit all over again. Three years with the RAF and now back with the Americans again, my own people. But were they? Now they seemed strange, odd, different, or maybe I had changed. Yes, I had changed all right, only the dead had not changed. I got up and went out across the drill square to the orderly-room. But I must go on fighting now no matter how much I hated it. It had to be won.

Inside the administrative office I found the private. While I was looking for him in the long room full of desks, and people bent over typewriters, someone dropped a ruler. Only a faint noise. I felt myself jerk inside as if someone had fired a gun.

The private said the Lieutenant was waiting to see me and would I come right into the Lieutenant's office, and what a good thing it was that he hadn't told the Lieutenant that I had re-fused to come, because the Lieutenant was often a very difficult man. I went in, closing the door behind me.

'Tech. Sergeant Norton?' the Lieutenant's flat, severe voice. He was seated behind a desk. He did not look up at me. A neat way of dominating, I thought, having seen the method used before. The Lieutenant was a young man with a red face and a small blond moustache. 'Tech. Sergeant Norton?' he asked again.

'Yes, sir.' (Who the hell does he think I am – Eisenhower? Didn't the private announce me?) 'Did you want to see me, sir?'

'Yes, Sergeant. I'm sorry to hear we're having trouble with you.' (What kind of a sweet approach is this, I wondered.) 'You were not on parade yesterday, Sergeant, and you refused to help sod the skeet grounds. Sergeant, you might as well realize you are no longer in the Royal Air Force.'

'I know that, sir.'

'I don't know why you seem to regard yourself as a privileged character around here,' the Lieutenant said in a nasty voice. 'After all, we didn't ask you to transfer.'

I gave a little cough.

'The Royal Air Force always seemed to have something better for me to do than sod lawns, sir. After all, if you don't mind me saying so, sir, I hope I haven't been an air-gunner for three years to suddenly learn that my experience fits me for gardening.'

'Do you see that, Sergeant?' the Lieutenant pointed to the Air Medal on his chest. 'Maybe you would like to go on operations. I can tell you you wouldn't like it. I've been on five trips.'

'You're quite right, sir,' I said. 'I wouldn't like it. I've been on thirty-three raids.' (What a way to get satisfaction, I thought, bragging, bragging, to each other.)

'You'll have to settle down, Sergeant,' the Lieutenant said. 'I don't want to discipline you. But you really must settle down.'

'Guess I'm just nervous,' I said. 'I'll be all right.'

But when I got outside I knew I would not be all right. I just said those things to put off realizing I wouldn't be all right.

I went back to my room and found a book, and lying on the bed tried to read, but it was no use. I could not keep my mind on it. People going to town for the evening passed my window.

The war. When would it finish? It must be won, but when?

Then what? The continual flying and what I had seen left me restless. I did not do anything very long now before it bored me. It had never been that way before.

Would there be a 'call on' tonight if I was back at the squadron? No use thinking of that now. No good. I could not go back to that life because the good part of that life was worn out. Maybe I was worn out. But what had done it? I met old friends from the squadron and they were all the same, glad to finish operational flying, then bored, fed up soon of being instructors. We had all lived too often in a state of false exhilaration. The MO said I needed a rest. But rest did not seem to come any place any more. I just went on, as if I were waiting for something, but what? where? who?

The future, the rest of my life ahead of me? What would I do with it? I can come home after the war, they wrote from America, and get my old job back. And be nice, I thought, to those people in the office I'd once thought it important to be nice to; that horrible Swanson, the manager, and Walker, one of the publishers. How ridiculous it seemed now that I had ever considered it important, or regarded them as anything but terrible people, always blathering about what they called the 'important things in life', which, as I saw them now, meant only the sale of more newspapers.

I wondered if it would do any good to go to town tonight with some of the fellows and tie on a good booze-up. When I was in the squadron, and to celebrate a successful raid and the rather miraculous fact that everybody had returned safely, everybody drank together in the same country local, night after night, and were happy because they were back. But the people here in this camp were not the same, and whatever experience had been the bond between friends and myself on the squadron was gone, and as sure as there were many friends gone for ever, that bond would not come again.

Düsseldorf, June 1941, I thought. Barker. He did not come back. Nor Evans. Where were they now? Buried? The North Sea? Somewhere near the Rhine? Gone. All gone. No, it was foolish to think that way. I'd get up and go out tonight ... This experience must not become more important to me than myself.

Seven more days here, seven more days until leave, and then London. There were only a few people left in London that I knew, and now when I went there things were different, not so gay. Girls. I could telephone some girls. Yes, that would do it. Always a few around town. Yes, that's what I would do when I got to London.

I closed my eyes and lay back on the bed.

(*I heard now in my mind the sound of engines in the dusk and then saw them again, big and dark and the four blurs of propellers turning on to the runway, and then they went tearing along between the flickering flare pots, taking off, one at a time. The sky full of them, circling, setting course in the soft green twilight. Johnny came up to me that night. It was our rest night and we were standing down. 'How many do you think we'll lose tonight?' Johnny said. When they came back in the dark hours sitting in the briefing-room, and when Johnny came in smiling I said, 'They're all back,' I did not believe it, but I smiled and felt relieved that they were all back. It was Essen. A hell of a tough target.*)

I opened my eyes and looked at the ceiling.

London alone without Diana. The girl I would have married. Her dark hair rolled up tightly under her ATS hat. The girl I loved. That night I might have been walking in the cool leafy darkness of Berkeley Square with her, or under the trees, spring, sky and stars overhead, moonlight showing through the branches on to the ground. Live in the States after the war. Have a wonderful happy time, and I would show her all the things at home that I now loved. And forget the war and have a long quiet life playing tennis in the long summer afternoons by the lake, and dancing on summer porches, where I had danced a long time ago; in the thick warm darkness that July the bands played *Begin the Beguine* and the war was only another headline in a mid-western paper. Do all those things and many other things, and in the winters go to New York and see the plays. But now we would not do any of those things together. Never. In my mind now I tried to stop picturing the raid again, sound rising out of the dark, the running, and the explosion, and then the waiting in the inn, watching the sunrise, knowing it wouldn't do any good to wait any longer, knowing she was dead, sitting on there in the hall until it was light outside, until the proprietor came along and handed me a cigarette, and then finally walking away, not knowing the cigarette was in my hand until I was sitting somewhere eating breakfast . . .

Go back on 'Ops' with the Americans? . . . Chances of finishing a tour with them? Two tours of Ops. No. One was enough. I had done one tour. But they would say I wasn't patriotic thinking of my own skin. Must win the war.

But the people who did not think of my skin. Sleek and well-fed, ruddy-faced with good living, standing chatting in the matinée lounges of London theatres. No, they did not care about me and my kind, George and his friends. Forty of our bombers did not return. I could see them ruddy-faced with good living, sitting in bright Bury Street restaurants ordering good food, reading the *Daily Mail*: 'I say, frightfully successful raid last night, wasn't it? Give anything for a crack at those Jerries myself, wouldn't you, old boy.' Well, they were welcome to the chance. I would be big-hearted: 'Madam, sir, you may have my turret tomorrow night. Don't forget to test the guns, madam, on crossing the coast. Oh, yes, quite necessary, my dear.'

No, none of them cared. But I could be sick on this bitterness. When you were gone they said you would be remembered. How very satisfying! A nice little cenotaph in the Ritz lounge, if you please, sir. Not too ostentatious, mind you, and well lit after eight o'clock. A nice beacon on it flashing S for sugar. Only a precaution, sir, I assure you. We must protect the lucky alcoholics from bodily injury . . . I dozed, dreaming.

(Gerald pulled the control column all the way back, hard against his stomach. The searchlight beam, probing, sabring in the dark, passed underneath. Gerald pushed the control column forward. There was the dull shocking boomph of heavy flak bouncing the aircraft. 'Weave! For God's sake! They've got us predicted!' A wobbly string of light red tracer came snapping upwards under the wing-tip. They were diving. I felt pressed down in the turret. Stars wheeled. Moon disappeared. Searchlights and bursting flak far behind. The flying straight and level, the naked full moon hanging high above the rudders.)

Keep going, they told you. Chin up. *Per Ardua ad Astra.* Towards the Stars. I wondered what smooth brand of scotch the author of that line used.

Get married. That was the antidote. 'I am a lonely young man. I am tired of war. Would you care to marry me?'

'But I don't know you.'

'My dear woman, don't be ridiculous. The love of a good woman cures all. Come, come, my dear, have faith.'

Marry and find a new meaning in life. You too can be happy. Read *The American Boy.* Get yourself a formula for happiness. Hey! Hey! Join our dear happy troupe.

Maybe it would stop everything for a while if I attached myself to something. Perhaps if I take up religion, I thought, or politics. They are less expensive than women, and so much easier to be rid of when bored.

I opened my eyes and looked at the logbook on the desk, near the bed. Two hundred hours of fear, worry, and strain. An itemized list of targets attacked in Europe.

Those hours, the destroyers of care. But now an end. Now nothing more to learn about living and dying, learning and changing under the strain and tension of operations. Maybe I've learned too much, I thought, too much, too fast.

But what can be regarded as serious, I thought, after I've been near death too much; they said there were more important things than death. But who could free himself from the memory of the dead while the old powerful ones who were alive, the sleek and the fat who knew that, and while others were afflicted by it, bulwarked themselves against it, and safe among themselves

171

carefully stayed out of the game to the end of time. Now, always, for ever.

So where lay the answer to honour? I wondered. To glory? To death? Where lay the meaning? Who knew? Who could tell? Find the key? The open way? For there would always be those whose actions killed the meaning of all words, who took the meaning away from others.

An aeroplane droned high overhead, sound dying away across the sunny air.

I looked at the letter from Jennifer, a vague friend in London. Safe behind a typewriter in a London embassy. WAAF and ATS were now returning in the evening all over England to lonely drab billets, and Jennifer, gay and charming, without a sense of guilt because, 'Really,' as she explained, 'there's actually little one can do about one's position. Actually they do need us badly at the embassy. And really, darling, it would be literally frightful in the Services. You know what I mean – living with all those people.' Yes, I thought, the machine was too big and smooth and too well run, and you could never really change it. The oil-can and tools to make it run are always in the same hands, I thought, now and always will be.

But it's no good thinking like this, I said to myself, I need something, somebody. No, I knew that was a lie. I did not need anybody. I needed only illusions and not the knowledge of how people really lived and died. George did not know yet. Would he learn, and then would George in time laugh at values he had once taken seriously, then laughing himself around in a kind of circle, laughing himself empty, begin soberly from the beginning asking himself the true reason for every human action, and have only the emptiness to go on, only the emptiness to tell him there were no true answers. Fate and ourselves conspire against us. 'Believe in something,' they all say; 'believe and you will find.' But of the darkness of a world of only hope and despair there comes only a mocking disbelief, for what in life can compare to the unceasing knowledge of your own possible death in the night to come, or in other future nights, alone somewhere in the dark.

Another aeroplane passed high overhead.

Great God, I thought, some day they will all be up there, everybody, and maybe they will all kill each other. The perfect mêlée. The final and complete victory.

'Come on, Tom,' a passing voice called to someone beyond the window. 'Hurry up. We'll miss the last bus to town.'

It would be nice in town, with a cool pint and a piano playing somewhere in the room, I thought; but no, I had been through that stage. No, there was nothing there for me any more in a bar with a cool pint in one hand. I would not know anyone and I would only end up trying to pick up some woman, and then standing in a doorway making love, trying to kill the emptiness and the thinking. Would they be going in to briefing now on the squadron? What time is it? Karlsruhe, Berlin, Hanover, Stettin, Nuremberg, Essen, Rostock, the Baltic, the North Sea. Did I want to return to that? And did I need all that again like a kind of old cocaine habit? No, I was only fooling myself. I knew that part of my life was ended, that I did not want to go back, that I was afraid to die now. But what do I go on to? No returning . . . Must find something, a new interest, and I must desire. Yes, that was it. For now in a single blinding flash of light of all your time you see, maybe for an instant behind everything, I thought, and you know then for a moment that the only meaning of your life is your own death, the end of all desire. And so it was all only desire and death. On and on. For ever changing yet remaining the same. But that is the only way there is for us, I thought, our only end and means, Desire and Death.

George knocked, and opened the door. 'Letter for you, Mack.'

'Oh, thanks,' I said absentmindedly, and opened the envelope and read. '. . . Simply must get up to London on leave . . . the 20th . . . marvellous party . . . bring some friends . . . Everybody is in town . . . Love, Jennifer.' I remembered now when such an invitation was exciting, interesting. Now it seemed empty. I could picture the party, a series of dances, different partners, drinks, smiling teeth and lips, more drinks, smiles and teeth, the fixed grimaces of our beautiful living. And God! Talk! There would be oceans of it, strings of words, like writhing eels, swimming through the air in long endless coilings and uncoilings, twisting and turning, non-stop, unceasing for ever and ever, all that night. No thanks . . . I will sit this one out, please, I thought.

I tossed the letter on the desk. I became aware of George's presence.

'Well,' I said harshly, not knowing why, 'what the hell do you want?' It made me angry seeing George looking so eager, so ready to enjoy everything.

'Say!' he looked astonished, very young.

'Do you have to look so pleasantly simple?'

'Well, Jees, I just dropped in to see if you wanted to go to town.'

'No!'

'Well, you don't have to get tough about it.' Hurt, George got up to go.

'I'm sorry,' I said, not looking at him. 'What were you going to do tonight?'

'Oh, just a bunch of us going to town for a few beers. Guys I came over with. I told 'em about you. Thought you might like to come along.'

'I wouldn't be any good,' I said. 'I am one big dope tonight.'

'Well, I just told the guys,' George said hesitantly, shyly. 'You know – I told 'em you might come along and give us some gen.'

'Seven easy lessons. You too can win a Victoria Cross,' I said, laughing, and suddenly felt better, released from myself. 'Norton's School for Heroes. Right this way, my boy! DFMs guaranteed with our special four-week telescoped set of instructions.'

And now I felt better, I did not know why, unless it was that I had suddenly stopped thinking and that I was suddenly back in a time when looking forward to an evening like this had pleased and excited me. Maybe I am having a nice temporary mental and moral transfusion, I thought, and grinned at George. 'Three pints to your one? What do you say?' I pulled on my tunic, smiling. 'Three to one! Show you how. A bet?' I smiled, feeling happy, gay.

'Don't come if you don't want to, Mack,' George said soberly. 'Don't make believe you want to come just for my sake.'

I laughed. An old gaiety was on me. 'But I want to come, George! My God, do I ever! This stinking room! Phooey!'

I grabbed George's arm and, racing him all the way to the camp gate, jumped on the bus just as it was leaving.

In the warm summer evening the beer was strong and cold, and in the pub, in the smoke and talk, it was like the old times again, in the early days of a strong bond of friendship among those with whom I lived and flew, but in a little while I remembered again those days, and the same talk here that once I had felt to have meaning, and a wonderful quality among the people of the squadron, now seemed as vacuous and pointless as that party at home long ago, only empty brassy noise among these new people. And in the dark I went quickly on home, glad to be alone, thinking in the night of all those who were gone, knowing now I was for ever caught in the memory of their living days.

NEL BESTSELLERS

T035 794	HOW GREEN WAS MY VALLEY	*Richard Llewellyn*	95p
T039 560	I BOUGHT A MOUNTAIN	*Thomas Firbank*	90p
T033 988	IN THE TEETH OF THE EVIDENCE	*Dorothy L. Sayers*	90p
T040 755	THE KING MUST DIE	*Mary Renault*	85p
T038 149	THE CARPETBAGGERS	*Harold Robbins*	£1.50
T040 917	TO SIR WITH LOVE	*E. R. Braithwaite*	75p
T041 719	HOW TO LIVE WITH A NEUROTIC DOG	*Stephen Baker*	75p
T040 925	THE PRIZE	*Irving Wallace*	£1.60
T034 755	THE CITADEL	*A. J. Cronin*	£1.10
T042 189	STRANGER IN A STRANGE LAND	*Robert Heinlein*	£1.25
T037 673	BABY & CHILD CARE	*Dr Benjamin Spock*	£1.50
T037 053	79 PARK AVENUE	*Harold Robbins*	£1.25
T035 697	DUNE	*Frank Herbert*	£1.25
T035 832	THE MOON IS A HARSH MISTRESS	*Robert Heinlein*	£1.00
T040 933	THE SEVEN MINUTES	*Irving Wallace*	£1.50
T038 130	THE INHERITORS	*Harold Robbins*	£1.25
T035 689	RICH MAN, POOR MAN	*Irwin Shaw*	£1.50
T037 134	EDGE 27: DEATH DRIVE	*George G. Gilman*	75p
T037 541	DEVIL'S GUARD	*Robert Elford*	£1.25
T042 774	THE RATS	*James Herbert*	80p
T042 340	CARRIE	*Stephen King*	80p
T042 782	THE FOG	*James Herbert*	90p
T033 740	THE MIXED BLESSING	*Helen Van Slyke*	£1.25
T037 061	BLOOD AND MONEY	*Thomas Thompson*	£1.50

NEL P.O. BOX 11, FALMOUTH TR10 9EN, CORNWALL

Postage charge:

U.K. Customers. Please allow 22p for the first book plus 10p per copy for each additional book ordered to a maximum charge of 92p to cover the cost of postage and packing.

B.F.P.O. & Eire. Please allow 22p for the first book plus 10p per copy for the next six books, thereafter 4p per book.

Overseas Customers. Please allow 30p for the first book plus 10p per copy for each additional book

Please send cheque or postal order (no currency).

Name ....

Address ....

....

Title ....

While every effort is made to keep prices steady, it is sometimes necessary to increase prices at short notice. New English Library reserve the right to show on covers and charge new retail prices which may differ from those advertised in the text or elsewhere.